Chinnery in China

Chinnery in China

A NOVEL

KATHLEEN ODELL

JOHN MURRAY

Printed in Great Britain by
Cox & Wyman Limited
London, Fakenham and Reading
0 7195 2433 4

FOREWORD

George Chinnery, portrait and landscape painter, was born in London in 1774. He spent most of his working life in the East, and died in poverty in Macao in 1852. Little is known of this long life beyond the outlines, how he went as a young man to India, his brilliant but eccentric career in Madras and Calcutta, and his hurried flight from Bengal to China, from which he never returned. He had a wife, from whom he soon parted, and there were two children of the marriage. He also had two illegitimate children. Much more information must be scattered, like his very considerable output of works, in far-flung places, and awaits a biographer.

The story which this book relates is entirely imaginary and the names of the characters, other than Chinnery himself, will not be found in the list of foreigners resident in Macao, although students of the period may find resemblances to some of them in contemporary accounts.

Part One

CHAPTER 1

I did not need to open my eyes to know that I was in Macao, that it was seven o'clock in the morning, and that the summer season would shortly be upon us. Outside the closed shutters, in the branches of the tree which overhangs my garden wall, I could hear a clattering and bustling as though a tribe of monkeys were out there at their usual game of destruction. But I knew it was birds, not monkeys. I opened the shutters and stepped on to the verandah to have a look at them. They are migrants, and arrive every year in flocks in the early part of May. They load down our trees to breaking point and utter one hoarse, repetitious cry calculated to rouse the strongest sleeper, and as soon as I hear them I know that the south-west monsoon has set in. At intervals it dies away, and a cooler spell supervenes for a few days, but these intervals become more and more infrequent while the monsoon increases in heat and humidity, until they cease altogether and summer is at its height. After September the cycle goes into reverse and the north-east monsoon blows, with occasional reversions to summer weather.

I suppose the number of trees on the peninsula of Macao, compared with the mainland, must attract the birds, as well as their comparative immunity here. I was sketching on the Penha Hill a few mornings ago, when a whole troop of the same species suddenly alighted in the trees, large booby-like creatures with imposing crests and tails. This magnificent plumage seemed to make it difficult for them to fly. They flopped from branch to branch in the most ungainly way, uttering raucous cries: Soldier was wildly excited and chased them from tree to tree, gazing hopefully upwards and

7

uttering even louder barks. Mr Bell, my fellow resident, who possesses a famous aviary, has told me what their name is, but I have forgotten it. Mr Bell has some great rarities in his aviary, and is always willing to show them off to any visitors who may come. It is an agreeable way of spending his old age, and he bears his misfortunes very well. As long as his creditors will show forbearance enough to leave him in his house for the rest of his life, he will be happy. He has one of the finest houses in Macao, in the old Portuguese style and very comfortable inside, but in the centre of town, a situation I don't care for. I prefer to look out to sea, whatever the typhoon danger may be. We have not had one in the five years I have lived in Macao, and in any event, I do not possess anything that would take much harm from a wetting. I have my old chair, my old companion, which I brought with me from Calcutta as furniture for my cabin, but everything else is bought cheaply from the bazaar and could be replaced in half an hour. When I think of the solid mahogany, marble, etc., which filled every house in India, I wonder that we took so much trouble to bring out from England furniture so little suited to the climate when so much could be got near at hand. But then I do not entertain, and so have no need for the obligatory two dozen chairs and table to match. I am invited out, to entertain the guests, but am not expected to return the hospitality.

On the last such occasion, the dinner was at the East India Company's house. The dinner, as usual, was very fine, and the guests not at all bad: at least in a small place like this one knows their limitations beforehand. Most of the gentlemen are now down from Canton for the summer season, my young American friend Mr Harker among them, although his firm usually manages to keep its young men in Canton throughout the summer in spite of the Chinese authorities' prohibition, on one pretext or another. Harker has been seriously ill, however, and is to spend the summer in Macao with Mr and Mrs Fay at their house, Mr Fay being the present head of the firm. As Harker speaks Chinese, which is a great rarity, he is worth cherishing on this account, even if he were not for his own sake, being one of the most delightful young fellows you can imagine. The talk was all, of course, of buying and selling—tea and opium, opium and tea. This is a community of traders, and my paintings are merchandise like any other: in fact they are a shrewd investment. When the China trade is fully opened up, the pioneer firms will be placed very comfortably indeed, and they will be able to decorate their offices with portraits of their founders which they acquired at a most advantageous rate. I perceive that the best compliment this trading community can pay me is to treat me as one of themselves. One thing I like about the society here is that it is free and easy in its manners: we are not cursed with the petty dignitaries and the ceremonial bowing and scraping which went on all day in India, and made social life there so uncongenial and the pursuit of patronage so arduous. In their Factory at Canton the East India Company keep up their establishment in their usual style, silver plate, chaplain, library and so on, but their hospitality is no less warm. I spent many happy days as a guest of the Factory.

One of the topics of conversation was the prospect of an addition—two additions, rather—to our little society. Mrs Fay's young daughter is coming out to join her parents, and a niece or some other female relation is accompanying her. The age of the latter was not specifically mentioned, but presumably she must have reached years of discretion to be selected as a suitable travelling companion. The two new arrivals cannot be here before the autumn, but already there was considerable speculation about their attractions. The shortage of females here is acute. We have only one unattached lady in the person of Mrs Haverill, who has lived here alone since the calamity of a few years back, when her lamented husband died on board the ship which was bringing them both, for the first time, to China. Mrs Haverill reached Macao and installed herself in the house which had been prepared for her husband and herself, and which she liked so much that she has not made any arrangements to quit it and return to her

9

home and her relatives. She is a most accomplished woman, although not in her first youth, being I should say about forty years of age. She is evidently well accustomed to foreign travel and was one of the first to see a resemblance between Macao and the Bay of Naples, a comparison which is now quite fashionable. Although she is not particularly intimate with any of the other ladies (perhaps she shows a wisdom here, considering the deterioration of the mental faculties, and the increasing propensity for gossip which attacks women in these climates), she is universally admired, and a great ornament to our society. Rumour couples her name on an average about once a month with one or other of our bachelors, but surprisingly enough, with more hope than malice. So far, all expectations have been in vain.

Mrs Haverill, by the way, wishes to take drawing lessons from me 'if it is not ridiculous to expect to develop a new accomplishment at my age'. I do not find it ridiculous at all, and I have not the least objection to giving drawing lessons to ladies. At least they are not likely to set up in competition with me, as one of my Chinese pupils has already done. And Mrs Haverill is a charming woman. But if she has any expectations of tuition in anything beyond drawing, she had better abandon them. So far as women are concerned, I feel I am a burnt-out fire.

Young Mr Harker, who is one of the most energetic members of the community, has invited me to join him and others in an expedition to the Valley of the Ringing Rocks, on the Chinese island which faces the Inner Harbour. There is an element of excitement about this excursion (the novelty of the Ringing Rocks themselves having long since worn off) in that it has recently been prohibited by the mandarin, on the ground that Chinese graves have been profaned. When a party, which included ladies, made a trip a week or so ago they encountered great hostility from the villagers and were forced to beat a rapid retreat to their boats. There was a great hubbub, and many thought that the Portuguese should immediately have taken the matter up with the Chinese authorities, but nothing was done, and wisely, as I think. The Portuguese hold of this place is so precarious (although so tenacious) that it seems unwise to demand as a right what has been granted as a privilege, and for many years past the Portuguese have had no right to use Lappa Island, where the valley lies. Harker takes all this as a great joke. He makes frequent forays from the Factories in Canton to visit temples and places of interest (all completely forbidden to foreign residents) and if he gets into any trouble with the Chinese crowds, he just trusts to his heels and his luck to get him safe back to the Factories. However, I excused myself from the expedition, not from fear of the villagers and the mandarin, but because I am, at the moment, overwhelmed with work.

The biggest task I have is to put in the figures of the two Chinese (the Company insisted on *two*) in the portrait of Dr Morrison translating the Bible into Chinese, which the Company has commissioned from me. Then I ought to work up a big piece for London, but this is hard work, and will have to be put off until I have finished Dr M. The kind of subject which interests me does not interest them in Pall Mall: I mean the street scenes, the groups of coolies gambling at the corners, the old men with wispy beards who sit and smoke on the steps of the churches, the contrast between these oriental figures and their background of crumbling Mediterranean magnificence. I like to draw the junks lying at anchor under the scorching sun on a sea which glitters like a sheet of burnished metal. The little islands rise quite bare out of the sea, as if all life on them had dwindled and died under the pitiless sun (it is strange that there are so few seabirds here). In the morning a trail of mist lies across the outer roadstead, and the sound of a cock crowing or a dog barking on board a junk in the Inner Harbour carries up to the top of Penha Hill. I have made scores of sketches from the summit of the hill, usually in the early morning, or in the evening.

Now that summer is coming on, I will have to change my

11

plan of working. I now find it impossible to work in the afternoon at the height of the summer heat. I did it when I was in India and had important commissions on hand, such as the portrait of the Chief Justice of Bengal which I finished in three months, including a mass of detail which comprised the Sword and Mace, the patent of office with the Great Seal attached, and symbolic figures (Justice protecting Innocence) appropriate to the office of the sitter, but I did it at the risk of my health, which would have suffered permanently had I continued. Now that I am no longer young, and have found a place of residence which suits me and which is a refuge from the torments of an uncongenial married life, as well as the business difficulties which beset me in India, I intend to live what of life is left to me in my own way. After all, I do not need much: a roof over my head, friends with whom to spend my leisure hours—emphatically, I do not want any more women—and a dog.

I had almost forgotten Soldier, but he never forgets me for a second. He is really too big for the furniture of this house: with every wave of his tail he sends chairs and tables flying. I intend to get a special couch made for him for the summer, for if he sleeps on a bench raised a little off the ground, he gets considerable relief from the heat. It is no use importing into the country a dog bred to a cool climate and expecting the animal to withstand conditions here unless endless care is taken, or the dog will never be healthy. His feeding alone requires constant supervision: the best-trained servant in both India and China will grudge the animal food, and may even poison it to be rid of further trouble. I would not trust even Augustine, my steward, in this matter. The Chinese have two uses for dogs, both utilitarian: either they are fattened for the pot, or kept as watch dogs, usually on junks. It is an amusing sight to watch one of these archaic and unwieldy vessels set sail with her packed community on board, including the chickens and the dog.

Augustine would not like to be described as Chinese, however. He claims to be pure Macanese, whatever that may

12

mean, and comes, in fact, of a medley of all the races known to these seas. He speaks the local variety of Portuguese, Chinese, and English of a sort, having served English families residing here for many years. By local regulation it is necessary to have one of these Macanese functionaries to each household to act as steward and go-between with the Chinese shopkeepers. In fact, what the Portuguese population would find to do were it not for the English and American ladies and the children who live all the year round in Macao, and their menfolk who come here from the Factories in Canton to spend the summer season, I really do not know. The Inner Harbour is fast filling up with sand, trade gets slacker year by year, and many of the finest houses would stand empty were it not for the Canton merchants and their families. I also help, a little. The modest competence which my profession earns me enables me to live here in comfort, if not in any great style, and also to feel that I am doing some benefit to others in the shape of Mr Barretto, my landlord, Augustine, and the half dozen or so Chinese who complete my establishment, and whose exact duties are known to Augustine alone.

It occurred to me today to think how old I am. I find with surprise that I am fifty-six. I have survived a good many of my closest friends, and many of my contemporaries are already old men. I have been very lucky to have been so favoured with health and strength, but there must come a point when one reaches the summit, and begins to go down the other side. Or has that peak been passed for me, I wonder, and I do not know it?

CHAPTER 2

I have been recommended a dog boy by an English friend, who sounds suitable, and whom I think I will engage for the summer. In winter there is no problem, I walk a great deal myself, and Soldier accompanies me, to the amazement and terror of the bazaar. Although I know he would not hurt anyone, yet he cannot resist giving an occasional snap at those pigtails which dangle down so tantalizingly just within his reach. Bazaar dogs and beggars run away when they see him coming, as he is large and formidable looking, so that I am spared a good deal of annoyance in my daily excursions. In the more remote parts of the place he is a useful protection, for there are always a number of bad characters who would not hesitate to attack and rob a solitary European. But already the weather is getting too hot to make walking a pleasure, and my exercise on foot will soon have to be reduced to the minimum. With reluctance I shall have to stop climbing with Soldier to the top of Penha Hill and have myself carried about in a sedan, while the dog boy takes Soldier for a walk on level ground, which means leading him down some dusty street or other. It is useless to take him on to the Praia, because of the hundred and one dogs on board the sampans and junks tied up alongside. They all give tongue together with one voice, and Soldier gets into a frenzy trying to reach them. It is hard work for me to get him past them, and with a puny little Chinese on the other end of the leash I should think he would make a flying leap into some sampan or other, and sink it. Then the bill of costs to be settled would be formidable.

The other day he contrived to give me the slip. I don't know how it happened, but as I was returning from a friend's house, Soldier broke loose and was off in a flash. I hurried back home and reported the matter to Augustine, who sent off the Chinese servants in pursuit. I set up my Dr M and tried to work, but was, of course, completely distracted by this disaster. I knew only too well that if the dog were not caught at once, many rounds of money would have to be paid out in rewards to ensure his safe return. The morning went by, and no news of Soldier, or of my runners either. I foresaw horrible calamities, each one more expensive than the last, pigtails outraged, lily-footed ladies sent flying, market stalls overturned and so on. Meanwhile, the usual noises of Macao to which I have become so accustomed that I hardly notice them, other than as a soothing background to a morning's painting, became more and more intrusive—the piercing wails of the food vendors, the perpetual clacking of wooden clogs, always ringing two different notes, the noise produced by the man who knocks two bits of wood together as he shuffles round the streets, the shouts of the cat-seller, mingled with the wails of his captives as they crouch in the two wicker baskets suspended at the ends of his carrying pole. I continued to work, but with less and less concentration. Finally, late in the afternoon, the culprit returned, led by one of my servants, with a black-trousered individual following behind. Total bill—the price of one hen! Augustine dealt with the matter with his usual efficiency, and although the negotiations were noisy and protracted enough to have accounted for a whole market stall, a settlement was finally reached on this very moderate basis. But I shall have to be more careful in future, for if there are too many of these escapades the dog will be costing me as much as Mrs Chinnery to keep—his only saving grace being that I enjoy *his* company.

Fortunately, living is cheap in Macao. House rent is considerably less than what it was in Calcutta, and there is very little else to buy. My major expense is food. Meat is scarce and not good, but chickens can always be had (the scragginess of Chinese hens would be inconceivable to those who have not had acquaintance with the Indian variety) and rice, of course, there is in abundance. It is a great error to think that in a hot climate we need less food, or that we should eat only as our fancy takes us. The body needs to build up its resistance to the oppressive climatic forces and the dangerous miasmas which are encountered on all sides. How can a man who lives only on titbits, soups and so on keep his strength up? The greatest folly committed by Europeans in the East, which I have witnessed again and again, is to indulge too freely in wine. It astounds all my acquaintances that I do not drink anything stronger than tea: they do not see the spectacle of themselves and others shortening their lives by this habit, and in the process deliberately benumbing all their faculties. There are two principal reasons for this excessive drinking. The first reason is the solitariness which besets all foreign residents in the East. This may sound extraordinary to those who see only the superficial appearance of things, and to be sure there is always a jolly crowd to be found, all anxious for distraction and amusement and any joke which will pass the time away. There are riding parties, rowing parties, expeditions and games of all kinds. But the society to be found in such places as Calcutta, Canton and Macao is necessarily limited and different from what it would be in any large city in Europe, and though there are jolly companions to be met, they cannot replace the intimate friends of one's youth who have been left behind. There is a void which will never be filled, and a man has to learn to do with his own company— or seek that of a bottle.

The second reason why men drink to excess is that they hope in that way to overcome the inevitable deterioration of the faculties which the climate brings about. Gradually the languid airs, the luxurious life, the absence of all effort, physical and mental, produce a weakening of the frame and at the same time a loss of perception. Sight, hearing and sense all deteriorate. The effect of drinking is to stimulate the faculties temporarily and give the impression of restoring them to their old vigour, while in fact excess is hastening the process of decay. In my case, I cannot afford to submit to this process. I have to use my senses to their utmost. Many years ago, in India, I realised that if I were to continue to paint at all, I must give up the use of wine. To drink at all was fatal: it then became impossible to stop while the rest of the company wished to continue. At first I found it difficult to abstain. Then, when I saw my companions being put to bed by their servants evening after evening, I began to appreciate how much I had gained and what they had lost— the marvellous beauty of the night skies, and the hundred flowery smells, and the night noises. Now tea has become my habit, and the result of it is that I am in excellent health. I may be fat and ugly, but for a man of my age who has lived in the East for thirty years, I am solid. I shall outlive many of these young men now in their twenties. I sometimes wonder what I shall die of, and when. When I see the grotesque tiles perched on the roofs of the Chinese houses in this place, I think that one of those blowing off would do the trick —hence my habit of walking in the middle of the street.

From my long chair on the verandah of the first floor, I can look over the roofs of the neighbouring houses, for the street descends sharply, to the beautiful Bay of Macao, and the islands beyond. The roofs are covered with these same quaint tiles, and the houses rise out of gardens of palm trees. I don't know the inhabitants of the house next door: they are Macaïstas, and when the ladies get inside the courtyard, it is impossible to distinguish them by voice from their servants. They babble and gossip without cease. In addition, they keep a talking mynah bird which imitates the sounds it hears in a manner which would cause me to wring its neck. He is a large, active, glossy bird, perpetually on the hop although his cage is too small to allow him much freedom of activity. He must work off his energy in the noise he makes. I have good opportunities of observing him, for every evening his cage is brought out from the house and hung on a branch of one of the largest trees in the garden, in the rays of the setting sun, and I can see and hear him perfectly as he bows and becks. The ladies themselves never come within range of my eyes: all I am privileged to see is a hideous old Chinese amah who shuffles across the courtyard to hoist the bird into position.

All this used to excite Soldier beyond measure. Poking his head as far as it would go through the pillars of the verandah, which are made of green porcelain shaped to resemble bamboo, he would bark himself hoarse. Now he just thrusts his nose through and withdraws it again with a sigh which seems to come from the depths of his being. Then he glances at me and gives a tentative thump of his tail.

Placed at intervals on the balustrade of my verandah, and also on the floor are pots of flowering plants which change with the season. The pots themselves are of coarse earthenware, roughly glazed with green which has run here and there in streaks on their sides. Just now the pots contain red flowers and white flowers with wonderfully glossy dark green leaves, a pot of white flowers and a pot of red being placed alternately. All this is done by the gardener without any orders being given. Although I have nothing but a yard to my house, I never lack for flowers and do not envy my neighbours their great domains, not even the East India Company house whose grounds support a herd of cows which accompany the Company when they depart for Canton in the autumn.

I live on the first floor of this house, and a bell hangs below, for visitors to announce themselves, for I am the keeper, you might say, of a shop which has to be always open. A visit to Mr Chinnery's studio is included in the programme of all our visitors and I get a good deal of business that way. The bell also announces, by a prearranged signal, the arrival of my friends to whom I can shout, from my painting room above, to go away if I am busy and don't want to be disturbed. I don't mind young Harker even if I am working, and his conversation entertains me. He is intelligent and is vastly amused with life and his surroundings. He has just started making a collection of Chinese shop signs, which he takes down in his notebook when the proprietor has no trade card to offer him. I had no idea when I was making my purchases in China Street that the shop I patronised for tea is 'The Hall of the Ten Thousand and Midday Teas', or that I have been obtaining paper in the Macao bazaar from the 'Abode of Peace and Prosperity'. Harker has been searching for a sign appropriate to my establishment, and the best which he has found so far announces that 'Rich Customers are Perpetually Welcome'. I have no doubt that my landlord would think it very suitable, and that Augustine would consider it very undignified. Unfortunately, its peculiar significance would be lost on those who would most benefit by reading it—I refer to the clients who owe me money. The problem of making customers pay is one which I have never solved—hence all my difficulties in Bengal. I suppose that if all the money I am owed in fees after thirty-odd years of professional life were to be invested in the Funds I should have retired by now like a nabob, instead of being what the Bengal Hurkaru was pleased to describe as an 'absconding debtor'. It makes my blood boil to think of it. I—I, who am an acknowledged master of my profession, have exhibited at the Royal Academy since I was eighteen, who charged the highest fees of any artist in India and painted every notable there—in fact, it was impossible to be noted in India, if you had not been painted by Chinnery— to be described by a scurrilous little news-sheet circulating among a couple of hundred wooden-heads as an 'absconding debtor'! Practically every one of those wooden-heads owed me money when I left India. But they were not described by the Bengal Hurkaru as absconding debtors, or even as the rogues they were, not a bit of it. They sailed for home, laden with booty from years of peculation and pilfering, congratu-lating themselves on having in that booty a Chinnery which they had never paid for. I am glad to think they will have had to pay an equally dishonest Revenue Officer an extortion-ate sum to bring the picture into England.

What did they ever do for me, these potentates, who had all preferment in their hands? What did they do for my wife after I left India? What would they have done for my son, had he lived? But my son died at the age of twenty-one. He was not as strong as I am, an old ox who can carry any burden. The first Indian fever was the last. He had only just come out to Bengal from England. He tried to obtain a com-mission in the 47th Regiment, but it was given to another. The Company at first refused him permission to come out, and I obtained this condescension only after infinite trouble.

He was a very clever boy, and a good boy. When he arrived in Bengal I had not seen him since he was a child. I had so little time in which to know him, and yet I think he was very fond of me. At that time I was hard pressed for money (not an unusual state of affairs, but that time was worst than most), and had moved my abode temporarily into Serampur, some fifteen miles up-river from Calcutta, which was Danish territory. It was there my son joined me. New to the country, everything delighted him, and his pleasure was a source of constant delight to me. I had the highest hopes that the climate might suit him, and he was never ailing for a day until the fever took him. There was no woman at hand to make the sick bed less painful. Mrs Chinnery was spared the sight. She had remained in Calcutta. When I saw her again she had, for once, nothing to say to me. The loss of our son might have brought us together again, but that was more than could be hoped. An intimate friend once told me that I have behaved very ill to Mrs Chinnery. I do not think he was altogether right; I think I did my best in a situation not altogether of my making, until it became beyond all bounds of tolerating. But it is true that I failed, and we none of us like to find ourselves face to face with our failures. That is why I prefer to live here with Soldier.

CHAPTER 3

This morning I had no clean shirt to put on. Summoned Augustine. He was brief, and to the point. 'All shirts wash.' On inquiry, I elicited the information that I have less than half a dozen shirts left. Confound it, I shall have to press on with Dr Morrison, the heat notwithstanding. It was easier when I had a pupil or two in the studio to finish off these big jobs, but here I am all alone. I shall have to ask the Company for a little more on account: after all, the fee which they are paying is a ridiculous one for a work of this size and importance. It is detestable to have to worry always about money. Augustine asks me continually for money for the rent —I suspect he is related to my landlord and retains a certain percentage for himself 'all same old custom'. Let it wait. I know nothing of Portuguese bailiffs, but I suspect that they are fairly slow.

The Chinese tailor is another matter, I fear: he will no longer give credit. It is easier and quicker to get shirts made here than in London, and the stuff is as good. One only has to give out a shirt to the Chinese tailor in the morning, and back comes its fellow by nightfall, every bit as good. I believe if you were to give him an admiral's hat, a lord mayor's robe or what you will, he would bring you an exact duplicate by the next morning. The only thing you can't teach Chinamen is the law of perspective. At first I wondered if those slit eyes of theirs had some defect of vision which might explain their topsy-turvy ideas, and I even asked the Doctor about it. He discounted my theory, however.

I forgot my annoyance about the shirts, however, in walking with Harker. It was a beautiful morning with every promise of a hot day to come, and the air was still and breathless, but there was no mist. The islands were as clear as we see them usually only in the late autumn. We were so early that the storekeepers of the bazaar were still asleep behind their shutters, and the pedlars underneath their stalls. The boat people, the floating population, were all astir, however, and about their occupations. The sharp smell of the cooking fires which an old grandmother would be tending in the well of each boat, the shouted interchanges of conversation as men and women manœuvred their boats into position, and the shrill outcries of the children all carried straight to us on the still air, making up that compound of sound and smell which is waterfront life in this part of the world. We walked to the extreme limits of the bay, and before we turned to climb the hill we paused for a minute to watch the scene.

On the water some distance out a junk was lying at

anchor with her mat sails already hoisted while her crew drank their morning tea. Egg-boats manned by boat girls were already being paddled to and fro over the water. A dog on board an inshore junk set up a tremendous barking at our leaning there against the wall and making a leisurely inspection of his home, but he was a nice dog and barked with a broad grin on his face. Soldier at once jumped up on the wall to get a better view, trembling with eagerness. A duel of noise would have resulted had I not kept a tight hold of his throat. The boat dog, taken aback at the apparition of a foreign devil dog, retreated the length of the deck and eventually fell silent. The near-by sampans were populated only by old women, their decent black tunics and trousers faded with age and washing, and their scanty grey hairs screwed up neatly on their heads, and by many crawling children. The intermediate generations seemed entirely missing.

These old ladies looked at us with no very friendly eye, and we were just about to move off when an egg-boat grounded on the spit of sand alongside the wall with two very handsome young women on board. One stood at the stern and worked the single oar while her fine long plait of hair slapped from side to side with her exertions. This plait was tied with a coquettish bow of red ribbon which she proceeded to adjust, much in the manner of an English schoolgirl, as soon as she was free to relinquish her oar, while at the same time managing to flash a smile in our direction from under the handkerchief drawn over her head. The second girl sat amidships with a pile of fruit in front of her which she was sorting into baskets. The little round mat roof which covers the centre of these boats and gives them their name had been collapsed. This girl looked up at us, and ostentatiously returned to her work. Harker called out something to her in her own language. She jerked her head and uttered some monosyllable, but that was all the response. Harker tried again and got a longer answer this time, but she refused to look in his direction. Just as we were about to give up and go, she relented: standing up, she pointed to her fruit and called out something which I, of course, did not understand.

'She wants to sell us some fruit,' said Harker.

He tried a couple of sentences of double-Dutch on the girl. The only result was to send her into fits of titters in which her companion joined. The girl at the oar called out something which made them both laugh until they hid their faces in affected modesty. It was exasperating for Harker, the linguist, but he was determined to persevere, and he addressed the fruit girl again. This time she admitted to understanding him, and began collecting a selection of her wares. I wondered how she would manage for wrapping until I perceived that she had beside her a pile of large leaves, on one of which she laid her selection. Then came the problem of getting it to us—the boat could not come sufficiently far inshore for us to reach the parcel from the wall—but the other, with great ingenuity, extended her oar towards us with the leaf platter balanced on it. Harker threw the fruit girl a coin. She immediately put up two fingers and set up a clamour until he gave her another. At this the boat girl gave a final sally which appeared to refer to the two of us, then leaned once more to her oar, and the little craft shot off in search of other customers.

'What did she say?' I inquired.

'She said the young foreign devil was as mean as he looked poor, but the old devil must be rich: see how fat he is!'

Not exactly a bashful maiden, but the tanka-boat girls of Macao are not renowned for bashfulness, as many bachelors could testify. Independent, healthy and fearless, they are the only Chinese females except the very old to be seen freely abroad, and only they would flout the conventions of their race by embarking upon intimacy with a foreigner. Although the 'flower-boats' are a familiar sight on the river at Canton, and the inmates flaunt their charms quite openly before the foreign devils, no foreigners are permitted to resort to them, and even a near approach is resented. It is a curious light on the Chinese mind that they take it so violently amiss that a 'barbarian' should aspire to their public women.

The two girls were really quite handsome, the boat girl rather particularly so. Their faces were fresh and glowing with air and exertion, but the firm texture of the skin showed no coarseness or roughening. Their costume of loose trousers and looser jacket worn over them left a good deal to the imagination, but the girl who was rowing was delicate in build, and her feet and ankles were small and shapely. Nor did she appear to be bandy-legged which is a very common fault about here, due to the manner in which babies are carried in infancy, in a sling on the mother's back. I could make quite a good picture of her.

Harker returned to the American Company's house where he expected his teacher of Chinese to be waiting for him, and I set to work on Dr Morrison. I see that I shall have to resort to desperate measures if I am ever to have it finished before the hot weather really sets in—and we are half way through May already. There is no time to lose. I must return to my old tactics and shut myself up completely, with plenty of cold tea, while the working fit is on me.

Poor Soldier is terribly bored. He keeps wandering towards the verandah and sticking his nose between the pillars, and then withdrawing it with a sigh. He can't settle himself comfortably: if he lies in the sun he gets too hot, and if he lies in the shade he wants to return to the sun. Until I get through with Dr M I fear that he must put up with tedium, for I shall not have much time for him. The most I can manage, and that only in the early morning until such time as the heat makes it impossible, is my favourite promenade, the round ending with the ascent of Penha Hill. This is to me the most attractive vantage point on the whole peninsula. There is nobody else up there as a rule except a herdsman driving his goats on to the scanty herbage. One or two residents have summer bungalows on the summit, but the road up the hill which the Portuguese had begun to construct

24

earlier this spring was stopped by order of the Chinese mandarin, on the ground that the disturbance of their natural surroundings was unpleasing to the spirits of the near-by temple. I for one had every sympathy with the spirits, and was heartily relieved that the road got no farther.

On my next visit to the spot, I made a sketch of the southern front of Mr Bowie's deserted bungalow and of two goats which were reclining in graceful attitudes on the grass beside it, and went home to breakfast, at which Mr Bowie himself, to my great pleasure, joined me.

Mr Alexander Bowie, my old friend of Bengal days, came to Macao from Calcutta shortly after I did, and for very much the same reason. He was lucky enough, however, to have part of his fortune put away where his Bengal creditors could not reach it, so that he lives here comfortably enough, and has acquired a substantial business which seems to be thriving. But he is a real fish out of water, and never ceases to yearn for the old days of Calcutta. He makes me laugh, as some of his grievances are so comical. He was used to living like a real swell, trains of servants and peons running after him, troops of clerks at his beck and call, everything lavishly gilded and marbled, and he really enjoyed all this magnificence. The poverty, as he calls it, of his present establishment is a constant source of grief to him. I would myself prefer to be served by a couple of Chinese servants, industrious, ingenious and able to put their hand to anything, rather than by a rabble hanging on my footsteps and each performing a quarter of a task. The Chinese, in fact, would not condescend to become servants to foreigners at all, except for the purpose of becoming acquainted with foreign business, and thus bettering themselves. Bowie is shocked by this, as he is totally unable to comprehend it. He sees the Chinese as another race of Bengalis, slightly different in colour and dress, but placed on earth for the same purpose, and he is disconcerted when the nations will not fall into line with his conception of them. He retains all his Indian customs. He professes horror at the servants appearing before their masters with shoes on but with their heads uncovered, and has of course taken no trouble at all to find out what are the correct habits here, which I am sure his household has taken full advantage of. But he is the oldest friend I have, and I value his company greatly. In fact I find that his groans about the lost joys of Calcutta have a tonic effect on me. He does not get on invariably well with others for reasons which can easily be guessed. Young men such as Harker he tends to patronise on the assumption that he who has not seen Cossitollah or Chowringhee has never lived, and he relates endless anecdotes of the splendours of Calcutta society. Harker bears it all very well, but he considers that the Chinese name for Mr Bowie, which is 'the old story-telling devil' is entirely appropriate.

I have just found out, by the way, what my own appellation is. I am 'the old red-faced devil', and I have a reputation for a fierce temper. This is quite unjustified. In fact, there is no milder-tempered man than myself, provided I am not provoked. Since I spend my days endeavouring to live quietly and avoid provocation, it follows that if I am roused to anger, it must be the fault of someone else.

I understand Bowie, because when I first came to China I was as much at a loss as he and ready to compare everything to its disadvantage with the life I had left behind. Everything was alien to me at first—the sights, the sounds, even the smells seemed less spicy than before. The people around me were the wrong colour, and they wore unfamiliar clothes. After the passage of time, gradually I began to adapt myself. Little by little my eye became accustomed to the sober, uniform dress of the peasants and to the monotonous landscape of rice cultivation, interspersed with peaks of jagged rock. I became indifferent to the hostility of the inhabitants, while deriving pleasure from observing their way of life. But when I tell Bowie that there is as much interest for me in the Macao bazaar as in all the ballrooms of Calcutta, he thinks I have taken leave of my senses.

The crux of the matter is this, that in India we were living on conquered territory, among a subject race, while in this place we are living under the eye of the mandarin in the shadow of the vast territories of the Emperor of China, whose population has a traditional aversion to foreigners and their ways. It is this contrast which unconsciously affronts my old friend. But as Harker says, it is no use coming to China unless you are prepared to play the game, by which he means observe only such of the regulations governing the residence of foreigners as are strictly necessary to enable the rest to be evaded.

I attended at Mrs Haverill's house to give the lady her first lesson in drawing. She is an accomplished lady in every way. I was surprised to see, as well as an elegant drawing-room, a considerable library of books, all well kept. The lesson went quite well. The lady has sufficient application to make it quite a pleasure to instruct her, and if she settles down to work seriously she will have an agreeable and rewarding occupation. A taste for sketching serves to fill what would otherwise be idle hours in a tropical climate where most of the men and all the women I have known find it too much labour to read a serious book or engage in any form of study. Mrs Haverill, I learned this morning, has met this problem in her own way, with fair success: she looks after her late husband's library, collects native arts, and observes with interest what goes on about her.

I suggested Mr Bell's garden as the venue of our next lesson, where there is a pretty prospect and plenty of trees. This suited Mrs Haverill very well, as she has a pair of pet birds given her by Mr Bell and he has promised her another one which has not, so far, materialised. Mr Bell has become somewhat absent-minded in his old age, and Mrs Haverill, while not wishing to recall the promise to his memory, thinks that a little more judicious admiration of his aviary would put his mind in the necessary direction.

Mr Bell himself, however, was absent from his house when the day came, but we were readily admitted to the garden as he has given standing orders to his servants to this effect. The birds in the aviary were in fine form and Mrs Haverill was enraptured anew by them, especially with the famous bird of paradise, the pride of the collection. It took my fancy to see the two pretty creatures, one on each side of the bars, examine each other with mutual interest—for the birds are well used to admiration and perfectly tame. The garden is, of course, in the Chinese style with all the flowers in pots, but these are most artistically arranged to give gradations of colour. There are also walks cunningly laid out between rocks, and Mr Bell has as well a number of exotic trees, including a Bombay mango and a custard apple, and others whose names I do not know. I led my pupil to a seat near a banana tree, and told her to draw it. There were no other foreigners there, but I noticed a group of Chinese of a superior appearance standing near the house, deep in conversation with Mr Bell's steward. Of the old man himself there was no sign.

Mrs Haverill persisted bravely in her task for half an hour before she pleaded the heat as an excuse for desisting. I saw her back into her chair, and the bearers trotted off. I had no chair, having come on foot, and I turned towards my house down 'Bell's Lane', for so it has come to be called. Mr Bell arrived in China in 1785, and the house had belonged to his elder brother before him.

When I reached home, I asked Augustine where Mr Bell had gone.

'Gone to the village,' was the reply.

'What village?' I asked.

'Mr Bell's compradore have got house in Patane village. Mr Bell go to compradore's house. Today plenty Chinese men come to see Mr Bell. Compradore say, Mr Bell gone away, come another day.'

'What sort of men come to see Mr Bell?'

'Chinese men, all ask Mr Bell for money. Mr Bell today should pay. Mr Bell no have money today. So he go to the village.'

All was as clear as daylight. Today was a settling day, and Bell was unable to pay up, so he had tactfully absented himself. The convention was a convenient one so long as it was accepted. The village of Patane lies at most a mile from the centre of the town, but it was clearly far enough to secure Bell immunity, while the compradore exchanged the requisite civilities with the creditors. After all, there is little they can do against Bell—a man can't be ruined twice over, and his great age commands the respect of the Chinese. The trick made me smile—it reminded me of the old days in Serampur, only a day up-river from Calcutta, where all of us who were 'in difficulties' dwelt in perfect immunity, coming into Calcutta on Sundays to pay our visits.

The breathless heat of the day broke in a fine storm that evening. Standing on the verandah, I watched the junks and sampans in the open bay before the Praia Grande get under way. Propelled by mat sails and oars they made in the same direction, streaming along in a disorderly flock. They passed out of my sight under the brow of Penha Hill, but I knew that they would then pass the Battery Point, then the Ama pagoda, sacred to the Queen of Heaven, the beneficent goddess of seafarers, before crowding into the security of the Inner Harbour. The servants ran from room to room making fast the shutters—and then the wind and the rain arrived together.

Gradually the storm wore round, and about six in the evening I opened the shutters and emerged once more on to the verandah which was littered with leaves and small branches broken off the trees. In the street below my house all manner of debris was piled up in the gutters, where the storm rain was tearing down to the sea.

On the Praia Grande broken tiles litter the roadway, and children are picking among the flotsam cast up on the shore. But the sky is clear again, and the stark peaks of the islands rear themselves out of a sea which is rapidly subsiding back to its normal calm. The hot wind has gone tearing inland, over the paddy fields, hills and valleys of Canton province. There are fishermen wading by the edge of the water, their sampans bobbing beside them like riderless horses. They raise a shout of satisfaction when they recover a long tangle of net from just below the surface, and take no notice whatever of the foreign devils on the shore— the Portuguese ladies shrouded in their ugly outdoor draperies, with their escorts, and a handful of Englishmen chatting together, and exchanging notes of our experiences.

No one has suffered, but one of the Company's cow-herds, failing to reach shelter in time, was blown off his feet by the storm and carried down the hill, fortunately without injury to himself. The cows, more solid, remained earthbound.

The immediate aftermath of the storm has been a drop in the temperature. Of course, it will soon heat up again—we are in June—but the relief would be welcome, save for an unpleasant interruption. On the breakfast table there arrived a packet of newspapers, and a letter from Mrs Chinnery, all sent up to me by the courtesy of the Company. I could well have dispensed with the Company's kindness on this occasion. The mere sight of that letter spoiled my meal for me, as I knew that I should have to bring myself, sooner or later, to open it. There is always the possibility that Mrs C's letters may contain, beside the usual matter which I know by heart, news of my children, and I am not such an unnatural father as to cut myself off from them.

When Mrs Chinnery came out to India in 1819, we had not seen each other for very many years. I would have resisted her coming if I could. Our characters were not suited, and however much I needed a settled domestic life, I knew we two could never live together in peace, after we had been divided by so long a time and by such differences in our habits of life—although, whatever others may say, I can never accept that it was *my* conduct alone which caused the separation. She thought the fault was mine: I think it was no less hers. Feeling as we do, clearly it was impossible for us to resume domestic life after so many years. Mrs Chinnery, however, thought otherwise, and being a woman, and persistent, she got her way, and to India she came.

When we met again I know I did everything in my power to please her. I did my utmost to be conciliatory, I tried to modify my habits to suit those of a newly-arrived lady. It was all to no avail. Mrs Chinnery judged by her own standards, which are not and never have been mine, and by her standards she did not like what she found. Women are the devil to understand. Mrs Chinnery was not pleased to find that I had a pair of natural sons by one whom she obstinately persisted in regarding as an abandoned woman, but what really horrified her was the fact that at seven years old they had not been baptized! This she caused to be remedied without delay.

Mrs Chinnery was quite wrong about the boys' mother, but I myself knew nothing of her history. Sufficient to say that she was a good woman, and looked after me to the best of her ability. In those days when I first met her, I was a young man, and demanded nothing more of a woman than her sex. Rosa was a beautiful creature, and of the kindest and softest disposition. She accepted her position, such position as I was able to give her, and such security as I was able to offer her (at times precious little), with perfect compliance. I never knew why she had not been able to make a suitable marriage, which should have been easy enough. Heaven knows what would have become of her, had she lived, when my real troubles began. But she was spared them. A fever carried her off.

I ought to be accustomed to deathbeds, I have seen so many of them. It has been my fate to watch one person after another die young, all of them men and women I loved, my own son among them. I know what it is to leave a friend healthy and happy in the morning, and to see him carried to his grave before night. Then Calcutta mourns for one day, but each loss leaves a desolation behind it. I could not have known Rosa without contracting ties of custom, affection and respect—yes, respect, for it is impossible to live with a woman

31

without respecting her—which left me completely at a loss when they were broken. Work was my only consolation. Such was my condition when Mrs Chinnery came out to India.

The attempt to renew our domestic relations was hopeless, as I had foreseen. The effect on my work and my nerves was disastrous, while the expense of keeping up a suitable establishment was considerable. It became a matter of grave concern to myself whether I would continue to evade the persistence of my creditors long enough to appear at our daughter's wedding. However, the great day arrived, the pair were united, but not long afterwards I was forced to take myself up the river to Danish territory, to seek the protection of the King of Denmark until my situation should become less embarrassed. And money troubles never left me until I finally succeeded in making my exit from India.

Since I came to China, Mrs Chinnery has several times announced her intention of following me, and once she even took her passage. So far, I have always been able to dissuade her by a prompt remittance, but at the moment I am not well placed to ward off a threat by that particular means. If the letter contained a new menace, I knew there was nothing for it but to make a run for Canton.

However, when I broke the cover it was not too bad. Only the first degree of complaint: which means five hundred rupees. *That* means a call on Bowie, who, although he is a business man, has never yet failed me in a crisis. If he only knew it, it might be some consolation to him to think that the several pieces of my work which I have given him from time to time as tokens of friendship will amply repay him some day—although he may not be alive to see it. He has some good investments there.

CHAPTER 4

My dog, Soldier, has been lost. Everyone has been helpful. The Portuguese authorities have initiated inquiries, my friends have turned out in impromptu search parties and ranged all over Macao, Augustine has searched the bazaar, and Harker has drawn up numerous 'reward cards' which have been posted in the Chinese villages. These promise that 'even if the dog has been stolen—an inconceivable thing!', the finder will still be rewarded. But all this to no avail. No trace of Soldier has been found for a week, and it is no use continuing to hope. He is too large and powerful to be kept tied up somewhere against his will, and if he has not returned, it must be because he is dead. Nobody can say exactly when he disappeared. My last recollection is that he was lying near my feet in the painting room, occasionally turning an eye in my direction to see if I was proposing to make a move. Half an hour later, when I called him, he was not there. The servants must have let him out, but I shall never know the truth from them.

It is foolish, no doubt, to have one's life upset by the loss of a dog, but Soldier was rapidly becoming the partner of my existence. A ship's captain has kindly offered to procure me a pup of the same breed on his return voyage, and candidates have already been brought here for my inspection, but I don't want any other dog but Soldier. I would sooner keep a bird in a cage, like Bell.

Meanwhile, the summer advances relentlessly. Never before have I felt myself so much oppressed in Macao by the blazing heat which dances at midday over the harbour. This is so shallow that it might as well be a land-locked lagoon. There is no freshness from the water, only a dense humidity. Even to breathe the hot, heavy air is an effort. By contrast, the more languid I feel, and the more oppressed my nerves, the more I notice the inhabitants of this place become increasingly vociferous as the heat advances. Shouting, clattering, chatting, spitting, they carry on their occupations at every street corner. What draws the life out of us is the breath of life to them. As I pace the studio trying to work with my hands slippery with sweat, or lie on a long chair on my verandah praying for a breath of cool air, my ears are assailed by this fearful din. The background to Dr Morrison has become hateful to me: I hate the sight of the picture, yet I must finish it for the simple reason that I want to be paid what is still owing to me on it.

It was to escape from this that I agreed to make up a party with Mrs Fay, Mrs Haverill and John Harker to visit Green Island. The American Company supplied the transport, and the ladies, Harker and myself boarded their pleasure boat, while the servants and supplies followed in a fleet of sampans. Green Island lies in the Inner Harbour less than a quarter of a mile away, and we were there in no time. It may seem ridiculous to go to all the trouble of taking servants, furniture, and vast quantities of food, in order to go and eat it on an island within a stone's throw of home, but when one's life is physically circumscribed by the limits of Macao, these little expeditions have a tonic effect out of all proportion to the distance involved. Once ashore, the first step was to decide where we should establish our base. There are several well-known spots which are generally selected for this purpose, and the merits of each one were discussed exhaustively. At last the ladies made up their minds, and we proceeded in that direction. Green Island was formerly in the hands of the Jesuit Order, until they were dispossessed of it and all their other property and evicted from Macao. The Jesuits originally constructed some buildings, which were pulled down by the order of the Mandarin, but they continued to farm the island until the day of their departure. As a result, there are many exotic and beautiful trees remaining. A grove of these marked our chosen destination, a charming spot in the shadow of one of the ruined buildings, where a stone terrace still remained. All was very quiet and peaceful: we might have been a hundred miles from the bazaars of Macao. A few Chinese peasants were hoeing at the plots they had planted out in one of the abandoned gardens, but they took no notice of us.

Presently, finding the view a trifle restricted where we were, I wished to walk a little farther on and find a place to sketch. I made my excuses, and leaving the ladies to Harker, I skirted round the back of the ruined building, in which the servants were preparing a cookhouse. Several of the chickens destined to appear at our tiffin were tethered by the leg to convenient bushes. Following a path which was strange to me, I came out on a little bay on the north side of the island. Here on the shore was one of the boat-dwellings of Macao—an old fishing junk drawn up on the beach and used for habitation. A sort of gallery had been constructed on the landward side from which projected bamboo poles for the drying of washing. A lean-to roof made of palm leaves had been put up to give added accommodation, and innumerable little boltholes had been cut out and porches and projections tacked on here and there. An upturned sampan was drawn up on the beach, and several shaven-headed children in cotton clothes were playing round it. Of adult occupants there was no sign, until the inevitable old woman in rusty black garments, her trousers turned up above her skinny shins, appeared round the corner of the shore. She caught sight of me sitting quietly on the rocks above her and started to run, letting out a volley of piercing yells all the while. The children likewise took to their heels, and they all bolted for the shelter of their residence. I was not much surprised by this scene, and I settled myself quietly to sketch. Usually the inhabitants emerge once again when they have got used to the novelty of a foreign devil at close quarters, and sure enough, in about five minutes a woman appeared from some aperture and made her way down the beach, carrying two wooden pails of water. She was not the wrinkled old granny, however, but a much younger woman dressed in the smock and trousers of the boat girl, with a handkerchief bound over her head, and a big wicker hat placed on top of that. Placing the pails by the upturned sampan, she sat down and began to fiddle with something she took from the boat. All this time I knew she was perfectly aware of my presence, and I sensed that the glances which she was sending in my direction from under the rim of the big hat were not unkind. I got up, and strolled down the shore. As I got nearer, she gave me a quick glance and then dropped her eyes to her work again, very busily. What I could see of her was quite pleasing, although most of her face except her cheekbones and her eyes was deeply shadowed by the big hat. Her clothing was neat and clean, and a fresh white apron showed under her blue cotton jacket. There were bracelets upon either wrist—such slender wrists—and a magnificent plait of glossy black hair hung down her back, intertwined with red cord. Her little bare feet, brown and muscular but very slender, seemed to me the prettiest I ever saw. I passed as close to the boat as I dared and took a closer look. I was sure I had seen this girl before, but with the baleful eye of the grandmother bent on me from inside the hovel only a few yards away, I did not dare to address her. As I drew level with her it seemed to me that I descried a demure smile under the shadow of the hat, a smile which disclosed little white pearly teeth, but I was obliged to pass on and round the angle of the shore as if my sole object had been to walk from that bay into the next.

Once round the corner, I was surprised to see on the path above me the white figure of a woman, waving a handkerchief. I made my way in her direction, and found it was Mrs Haverill.

'I am quite lost,' she exclaimed, as soon as I came up to her. 'This is what comes of wandering away from the others. If you had not arrived, Mr Chinnery, I should by now be falling into a panic. I came so far, without realising it, that I have not the least idea how to get back.'

Well, the size of Green Island is such that the ordinarily active person could walk clean round it and arrive back at his starting point in the space of half an hour, but of course I did not point this out to Mrs Haverill. Instead, I volunteered to escort her back to the rendezvous. I offered her my arm for support, she took it, and we began to make our way through the groves of plantains and bananas which spread their fantastic leaves on either side. Mrs Haverill remarked on the heat: I replied appropriately, throwing in a compliment or two which Mrs Haverill received with charming simplicity. In fact, by any standards Mrs H would be regarded as a charming woman, and in the East that counts as a raving beauty. A fine figure, too: although how much is attributable to a good pair of stays is not always obvious on superficial inspection. When the path became steeper, I felt that a little more assistance was required of me. I ventured to shift my arm to my companion's waist, and made two discoveries, one, that Mrs Haverill was not wearing stays, and two, that I was not as indifferent to female charms as I had latterly imagined myself to be. I stole a glance at my companion's face: she was perfectly calm. I wondered that my agitation had not communicated itself to her, then I thought that I detected on Mrs Haverill's face a shade of self-satisfaction. She knew! When the path became more level, Mrs Haverill disengaged herself from my arm and thanked me in the most natural manner. We arrived at our destination with myself in a sweat as if I had run up a hill, and my companion as cool as a cucumber.

On noticing my heated condition, kind Mrs Fay at once asked me why I did not remove my coat, saying that the ladies would excuse my shirt sleeves, and I was obliged to explain that by reason of my tailor's obdurate refusal to deliver without seeing ready cash, my attire left so much to be desired that I could not venture to do so. Mrs Fay laughed heartily at this tale of a shirt, but Mrs Haverill turned her beautiful eyes on me with wordless sympathy.

Later I found myself alone with her again. I asked her permission to make a sketch of her. She was lying back in her chair with her face turned away from me, but the face is only one aspect of a fine woman, and Mrs Haverill's figure

37

was displayed to advantage by the attitude she had chosen (I have no doubt she knew it).

'Surely, Mr Chinnery, you can find a subject with more local colour—one of those peasants working down there.' She pointed.

'True, but you can't expect me to sketch a man a quarter of a mile off.'

'You could ask him to come nearer.'

'I expect Mr John Harker could, but he is not here.'

'You make a great many difficulties, Mr Chinnery. I see that I shall have to be the inadequate substitute.' She began to sit up.

'No, no, don't move, I beg you. Stay as you are, I like the attitude you are in, and I find the back of your neck, if I may say so, uncommonly expressive.'

'I am not to be flattered, Mr Chinnery, by one who has said that the true curve of beauty is to be found in the back of a Chinese pig—or was it a buffalo?'

'Pigs and buffalo are all very well in their way, and I don't usually find anything better on my morning walk, but you must not think that because I married the ugliest woman in the Orient, I am indifferent to the charms of the ladies.'

The answer came quickly—was it perhaps a shade too quick?

'I don't think you are very kind to Mrs Chinnery, to speak of her in such a way.'

'Not kind to Mrs Chinnery!' I exclaimed. 'Heavens, what more can I do for Mrs Chinnery than I have done! My kindness to Mrs Chinnery is the reason why I have no shirts.'

'Why don't you send for Mrs Chinnery to join you in Macao? That would save you the expense of two establishments?'

'I know Mrs Chinnery too well to suggest such a thing.'

'But suppose your wife comes to join you, you cannot refuse to receive her?'

'I shall do what I have done before when danger threatened. I shall fly to Canton and throw myself upon the mercy of the Company.'

'That must be an extraordinary life, with no ladies, no amusements, nowhere to go, no occupation beyond business. Whatever would you find to do there, Mr Chinnery?'

'I would have my work, just as the others have theirs. Believe me, most of the men enjoy themselves thoroughly. Six months' married bliss out of twelve is quite enough for many of them. There are several old fellows there who would not come away, if they had the chance.'

Mrs Haverill remarked that she feared they must be eccentrics.

Of course, that is true. Most foreigners in the East become to a greater or lesser degree eccentric. Some of them embrace the life around them to the extent of living on vegetables, or retiring into monasteries to devote themselves to the study of religions, but far more become stiff, cold and suspicious, the result of years of isolating themselves from their surroundings. When the newcomer arrives in the East, the first contact flashes upon him with a blinding light. He strives to capture and communicate it, so he paints, if he has the ability, or if he has none, he writes long letters home bursting with description. He tries to communicate his sensations to those about him, unconscious of the fact that his companions have long since reached the stage of indifference, but slowly this dawns upon him and he feels the first chill. Then everyone combines to tell him that the country is dirty, the natives are thieves, liars and perverts, and their rulers are beneath contempt. Soon he begins to say the same things himself. And so it ends. The infinitely rich and exciting life about him poses a challenge which he prefers to ignore. Instead, the foreigner lives in a world which he has made for himself, a little cage just big enough to carry on the daily round. All that is left to him is eccentricity. It is his only way of expressing himself.

I could have explained all this to Mrs Haverill, but I was

perfectly content to accept her gentle strictures, and all too soon the return of the others broke up our tête-à-tête.

There was a sequel, though, to this expedition. A few days later a packet was brought to me, and with it a note from Mrs Haverill. In the note, Mrs Haverill wrote that she ventured to hope that the garments enclosed, which she found among the effects of her late husband, might serve me until my tailor could be prevailed upon to resume work. The packet contained one dozen very fine linen shirts. I tried one on straight away, and found it a very good fit. I did not of course know the late Mr Haverill, but somehow I had never pictured him as a *fat* man. Moreover, the shirts seemed remarkably well preserved for garments which have been put by in this climate for a matter of years.

I was wearing one of the shirts when I called at Mrs Haverill's house to thank her. My heart was beating so violently that I was near to choking. I did not know what to think. Confound all women! A man is helpless before them, they have so much adroitness, such a way of dangling a man on a string while meaning nothing at all. For all I know, Mrs Haverill bestows marks of her regard equally among the bachelors of Macao. Yet I could have sworn at Green Island that she was not indifferent to me, and she could hardly have been unaware of my feelings towards her. I had bought in the bazaar a caged bird for her. It was a small finch, of a kind I had not seen before, with brightly spotted plumage. The vendor assured me that 'birdee velly good, he sing plenty-plenty,' and from time to time the little creature gave out a loud trill of song, then fell silent again. Mrs Haverill received it with rapture, saying it was a kind she had long desired to possess. We stood for quite a long time in front of the big cage into which she liberated it, to join a crowd of other brilliant twittering creatures. Finally I took her hand and led her to a chair.

'Madam, will you not sit down?' I said.

'You give me no choice, Mr Chinnery,' she said, with a smile.

'You must allow a short man his vanity, madam. Standing beside you, I feel no less than a fool. I am not a good match for your elegance and your beauty.'

Why I said this, I do not know, except that I was certainly carried away by the proximity of the lady. In truth I don't care a rap for Mrs Haverill's inches, or my own lack of them. This is not a defect which has ever troubled me where women are concerned. Mrs H was gazing at me in faint surprise. I went on:

'You must laugh at me, madam, as much as I laugh at myself.'

'I can assure you that I do not laugh at you, Mr Chinnery, although you must amuse yourself by making fun of us all, and of yourself as well. When you give these whimsical accounts of your own defects—and those of others—I never feel the least desire to laugh.'

'Madam, I gather that you do not approve of my conversation.'

'You are a wonderful artist, Mr Chinnery, and you cannot conceal that, but when you speak you seem to want to hide your other qualities.'

'I have never hidden anything from you, and you ought to know that. I am incapable of dissimulation where you are concerned.'

At this point I found it hard to continue, the presence of this charming woman at close quarters was having its effect on me. I raised her hand, which was within reach, to my lips; she tried to withdraw it, but I would not let it go. We were sitting on two chairs, side by side. Anything more uncomfortable and less suited to the occasion it would be hard to find. On the other side of the drawing-room was a sofa. I rose, still holding Mrs H's hand in mine, and led her to it. She was too astounded by my audacity to resist, and followed me like a lamb, with the result that we were installed on the sofa with the minimum of disturbance. I obtained possession of both hands, against token resistance. The sight of Mrs Haverill's bosom rising and falling under her light muslin dress did nothing to calm my state of mind. I poured out hasty words: I could not tell if she were angry or not, as she kept her face resolutely turned away. Her pliant waist invited my arm, but Mrs H gave me no encouragement and I could not tell if her reluctance was real or feigned. I flung myself at her feet while not relinquishing her hands, and by this move forced her to look at me. I obliged her to acknowledge that my passion was real, and it became evident that I had kindled a response. I was no longer detaining Mrs Haverill's hands by force, she no longer turned her head away from me—and at that moment her Macanese maid-servant approached along the verandah.

With indescribable presence of mind Mrs Haverill dropped a handkerchief from her sleeve to the floor. I recovered it from where it lay, thus justifying more or less my situation. I restored the elegant trifle to the lady and stood up, slightly blown. Very shortly afterwards I took my leave. Many emotions boiled within me as I left that house, and certainly relief was one of them. I knew that Mrs Haverill was not as innocent as she seemed. Her quickness when the maid interrupted us was incomparable, and could only come from long experience. That woman could make a perfect fool of me!

CHAPTER 5

A most irritating thing has come to pass in my establishment. I am well used to the depredations of cockroaches, lizards and beetles of all kinds, but in the last few nights a predator of much greater size and capacity has been at large in my studio. The corners of canvases have been chewed, likewise any oily rags which were within reach, and even my paints have been attacked. Augustine says it is rats. I detest these creatures, and the thought that they may next invade my bedroom is a horror. I held a conference with Augustine.

He said that the rats have come because there is now no dog in the house. I must replace Soldier without delay, or 'Much better catch cat.'

I still do not want another dog. The pain of Soldier's loss is too fresh. I do not particularly want a cat, but rats are infinitely worse, and if a cat will deal with these, then it can be tolerated. So I told Augustine to procure a cat. What drove me to this final step was being woken up by something running over my face, as I lay in bed. Half asleep, I jumped up and threw whatever it was away from me. It turned out to be a cockroach: this was bad enough, but it might have been a rat.

The cat duly arrived, and took up residence. It is a young female, thin and underfed looking, as are most of her kind in this part of the world. When I came back from my evening walk, I found her in the painting-room, tied by a string round her neck to the table leg. On seeing me, the poor creature immediately rushed to take cover under a big chair, so I could not attempt to make her acquaintance. I was rather taken aback to find her in my apartments, having assumed that she would be confined to the lower regions, through which the rats would presumably have to pass before they gained the upper floor. Augustine, entering then, made it clear, however, that the cat's post is above stairs, as the rats come up the outside of the house, and get into the studio by the verandah. I inquired whether the cat had been fed, and was told that it had had its rice. (This was no more than literally true, for Cantonese cats as a general rule live on rice.)

I proceeded to eat my own dinner, but the thought of the skinny captive in the next room smote me, and I took some chicken bones which still had a little meat on them, and with the bones coaxed her out from under the chair. The meat proved irresistible, and she fell on the bones, crunching them until only a few gnawed fragments remained. As she opened her mouth to its fullest extent to encompass a bone, her eyes crumpled up into slits which gave her a most comical expression of ferocity, in conjunction with her fiercely bristling whiskers. As the cord round her neck seemed to me to be uncomfortably tight, I took it off. She made no attempt to hide again, but sat up and embarked upon a prolonged toilet, so I was able to take a good look at her. Her thinness apart, she is a pretty little animal with a good deal of white on her face, extending over her chest and half way down her legs. Her back is nondescript in colour, rather more grey than brown and quite nicely marked. Her tail is long, but marred by a permanent kink in it near its tip. When I returned to the other room, she did not at once follow me, but jumped into a chair, where she crouched with watchful eyes. Later in the evening she ventured an exploration, and looking up from my book I saw her gazing at me from the threshold. She quartered the room in which I was and the bedroom with great thoroughness, investigating everything and sniffing into drawers. She stood on her hind legs the better to examine the bed. Finally she came back to where I was, and crouched down within reach of my hand. I reached out and stroked her warm, elastic fur. Immediately a purring arose which seemed out of all proportion to her small body, so I concluded that she felt herself to be at home.

When I went to bed, I put the cat back into the studio and closed the door which communicates with my bedroom, though this is usually open to permit a current of air. I felt that Puss had better take up her duties without delay. Hardly had I got to sleep, however, when a most persistent rattling of the door handle was set up, mingled with plaintive cries. I turned a deaf ear, and tried to compose myself to sleep, but I had reckoned without the ingenuity of a Chinese cat. There was a further outburst of rattling, and then in some way she must have managed to depress the latch, for the door opened of itself. The next thing I knew was that the cat had crept under the bedcurtains and was scrambling up on to the bed. With loud purrings she proceeded to establish herself on my feet.

Well, I could have put her back in the studio and locked the door, but this would have meant finding the key, and in any case I had no desire to be kept awake all night by her battling to get out. I decided to make the best of it as things were, and we settled down together. Puss was persuaded to move off my feet, and she curled herself up at the bottom of the bed. Once or twice in the night I must have touched her as I turned over, for a sleepy purr arose, but otherwise she was perfectly quiet until half-past-six next morning, when she woke me by scratching at the shutters, wanting to go out. I obliged her by opening them for her, half expecting to see her take a flying leap into the garden and vanish for ever, but no, she proceeded to make a minute investigation of the flower pots which stood ranged along the verandah, selected one in a secluded corner, and returned into the room to wait for breakfast.

Augustine later pointed out to me with delight that there was no sign of any visitation from rats. I did not disclose to him that the rat-catcher had spent the night sleeping soundly under my mosquito curtains. Perhaps the aura of her presence is enough. She gave an excellent demonstration of her skill, however, when I was dressing. A cockroach tumbled out of the garments I was about to put on, and in a flash Puss was on it. I have always thought the cockroach to be one of the swiftest living creatures, but it was no match for the cat. She allowed it to scuttle within a few inches of safety, and then flattened it with a contemptuous blow of her paw.

Puss's diet causes me some concern. Augustine says firmly that cats eat rice. The cat seems perfectly happy to eat whatever I do, but I consider that the proper food for cats is milk. Now cows' milk is a commodity in very short supply, as the only cows in Macao belong to the Company. I have therefore instructed Augustine to procure buffaloes' milk daily which he has now arranged, although plainly he thinks that I am mad. The cat drinks it avidly, and although she remains nearly as thin as before, her coat is wonderfully glossy, and her whiskers bristle more magnificently than ever. Meanwhile she is developing into an amusing companion. Unlike Soldier, and all the other dogs I have kept, she makes no effort to accommodate her habits to mine, although at times she shows a definite preference for my company. While I work she is usually to be found perched on the top of some cupboard or on a high shelf from which she can survey the studio, and at the same time keep an eye on what is going on in the trees beyond the verandah. She does not sleep, but squats with her forepaws straight out before her, looking like a Chinese god on a roof tile. As it gets on towards evening, she comes to life, yawns occasionally with a generous gape of her pink mouth, then licks a paw and finally drops on to the floor. She pads over to the verandah, where she sits staring into the darkness where the cicadas sound interminably. I have wondered what it is she watches, hour after hour, until I have retired for the night. Usually I have not been long in bed before she comes back, squeezes under the curtains, and takes up her usual place, but there are times when she stays out there all night.

I have not got another Soldier, but I see that I have acquired a companion who will not hesitate to adapt my ways to hers.

Part Two

CHAPTER 6

Today Dr Morrison was finished, the last touch was laid to the canvas. I am finished, too. I know this condition of mind, and body, and I know it has to run its course. It brings an immense flatness, a boredom and desolation in which I have to force myself to remember that life is beautiful, and the future a hope of more beauty. Nothing can drive away this awful sensation that my surroundings have nothing more to offer and that I have sucked life dry. I am afraid that I shall never paint another good picture.

No one in my household can share this mood with me. Augustine, harassed one would think by his debts, mothers-in-law, and no doubt hordes of dependants, is always smiling and imperturbable. Puss licks her sleek paws, dismisses the remembrance of yesterday's mouse, and concentrates on to-morrow's. In the meantime she drinks my buffalo milk, and lies yawning in the sun. This stranded town, washed up on a peninsula in the China Sea, has become my prison. Here I, Bell, Bowie and the rest of us tread our little round, and live out our days.

I have had this disease so many times, and yet I have never become immune to it—this horror of living in exile. I remember my other attacks. I had a bad one in Serampur, after the death of my son, John. Serampur is even smaller than Macao. The flag of Denmark flies over a little enceinte perched beside the river. The only Dane in the place is the Governor. Two or three streets at the most: the stone houses could be counted on the fingers of both hands. The Governor's palace, a gingerbread castle, with the Governor's lady's pet donkeys browsing on the lawn. Most of the stone houses belong to missionaries of the Baptist persuasion, who have made this place a centre of activity. They have even built a so-called College and filled it with little black Baptists. The population consists (or consisted when I was there) of debtors, missionaries and beggars. I know every inch of Serampur. Outside the walls a blank, dusty space, then nothing but the jungle stretching away as far as the eye can see: jungle, the river, rice fields, temples and more jungle.

Company is not a cure for my ailment. I feel too heavy-hearted to pursue my flirtation with Mrs Haverill. The cure must come from within. Good meals are a help. Exercise is also good.

This morning I abandoned Penha Hill for another route. I walked through the town, past the shuttered shops, past the closed grilles of the churches, the Senate House bolted and barred, and on to the Praia Manduco, the quayside of the Inner Harbour. The Praia is lined with godowns, foreign and Chinese, and the waterside is lined with junks, several rows of them, and at every landing place there jostles a crowd of tanka-boats. Coolies sit in the dust with their carrying poles at their feet, waiting to be hired. They sleep, they wake, they eat, they spit, they gamble; every want is supplied by the hawkers who are constantly on the trot with their portable stoves, shouting their wares and banging their clappers. The boat girls chatter among themselves like a flock of magpies, while every now and then one of them bends to her single scull and sends her little boat shooting out into the glittering harbour. At dawn today the boat people were letting off fire-crackers in honour of some auspicious occasion, and the smell of burnt powder still hung heavy in the air as I passed by. There were large red characters pasted up on the godown walls, but I could not tell what they signified. I walked on until I came to the American Company's landing stage which is at the far end of the Praia. There should have been a watchman, but there was no sign of him in his little hut. A single sampan bobbed gently beside the quay. The inevitable old woman crouched in the stern appeared to be sound asleep, while the baby slung on her back in a red cotton sling was either asleep or dead. A dog ran up to me, barked and ran away again. I drew out my sketch-book.

'Master!'

The voice seemed to come from below. I looked down and saw an egg-boat close to the shore, held there by a single oar in the hands of a Chinese girl—my fair unknown of Green Island!

'Master wanchee catch boat? Master wanchee go what side?'

As I walked towards the steps she sculled towards the landing to meet me. To my surprise I saw no other boats about: the usual flock of boat women who pester you if you go anywhere near the water were elsewhere. It was only later that I realised that it is prohibited for these girls to take passengers from any other than the recognised landing points, and the American Company's steps is not one of these. The girl worked the boat in as close as she could, and then began nodding and beckoning. From here we were quite hidden from the Chinese customs stations and from the main part of the Praia. I don't know what made me respond to the invitation, but I clambered into the boat and stowed myself under the little circular straw canopy. There was a low seat inside on which I squatted. The boat seemed quite clean. The girl fired off a string of names in Chinese. I could not understand a syllable, so I pointed to Green Island and the boat's head was turned in that direction.

The last time I had made this trip I was in convoy with a smart craft crewed by the American Company's boatmen. Now I was sitting alone in the bottom of a tanka-boat with the water running a few inches from my backside, in the charge of a Chinese girl of unknown capabilities and independent temperament. All I could see of her as I peered out of my straw cabin was her trousered legs and bare feet. From time to time as she swung to the oar her pigtail fell forward like a live black snake. Her little feet fascinated me as they shifted their position on the planks. I was watching them

49

as she ran the boat on the shore at Green Island so suddenly that I was thrown off my seat and fell on my back, which made her laugh, of course. I found that we had landed on the open beach in a little cove which I recognised at once: there in front of us was the banana grove in which I had wandered with Mrs Haverill. I climbed the beach and sat down. It was earlier in the day than last time, the air was fresher, the lights and shadows were different and the mountains not as stark and bare as they would show themselves to be in the blinding light of noon. No life was in sight. For some reason this secluded beach seemed to me intolerably oppressive. I had brought a sketch-book with me, but found no inclination to make use of it. I descended the shore again to where my Chinese girl was squatting beside her boat. To see if I could get a spark of interest from her, I turned over the pages of my sketch-book until I came to the drawing which I had made of the boat-dwelling, and showed her the page. I could not be sure that she recognised it—most Chinese cannot make head or tail of a European drawing or painting. True, she laughed, showing remarkably pretty, even teeth, but that meant nothing. As well as the pretty teeth, I noticed that her skin was not pock-marked. She had on bracelets of some stone which resembles jade. I was about to take the book back again when she began turning the pages. The first drawing which appeared to catch her interest was one of my own street. I attempted to address her in a way which she would understand.

'This b'long my house.'

She peered at it, turning the book this way and that.

'This one b'long *your* house.'

'Ha?'

I turned back to the sketch of the boat-dwelling and this time I think she understood it. But we were not able to go on from this promising beginning for someone, unseen to me, must have come into view in the banana grove and the girl backed away, beckoning me to follow, saying something about 'Go home.' She pushed the boat off and I had no option but to get in, wetting my feet thoroughly in the process. I got no sympathy, of course, from the heartless girl. She herself was wading to get the boat out and then lightly sprang on board, with her cotton trousers wet to the knee. Directly we were under way, and heading for the distant Praia at a smart pace. Nearing the shore we entered a dense mass of sampans and egg-boats, but my girl threaded her way between them with a wonderful dexterity, and brought the stern of her boat against the public landing steps. I fumbled for my purse and handed her a coin which she seized and examined. 'Two piecee,' she hissed, barring my escape to the quay.

I shook my head and made to pass her. The boat rocked violently.

'Two piecee.'

The boat gave an extra violent lurch and I clutched at the oar which the girl had just stepped and which effectively barred my progress. I am quite sure she did it purposely. The inhabitants of the surrounding boats were beginning to take an interest as were the passers-by on the Praia. The girl began to talk vociferously, no doubt about the enormous distances she had rowed me. I looked round in desperation. Of course there was no sign of an English-speaking Chinese, and the mandarin's men who are supposed to control these girls and the fares which they charge were asleep in the hoppo-house. I was in a predicament and she knew it! There was nothing for it but to produce the only other coin my purse contained, which I knew was far too large. The girl took it with only a token protest, and while she was examining it I hastily stepped ashore and hurried away in case she should follow me. When I looked back from a safe distance, I could not distinguish her in the swarm of boat women rocking on their oars, all as indifferent to the foreign devil as if he had never existed.

The way I had taken, the first which came to hand, led me through the Chinese bazaar. I stopped to recover breath before a carpenter's shop and peered into the dim and odoriferous interior. The occupants regarded me with hostility but without interest: the same thing happened in the shop next door which was devoted to the Chinese pharmacopoeia. Only in the larger shops frequented by foreigners which sell such objects as ivory figures, fans, carvings, lacquered boxes and so on, is any effort made to attract the visitor by offering a show of civility.

I turned down the lane leading into the centre of the town via St Paul's Church. Between here and my house I passed St Domingos, St Peter, St Augustine, St Joseph and St Lawrence. By making a trifling detour I could have included Saints Clara and Francis, still leaving over St Antonio for another day. All these churches minister to a Portuguese population officially reckoned at 4,000 souls, and Heaven knows what is reckoned to be Portuguese here. The afternoon siesta produces some very curious progeny.

The sun was beginning to pour heat into the streets as I climbed the narrow lane to my house—the stairs were a final effort. It is very pleasant to lie on a rattan chair on my verandah while my little cat crouches on the balustrade sniffing the warm, lazy wind which will drop as the sun mounts to its height in the sky and annihilates us with its glare. In the afternoon the shutters will go up, as my neighbours retire inside their houses to drowse. It would be pleasant to go on sitting here, but I must get to work. Dr Morrison and his disciples are finished, the canvas is gone, their place is empty. I must fill it by painting another good picture, at least painting as well as I know how. Left to my own choice, I should paint a landscape, but a fancy portrait sells better and I have the subject ready to my hand: my Chinese lass from the boat!

As soon as possible I acquainted Mr Harker with what I had in mind. He joined in the idea with enthusiasm, and made light of all difficulties. First of all, as to finding the girl, Harker was certain that this could be done through the offices of the American Company's boatmen. He pointed out that Augustine would be useless as an intermediary with the boat people. The only contact could be through another member of the same tribe. When the girl was found, as he had no doubt she would be, it was only a question of settling the terms with her, of bargaining, in fact. Harker thought the girl would be perfectly ready to sit for me, for a consideration. The boat-people are hardly under the hand of the civil authorities: bold, hardy, resourceful, and possessed of mobility and independence, they pretend to bow before the will of the mandarins but in fact do pretty much as they please.

Much Hodgson's Pale Ale was drunk while we debated ways and means. Harker asked if it had to be that particular girl: I answered Yes. In the ordinary way one Chinese is as good as another, so much alike are these people in all their characteristics, as witness the variety of roles in which my cook has appeared, but in order to produce the picture which I had in mind, some flash of spirit would be necessary to illuminate the dull countenance of the average boat girl—and that flash of spirit my girl certainly had. I felt immediately drawn to her as a subject. My boat girl was the only Chinese woman so far to attract my attention, and it would be only honest to admit that she is the only Chinese girl who has ever looked twice at *me*.

'That is settled, then,' said Harker. 'My head man will find her and discuss terms. And now where do you think you are going to paint her?'

I replied, in my studio, naturally.

'That is out of the question,' said Harker. 'Your house is right in the centre of the town. She could not fail to be seen.'

Of course he was right. It could not be publicly known that I was painting the girl. The mandarin would want 'squeeze'; if not, there would be exactions on all sides to prevent the girl being reported to him, and her services would become very expensive indeed. My own servants and Augustine, although not parties to the transaction, would also expect to get a share. My heart sank at the idea of all this trouble and expense, and I was ready to abandon the project when Harker suggested that I should bring all my gear down and paint her where we were, in his own house.

I must explain at this point that Harker had left Mrs Fay's house and our conversation was taking place in another house which the American Company rented on the Praia Manduco. Part was used for the purposes of the office, but there were living-quarters which were occupied by the bachelor members of the firm when in Macao. I fancy that Harker, now fully restored to his normal state of health, was not averse to regaining his freedom, but the reason for his move was that Mrs Fay was getting the main house ready to receive her daughter and niece, those two rare birds who were expected to arrive very shortly, and his rooms were required for the young ladies.

'This house is capital for the purpose—look at the number of ways there are of getting in and out! The girl can be brought in without the servants seeing her at all, and if there's an alarm she can slip out through the office and be back on board her boat in a wink, while we could stand a siege up here!'

These words, I must confess, made me feel decidedly uneasy. I pictured in my mind's eye the mandarin and all his braves surrounding the house and bringing up their painted artillery while Harker ran up the American flag: but it was too late to draw back. Instead I began to worry if the girl would insist on bringing a chaperone. I could not stand some hideous Chinese crone staring at me while I worked.

'If she agrees to come at all, I do not expect she will insist on formality,' was Harker's view.

I told him he would have to stay by, and interpret for me. I have known in my time quite a number of misunderstandings with female sitters, and I know one cannot be too careful. I am becoming much too deeply involved with Mrs Haverill. Yesterday we were sitting alone together in her drawing-room. I had only to put out my hand . . . but thank

God, some prudence restrained me. I do not think there would have been opposition to my advances. But there would, afterwards, have been such a confounded *fuss*. Mrs H is a very fine woman, she is completely wasted in Macao where there is no one to appreciate her real worth, she has been kindness itself to me, but she would run my life and that I cannot abide.

To return to the girl, I am really a little frightened of what I have undertaken. Yet I am anxious to make a start, while the idea is fresh in my mind. There is nothing for me but to go home and wait for news from Harker, that the affair has been arranged.

Well, the thing is done. Heaven alone has kept count of the go-betweens, aunts, sisters and mothers who took part in the negotiations, but at last terms were agreed and the young woman came for the first sitting. It was not at first very promising. At first she giggled without cease, and then became awkward beyond all words. I was about to give up in despair and send her away, when she became bored with her own antics and by chance fell into almost the pose I should have chosen, sitting on the ground, or rather, on a little low stool hardly worthy of the name of seat, with one foot advanced and her arms folded on her hat placed at the side of her. Her head tilted at just the right angle. She was wearing a clean cotton tunic and trousers, the latter being so voluminous as to resemble a skirt, and a freshly laundered white under-jacket of which part could be seen. On her head she wore a handkerchief folded corner-wise with the two long ends tied under her chin. The effect was charming.

After I had got the girl settled it was easy enough. I worked quickly and well, undisturbed by the comings and goings in the background, for in spite of all that Harker could do, the inhabitants of the house were each anxious to catch a glimpse of what was going on. When I had done as much as I could, I told the girl to go, and arranged, by Harker, when she was to come back (she had no difficulty in understanding him now, I noticed). She gave me a final smile, then pulled her kerchief over her face and padded out on bare feet.

She is a pretty little thing, and I think the picture will be effective. I have been considering the background and this morning the idea came to me—what could be better than her own boat-dwelling on the shore. The girl seated at the side of that, with the sea and the mountains behind her. That will make an impression in the Academy.

CHAPTER 7

Only half way through July.

Heavens, what heat! All Macao is breathless, gasping, helpless under the sun. Nothing moves, except the air endlessly jumping and quivering. The trees shed a heavy shade but no coolness. The birds are silent now all day, except for the solitary sea hawks high up in the sun, slowly circling and screaming their thin cry. The shallow bay in front of the Praia Grande literally steams. The water hardly moves against the granite blocks of the promenade. The black African soldiers on guard in front of the Governor's palace are now quite asleep, instead of half so, as usual. The nights, I may say, are hardly any better than the days. Last night I woke between two and three o'clock to find that my little cat was not in her usual place at the foot of my bed, and I suspect she has been out most nights this week. From the garden below was coming the most terrible squalling. I went out on to the verandah and looked over. The moon was high, and I could see Puss sitting on my garden wall, immaculate and composed, while from opposite ends of my domain, two tom cats were advancing on her. I have never seen such enormous cats before. It may have been the moonlight which distorted them, but I do not think so. They were really wild creatures from the hill, not domestic animals. One disappeared into a patch of shadow. The other continued to advance in full moonlight with a deliberate, stealthy pad, his head held low, his body all powerful shoulders and lean flanks. I could see his rough coat and torn ears and could guess that he was a veteran of many battles. The unearthly squalling broke out once more and then abruptly stopped. The rivals had evidently seen each other.

I went back to bed and lay down again on my bamboo mat, leaving the three of them to their nocturnal life. Eventually they left the garden and went up the hill, as I could still hear their cries faintly from far away. I was wondering if I should ever see Puss return from the clutches of those savages, but she was home again by breakfast time, and then slept most of the day. I have never before lived at close quarters with an animal so completely absorbed with its own affairs, and so self sufficient. Puss lies stretched on a chair, probably not even dreaming of her bridegrooms, the wild cats in the hill, but simply immersed in a methodical and reviving slumber which will give her new steel springs of energy. At the slightest alarm, however, the machine would be alerted and Puss would be ready to take flight, or to come lazily to my side. My wishes are nothing to her: in fact, they don't exist. My function is to open doors and shutters when required to do so, or to flick bits of paper, dry leaves and such when Puss is in the mood for play. My cat has better manners at table and is far more scrupulous in her toilet than many residents I could name, but nature has also equipped her to live like a savage in the jungle. If life is wonderful to us men with our limited senses, what must it be like to such a creature as her? When I stand on the verandah on a moonless night I can hear rustlings and scratchings, but strain my eyes as I may, I can see nothing, while the cat crouched on the wall can see the beetle crawl in the grass stems. There must be a whole host of strange nocturnal creatures of which we know absolutely nothing: I hear them squeal, yap, cough and rustle beyond my garden wall all night, but I never get a glimpse of them. Then just think of the smells! The air is thick with them: the heavy smell of newly turned earth;

the fugitive odours of flowers; the all-pervasive smell of the bazaar, burnt gunpowder, sunflower-seed oil and cooking fires. Even dull-nosed humans could tell their way blindfold to the street of the carpenters, aromatic with wood shavings, but to a cat each casual whiff of breeze must carry a message.

From my bed I can hear the night wind rustling through the branches and I can tell what direction it comes from. I hear the rain falling, first in single heavy drops, then in a pelting tumult, and I can see in my mind's eye the teeming gutters and the streets sheeted with wet. The sound of the gong from the Chinese temple comes faintly to my ears, but I do not know what is going on there. Puss knows: the night is as familiar to her as the day to me. She slides down over the verandah in the teeth of the downpour to keep some rendezvous. From some fastness in the hill she watches the temple ritual behind the courtyard walls and then comes back to my house when light breaks. What she has been doing, what she has seen, she keeps to herself. If she could think about it at all, I am convinced she would have nothing but contempt for me as a creature who can smell nothing, hear nothing and taste nothing, on whom half the riches of life are wasted.

To return to my picture. I have made no progress in the past week: the reason is that I have been working, toiling rather, on portraits to keep the pot boiling. This hottest of all weeks, when we would welcome a typhoon to blow away the stagnant air in which we are suffocating, has brought a sudden accession of clients. It is always the way; merchants never want to sit during the cold weather when they are all far too busy sampling tea or turning opium into gold at the Factories. Also the first ship of the season has come into Typa Roads, a country ship, a real old tub, but she has beaten her smarter rivals on the run from Calcutta. The first ship is always an event: there was a magnificent banquet attended by some fifty guests, including myself, at the Company's house. In addition to her cargo of cotton, rice, tin and pepper, she has two gentlemen on board who have taken passage to

China to see the world. They have already visited the studio and both have commissioned portraits. One of them—referred to as 'the Captain'—could be interesting: strong bone structure, high colour shows signs of coarsening; self-confident, probably a bully. The sort of man I don't get on with, but a good sitter. His friend is a nice gentlemanly fellow, but insipid: a pot-boiler. It will be difficult to prevent him from looking what he is, an amiable nonentity. 'How can handsome face make when handsome face no have got?' as one of my professional colleagues—or rivals—in Canton once remarked to a disgruntled client. I envied the Celestial his eminent common sense.

August: and the first dinner party of the month last night, at which I noticed our visiting Captain (Galbraith is his name) making himself very attentive to Mrs Haverill. It was sweltering hot, but she looked quite cool with her gown cut half-way down to her waist: the fashions are convenient indeed. Galbraith was enjoying what he saw, no doubt. I did not interfere: it will be a pleasant change for her, a fresh, lusty fellow just newly arrived. She has mourned her husband quite long enough for decency and decorum to be satisfied. The pair were some way off from myself and I could not hear their conversation, but every now and then Mrs Haverill gave her tinkling laugh at some sally of wit. As usual I was fully occupied. There was plenty to drink, and the company were filling their glasses pretty frequently, so that the task devolved upon me, as it always does, of keeping the conversation going while the guests proceeded to fill themselves with wine. It is not difficult to acquire a reputation as a brilliant raconteur in such circumstances. And my conversation is always suited to ladies, unlike that of other men who pass as dinner-table wits.

I was talking with Mr Harker and others after dinner was finished and the ladies had retired, when Captain

Galbraith joined us. A glance showed me that he had reached the first stage of truculence. Harker asked him out of civility how he liked Macao.

'I like it as little as I like any place,' was the reply, 'where the women are all so unapproachable.' Harker replied politely that he was sorry to hear this.

'The white ones, anyhow,' continued Galbraith. 'I don't yet know about the yellow ones. I have not had any experience of them so far, and there is the language difficulty to get over. Still, in my experience, some languages are universal. It is just a question of getting a hearing. Now I hear that Mr Harker actually speaks Chinese. Where do you gentlemen, with your wealth of experience, advise me to start?'

He looked round, grinning at us.

'The difficulty *is* to get a hearing,' said Harker very seriously. 'Most Chinese think a foreigner so extraordinarily funny that they burst into laughter at the mere sight of him.'

'Funny—what is funny?' asked Galbraith, frowning.

'Everything, my dear sir.' Harker was becoming expansive and beginning to enjoy himself. 'Look at your skin, it's the wrong colour.' Galbraith, in spite of himself, glanced at his hand. 'Whoever saw a human being with a skin of that colour? And your nose—just a huge protuberance! No Chinese, that is to say, no civilised man, would have a nose as big as that. Then there's your hair, all curling like an animal's bristles. Everything about a foreigner is wrong, including his clothes. Foreign men dress like women, and women like men. We even button our coats up on the wrong side. You can't expect a Chinese girl to have anything to do with barbarians like ourselves.'

'Now wait a minute,' said Galbraith. 'You say that all Chinese, including the women, have no use for us. When we came ashore here, we were brought off from the ship's boat in a couple of funny-looking little punts, rowed by girls. I would swear they were not disinterested. Mine was flashing her eyes at me, I can tell you.'

60

'You were very fortunate,' murmured Harker. 'Ah, but those were boat girls, "water chickens". They are a different race altogether and in fact are not Chinese at all.'

This sounded nonsense to me, and I said so. These girls look pure Chinese to me. But Harker insisted that they were of another stock, and to prove his point embarked upon a long discourse on the origin of the inhabitants of Canton province, to which Galbraith paid scant attention. Finally he broke in and asked Harker directly how he could get hold of a 'water chicken'.

'You must put that question to Mr Chinnery,' said Harker with a sly look at me. 'His experience as an old resident of Macao greatly exceeds mine.'

'My experience, dear sir, of Macao matters is confined to those objects which please the artist's eye. So far I have found nothing to better the Macanese pig, which has the most elegant arch to its back of any in animal creation. You can keep your water chickens.'

At this point we were called upon to join the ladies, and the conversation lapsed. Galbraith made his way to the side of Mrs Haverill, hoping no doubt for the opportunity to touch hands, mingle breaths or glance down the neck of her gown, and stayed there for the rest of the evening. The other men hung together as they usually do and talked of the topics which interest men in these parts—tea, opium, and trade. The room grew hotter and hotter and the voices thicker and thicker as the gentlemen refreshed. At a fairly early stage Mr Bowie was assisted to his sedan chair and piled inside. He had been telling tales of Calcutta all the evening, to anyone who would listen.

It was late when the party broke up but I was, of course, perfectly sober. It is no distance to my house, and I decided to walk home. This, I can assure you, is unheard of. In the East, no gentleman walks to his home, even if he is in a condition to do so. However I insisted, and my companions let me go, Harker promising to come and see if I were there in the morning. I deliberately lengthened the walk by going

61

down to the Praia, where the sea was gently lapping the granite blocks. I could only hear the water, I could not see it beneath my feet. The water was quite black, but the middle air seemed to hold a little reflected light, and after a while I could make out the shapes of the fishing junks at anchor some way out from the shore, and the loom of a fish trap running out into the bay. Even at midnight, the air had no freshness. It carried all the stale smells of the preceding day and the promise of more tomorrow. I threw open my coat and shirt, but no breath of air came to my skin. Standing there by the shore at midnight, breathing in the warm, odorous air, so evocative of sights, sounds and sensations, all sorts of regrets and recollections invaded my mind. Do I do wrong to thrust them back again? They are part of my past, I cannot disown them; but what is done is done and I am living in the present with the future as yet uncompromised. So I tell myself: yet there are times such as this, at midnight on the Praia Grande, when my past cannot be held at bay, and all my being is pervaded with sadness from my past failings. Failings as a husband, failings as a father—these haunt me, and the ghosts of people who need not have died. My answer is that I *had* to act as I did, that it is given to no man to change himself, we all have to justify our existence, and I have done so in the only way I know. Tonight I give myself this answer, but I cannot convince myself.

If I were Bowie I should get drunk and then I should not feel like this, but it is important to me not to get drunk. I am sure that Bowie has done plenty of dirty things in his life—some of them I know of—yet he never feels the slightest pang of conscience or remorse, nor does anyone think a ha'porth the worse of him. Not that his money has done him much good. Here he is, not much older than I, played out, with a hideous old Portuguese half-caste woman. It all comes of stupidity. I may not have kept my money, like Bowie (I am certain I have made more), but I am not stupid, and that is the difference in us.

It is not wise to stand so long in a lonely spot like this.

I must go home. The street is perfectly clear up to my door, the houses on either side are caves of darkness, the marble steps of the church at the corner glimmer faintly. Everything is shuttered and silent as the grave, except for the far-away boom of the temple gong. Only the cats of Macao are awake and promenading on the marble steps and picking their way along the porcelain balustrades among the pots of flowers, now closed and drooping. My cat must be out there. At any rate, when I go into my room, her place on the bed is empty and she does not come in all night. I wonder when she will have her kittens—she has been looking at bursting point for the last few days—and what I shall do with them.

The bed is empty, and for the first time for many months I notice it. For a long time now I have been used to sleeping without a woman. I have declined Augustine's offers of his aunt, his sister, his daughter. This is Mrs Haverill's doing, of course. She knew quite well what she was doing, that woman, when she led me a dance. Perhaps it is as well that she did: to tell the truth, I have been disturbed at my own lack of interest these past months in the fair sex, something which has been quite new in my experience. Perhaps Mrs H is now also regretting her empty bed—unless she has our lusty soldier friend, Captain Galbraith, in it. He was determined to have her, willing or unwilling. I could never do that. If a woman was beautiful, no matter if she was not yet willing, I admired her with all my heart and soul and I would have laid myself down under her feet as her devoted slave. I could never conduct myself like the Bowies and Galbraiths of this world, who take what they want and probably never even say thank-you for it.

Just now I would welcome the company of even Augustine's aunt. To be awake and watchful at three o'clock in the morning is something which has not happened to me for a long time, and it is terrible suddenly to be afraid of oneself, to be afraid of sleeplessness and night terrors. Confound all parties: I must never go to one again. They ruin the nerves, they undermine all that has been built up in months of

63

careful and sensible living. It is all right for the merchants to roll into their beds in the small hours night after night and wake bleary-eyed at midday, but that sort of life does not and never can suit me. If I could afford to cut out their company altogether, I would do so with pleasure, but I have to sing for my supper. To this I am reduced for lack of a few lakhs! It often amuses me when I look round the table to think that each of these fools will probably go home with a fortune and here am I, after thirty years in the East, as poor as when I first came out.

The most extraordinary thing has just happened. I was just about to close the shutters and try to sleep when I heard a muffled but urgent miaow from my cat in the garden below. Fearing that in her corpulent state she might have got herself stuck in some precarious situation, I went downstairs to find her. I opened the door into the garden with the greatest difficulty, for Augustine barricades the house at night, and peered out into the darkness. Puss flashed past me into the house and was up the stairs as fast as she could go. I could only see that she had what looked like a mouse in her mouth. I followed her up and into the studio, and found her scrabbling at the door of an almirah, trying to get it open. The object in her mouth was not a mouse, but a new-born kitten.

Well, I opened the door for her and she jumped in at once, deposited the kitten and was off down the stairs again. There was an absence of about ten minutes and then she reappeared with another kitten which she placed with the first. This time she showed no disposition to go out again, and after waiting for a while, I refastened the door. I dared not look into the almirah to see if the kittens had survived this transplantation, but when I addressed Puss through the door she answered with a steady purring: so I went to bed and after all this excitement at last slept soundly.

We are entering September, but there is still no relief from the heat. The only marked difference is that the humidity has begun to drop a little. I do not myself draw from this the satisfaction that others do. I have not the same objection to a state of perpetual dampness, and in fact I find the next two months when the sun continues to blaze furiously while there is not an atom of moisture in the air exceedingly trying to the nerves. There is a brazen smell in the air, and the gongs in the Chinese temple seem to keep up their din most of the night. It is possible that the infection of restlessness passes through the local population as well. Certainly their voices never sound so strident, nor are their exchanges as long and acrimonious, as at this season. To my chagrin, I find myself uncommonly wakeful at nights. I have not succeeded in recapturing the peace of mind which I lost at the English dinner party. I have made a start with the portrait of Captain Galbraith. I dislike him more intensely with every day which passes. He is amusing, but cynical and brutal. He continues to flirt quite outrageously with Mrs Haverill, who encourages him while contriving to maintain that cool and decorous manner with which she greets the world. I suppose she is flattered, for he is a handsome fellow in his way.

To return to a more rewarding subject, I must note that my three cats are thriving. I now have two females and a male, so we are a partie carrée. The tom is approximately six inches long and has just opened his eyes. He has no tail, merely a stump, but Puss sees no defect in him and lavishes attention on both her offspring. She rarely stirs out of the house, but when she gets too hot and feverish from nursing her kittens, she comes and stretches herself out on a chair at my side, and bestows a little desultory attention on herself. Augustine was all for murdering the kittens as soon as he set eyes on them, but that I felt I could not allow. I would never have been able to look Puss in the face again. In any event, they amuse me and they cost me nothing.

Day after day continues to pass with no break in the weather. This calm cannot last, and I feel a suspense in the air. This is the kind of weather in which anything could happen, yet the typhoon season is supposed to be passed. This morning I went for an early walk, my usual walk, up Penha Hill. I climbed slowly, dripping with sweat. On the summit a light breeze—how grateful I was for that light breeze!—was blowing. I looked back at the quarter from which I had come, and saw the palatial white houses set in well-tended gardens with terraces where I could see the huge cartwheel hats of the gardeners, and nothing else, as their wearers squatted on their haunches over the cherished plants.

This place is really all so beautiful, why am I filled with discontent? It is better to turn my eyes away from the habitations of men to the wide sweep of sea and islands which surrounds me on all sides but one. The islands are not beautiful, perhaps, to some eyes. They rise out of the sea without gentle slopes or beaches. They are cliffs of rock from which the burning rays of the sun rebound, there is almost no vegetation and certainly no life on them other than a fisherman's hut rigged up to give him shelter while he dries his catch. In some lights the islands look like painted toys floating on the surface of the water, and the cloud shadows which pass rapidly over them, too quickly to be captured by my pencil, are like flashes of lightning on a stage scene. I can now see, pinned down on the water at the entrance to the harbour, a number of junks which are struggling to get under way, but the breeze is too light to fill their heavy mat sails. If I turn myself round to face the mainland of Canton, the pagoda lies beneath me, half concealed in its heavy screen of trees. The hill top is not for me this morning. I will take the path which winds down the side of the hill by the pagoda to the Inner Harbour.

This was quite a scramble, but eventually I arrived in the road which follows the shore, at this point very pretty with its picturesque rocks and overhanging trees. For some super-stitious reason there are always trees sheltering Chinese tombs and temples, although apart from these there may not be a tree to be seen for hundreds of miles. There is a little sandy beach at this point where usually a few tanka-boats are to be seen rocking at anchor or drawn up on the beach. At some distance to the south is the big beach below the temple steps where two Chinese banners are always hoisted on long bamboo poles. There were plenty of Chinese here, but on the small beach I could see no sign of life except the figure of a solitary European. I must confess I was not best pleased when this figure turned and hailed me, and I recognised the Captain.

He was carefully dressed and wore a broad-brimmed hat. He still looks a fine, upstanding man. Dissipation has not yet begun to tell. Very soon, thought I, he will begin to grow fat (like myself), but unlike myself he will have himself carried everywhere in a chair.

He advanced towards me, swinging a cane and smiling.

'What are you doing out so early, Mr Chinnery?' he asked.

It seemed strange to me that I, as a resident of Macao, should have my habits questioned by a total stranger and a visitor to boot, but I answered, 'This is my usual time for a walk, but I don't usually expect to meet any of my acquaintance.'

'My host is still asleep and likely to remain so till noon, so I have been obliged to come out and find my own entertainment. I have just been up to that place which looks like a temple and endeavoured to see inside, but the filth and the gloom defeated me.'

'Apart from the peasants and the fishermen, these people are not early risers. Probably the guardians of the temple are still snoring.'

Galbraith looked round him, and his eye lighted on the tanka-boat. 'That is an odd-looking affair. What do you say it is called?'

I answered that craft of this kind were called egg-boats, on account of the conical mat roof, which resembles an egg in shape, and it was in one of these craft that he probably came ashore.

'And here comes the owner, by the look of it,' exclaimed Galbraith, 'who the learned Mr Harker would say is not

Chinese at all but some kind of aboriginal. If it were not for the costume I should say she is too pretty to be an aboriginal.'

True enough, the boat-girl who was coming towards us was pretty. Her head was uncovered and her long, glossy plait of hair shone in the sun. A red flower—I could not see whether it was made of paper or was real—was tucked into it. Her feet, which were almost hidden by the flowing trousers, were bare and soundless. At first when she saw the two foreigners the girl slowed down, and I saw her look at the rocks as if in doubt whether to make a detour. As I have become accustomed to these people's ways, this did not surprise me, but the girl continued straight towards us and I saw that it was my little friend, my model girl. I then concluded that the display of shyness was entirely for the benefit of Galbraith, for to my knowledge no bolder little minx ever stepped, and as she came right up to us to get to her boat, I detected on her face, carefully turned away from us, the same enticing half-smile. Galbraith deliberately advanced and placed himself in front of her.

'Aren't you going to offer us a ride in your boat?' he asked.

The girl turned her head and vouchsafed him a look of supreme contempt, but no answer.

'I am sure she can understand me perfectly well if she wants to, so let us see what this can do.' He took a coin out of his pocket and held it up for her to see. She made a move as if to extend her hand and then dropped it again. Galbraith burst into laughter.

'Listen, I just want a ride in your boat. You are a very pretty girl, you know, and with beautiful bracelets, too.' He made as if to take her hand and examine the bracelets which she wore on her arm, but the girl recoiled with a look of consternation, exclaiming, 'No, no!' Her eyes swept rapidly up to the road, where I could see nobody but a pedlar passing with his two baskets slung over his shoulders. The girl began to splash into the shallow water to regain her boat.

'I am not going to get my feet wet, thank you,' said Galbraith, turning in the direction of the road. 'What I have been told about the characteristics of boat girls is evidently wrong. I take it that there is nothing more to see in this direction, so I'll leave you to your inspiration, Mr Chinnery. Good day to you.'

He started back along the road, his whole bearing indicative of bad humour. I lingered to assemble my sketching materials which I had abandoned on a rock, and when I looked up I found to my surprise that the girl was there. She gave me a delightful conspiratorial smile. 'That man no good. B'long one bad man. Master no send for me any more? Long time I wait.'

I tried to explain that I was still busy painting Galbraith, and others, but that soon I would send for her again and resume the sittings.

'I understand. Day-time no wanchee me. Night-time more better—no man see. Night-time I can come your house. This night I come.'

This was wilful misunderstanding with a vengeance, but there was no time for explanations, before the girl was gone. She jumped into her boat and left me foolishly standing there. I sat down on a rock to ponder, until a number of Chinese urchins appeared. The presence of the rocks to shelter behind gave them courage and they approached quite near, shouting and making unpleasant gestures. How I missed Soldier, who would have scattered them in a trice. I shook the hellish brats off only by beating a retreat from the spot.

The day passed as slowly as a day has ever passed. The heat at noon resembled a furnace, and I worked desultorily, read a little, and saw nobody. It was Mrs Haverill's day for a drawing lesson, but fortunately she sent a message with her excuses to say she was not well. Towards evening a growing sense of flatness and heaviness oppressed me, the result of waiting all day—for what? Ten to one, the girl would not come. And if she did come, would I want her?

It was after I had eaten my last meal and quite dark when Augustine appeared and announced to me on the verandah, in a voice of the deepest disapproval, that the tanka-girl was here and in my bedroom.

I nearly told him then and there to send her away: to arrive after I had waited hours was too much. Then man's curiosity reasserted itself, the warmth of the evening which had before brought only lassitude now began to run pleasantly through my veins, carrying a familiar message with it. It was reassuring to be aware of my body, that old and trusted companion, making its patient and not unreasonable demands, so easy to gratify since the girl was there, waiting. She was sitting on a chair beside my bed, her hands on her knees, her head slightly bent, and on approaching I thought I could see in the light of the candle which Augustine must have lit, the smile at the corners of her mouth.

It would be wrong to suggest that I have not had encounters with native women fairly often in my life. When I was a young man, and had the appetites of my age, I frequented Indian women as most of my contemporaries did. I did not love these girls, or respect them, although I do not doubt that many of them were worthy of love and respect. They seemed to me the product of a sultry climate, bred solely for the pleasure of men. I could admire their grace, the colour of their skin and of their hair, their bright dresses and their insatiable appetite for gaudy ornaments, for tinkling glass bangles, gold rings and trumpery jewels, without wishing in the least to see the girl a second time. There was a time, shortly after I came to Calcutta, when I might have been forced by loneliness to take one of these girls into the house, but then I met Mrs Delaney, and that took up all of my mind and all my energies.

God, what a time that was! How unhappy and yet how happy I was. I pursued Mrs Delaney for a year, I eventually possessed her, and for a year was completely happy in my possession. Everything combined to throw us into despair. Her husband was a drunken brute, he was jealous, suspicious and violent. Mrs Delaney had no money of her own, and I was making at that time very little. We could not see any way out of our predicament, and the fact that the sands were running out only made our love more desperate and our stolen meetings sweeter. Finally the blow fell. Mr Delaney grew tired of Calcutta, and suspecting that his talents (he was a pleader of an indifferent kind) were not appreciated as they should be in the East, determined to return home and to take, of course, his wife with him. There was no escape: we had an agonised parting, Mrs Delaney was conveyed on board ship, more dead than alive, and I—I met and set up house with Rosa.

What followed was perhaps the most tranquil period of my life. I have, I think, a natural bent for domesticity which Mrs C never succeeded in satisfying. I would have made a very good husband to any other woman who gave me children and made a home for me. To hear that the Chinese girl was waiting for me was to go back twenty years, to the remembrance of encounters with girls as passing as birds of paradise, and to the anticipation of the touch of an unknown dusky skin, and an unfamiliar fragrance. Every time it happened I could not have told you afterwards what the woman looked like, but I have never forgotten the fragrance of her hair and skin.

But to return to Ala—for that was her name—sitting on the high chair by the bed. She offered herself at a time when I needed her to release me from the state of frustration and discontent into which I had fallen for the past few weeks. Perhaps I should have taken the remedy before, and not disdained the offer of Augustine's sister and daughter. The coy flirtatiousness of Mrs Haverill, and the glimpses of her still elegant figure afforded by her low gowns, are no substitute for the embraces of an Oriental woman, however matter-of-fact these may be. Ala was quite devoid of sentiment in her dealings with me—indeed, why should she exhibit any?— but she showed a willingness which made her an active accomplice in the business, and it was the smile of complicity which I detected in her eyes, by the light of the flickering candle. It was my first encounter with Cathay in the shape

71

of a Chinese woman, and at first I found myself cast on uncharted seas, so unfamiliar to me were the garments with their myriad fastenings, and the snake-like rope of hair. Then I found my bearings, got on the right course, and came into a familiar harbour, thanks to the Goddess of sailors and tanka-girls, whose temple stands on the shores of the Inner Harbour, where Ala daily offers her pinch of incense. Finally the candle guttered and went out altogether, so that I could not see if I had managed to bring a little tenderness into those unfeeling eyes, eyes which might have been painted upon glass, so clear and unwinking were they, and before the next morning's light had come, Augustine must have come in and fetched her away.

I must write down now, before I can forget the pain, the story of my romance, if you can call it that, with Ala. It was a Thursday night when she first came to me. I remember that the next day dawned as hot and breathless as ever. The sky was beautiful, pearled with cloud, and although I streamed with sweat as I worked in the painting-room, none the less I felt refreshed and invigorated. I have lived too long without a woman, I thought to myself, I should have found an Ala before. It was a day when I ought to have felt burdened and bound down with cares. Augustine, piqued no doubt by my having settled this matter without his intervention, was murmuring about money for this, that and the other, and my pockets were empty. The season's ships would soon be arriving in number, bearing without doubt letters of demand from Mrs C, if not the lady herself—in which case I would be forced to beg a passage to Canton and take refuge once more in the Factories. The newspapers, those inventions of the devil, would also be arriving from Calcutta, and they always contain something to put me in a rage. I had accepted the commission to paint the portrait of Captain Galbraith, Gloomy prospects indeed, yet with my restored energies I made light of all the difficulties. As regards the portrait, I

72

successfully obtained payment in advance, and the sight of ready cash quite reconciled me to the obnoxious sitter.

I set to work again that day. It was clear that Galbraith was in the blackest of moods, and he was barely civil. I had him at a disadvantage, however, pinned down in the studio chair, and teased him not a little, asking for a pleasant expression when it was clear that a scowl would have been more appropriate to the Captain's feelings. A painter and a tooth-puller both have the same advantage—they cannot be answered back. I suppose I might have sympathised with what the Captain must have been enduring at the hands of Mrs Haverill, but I did not. Let him stew, I thought: whether he has had his hand up her skirt yet is no concern of mine. He is one of those men who would look a ridiculous figure when ——. I may say that I painted a remarkably fine likeness of Captain Galbraith posed in front of an open window with a glimpse of the harbour behind. All the time I was painting him, I could see the Captain in my mind's eye in a series of much less elegant postures, and I felt like laughing aloud. He really is a coarse and uncouth brute.

She came to my house again the next Monday. Never had I been in such a curious position with any other girl of my acquaintance. I sent for her on Saturday—that is, I told Augustine to send for her. He reappeared and told me she could not come that day but would come in two more days' time. On Monday evening I supped as usual with the Company. I felt carefree and as young as any of them there. The solemn faces of the merchants, the scowling black looks of Captain Galbraith who was there as usual with his pallid companion, tickled me, and I set myself to amuse the guests in return, especially the ladies, with particular emphasis on Mrs Haverill. I soon recaptured her attention: I thought to myself that that was not too bad, seeing that Galbraith was at least fifteen years my junior and I was never a handsome man. It made me laugh to think of Galbraith going to his lonely bed, unless he accepted a Sino-Lusitanian-Malay companion for the night.

73

When I returned to my house, Ala was lying on the bed eating lychee fruits from a bowl beside her and throwing the rinds on the floor. She continued to reach for lychees while I embraced her, and the big black stones appeared for a moment between her white teeth like the tongue of one of the black chow-dogs which guard the fishermen's junks. At one moment Puss, all unsuspecting, jumped into the verandah on her return from some outside expedition, and fled in horror at the sight of the little savage I had taken to my bed.

The kittens were at this time getting fat and bold and they amused Ala. She encouraged them to scramble about the bed and tickled them with her bare toes and hid her face in laughter when they bit her in retaliation. If I had not watched her closely, she might have popped one into her basket and taken it home to her boat to cook it for dinner, but she behaved quite nicely to them while she was under my eye. Perhaps I need not have had any fear. The cats and Ala, it is true, may have understood each other better than I understood them. After all, they were all Chinese.

I find it very difficult to describe Ala and her sentiments for me. The picture of her body, of course, it would be easy to summon up, although I never saw it except by the light of a flickering candle. Her skin, though slightly deeper in pigmentation than that of a European, was finer in grain and wholly without blemish. It shone like ivory. I never ceased to admire the slenderness of her ankles and of her wrists, encircled by the jade bangles. The slenderness was rounded, not attenuated, and the limbs in spite of being slender were very muscular. Her hands, for instance, were the hands of a boat woman, accustomed to keeping her craft on its course in the tricky tides and shoals of the harbour. Ala used various oils and unguents which she applied to her body and to her long black shining plait of hair. I do not know what they were made of, as she refused to divulge any of her secrets to me, but they certainly were efficacious. The

74

scent was distinctive and memorable, although not wholly pleasant to a Westerner's nose.

So much for Ala's body, but what of her mind? I knew very little of that, after our few meetings. I am a man who cannot have a repeated connection with a woman without feeling tenderness for her and a desire to see into her thoughts —in other words, to possess something of her beyond her body. It is women who are usually the tender sex and it is they who are supposed to fall in love with their lovers. Ala did not seem to have heard of this convention. I suppose she must have liked me—although why, heaven knows, old, fat and ugly as I am—or she would not have come to me in the first place. Or the reason may simply have been that by Chinese tradition a fat man is a rich man. I must confess that after she had offered herself to me I was frightened that it might be difficult later to break off the connection. I have heard stories in which the Chinese woman manifested a most tenacious passion. I feared that I might end up poisoned with ground glass, or find the corpse of the girl, strangled with her own handkerchief, upon my doorstep. I knew enough about the East to know that *that* situation would call for a speedy removal on my part, out of the reach of the relatives.

I need not have entertained any such fears about Ala. She came and went as she, not I, desired. If I had told her on any day to come tomorrow, she would have refused: in that, she was fiercely independent. While she was in my house she was gentle and gay, she manifested the charming compliance of the oriental woman who bends to the will of superior man, but of tenderness I never discerned a trace. She laughed at me, corrected me, and no doubt in her heart of hearts despised me. She was practised at her trade, of course—and yet those words do not describe her truly. She was not what I would imagine a flower-boat girl to be. For one thing she did not wait to be chosen—she chose.

How it would all have ended if it had not ended as it did, I know not. Perhaps I would have tired of her just by reason of the very limits of our relationship and told Augustine to

send her away and thereafter to introduce another woman—
any woman—into my bed when necessity demanded. On the
other hand, perhaps I would have tried more desperately to
get inside her mind and to make her my companion, which
would have ended by my bringing her into the house to live
with me. And if she had consented to such a step, to cut
herself off entirely from her own race, and to cast herself on
the mercies of a foreigner living on sufferance in her country,
would she not have tried to take possession of *me* entirely?

I have counted up the occasions, and she must have come
to my house less than a dozen times in all, but I can remember each and every occasion, for there was something memorable about each one of them. The rising of the moon, the
gentle rustling of the branches outside the shutters like the
feet of wild creatures slipping through the moonlight (every
time I got up from the bed and pulled back the shutters to
see the progress of the moon I expected to see strange furry
beasts whisking into cover, or else staring at me with unearthly, glowing eyes) were familiar to me, but with Ala
there they took on a different quality. One night the rain
fell not in drops, but in cupfuls, and a great wind burst the
shutters open so that the rain fell in a wide arc into my
bedroom and soaked the boards, until the girl left the bed
and went over and closed the shutters again. One night a
cockroach ran across the pillow, and the girl laughed at my
revulsion when I knocked it to the floor, and she put out her
foot and would have crushed the cockroach beneath it. She
also told me that cockroaches dried and powdered cure fever.
Ala was not at all impressed by my house or anything in it,
she only cared for the pots of flowers and touched them
lovingly (although the flowers which she wore in her gleam-
ing plait of hair were made of paper). Everything else was
foreign and thus exquisitely funny to her. She laughed at
everything, from the knives and forks to the way I buttoned
my coat.

I can hardly bear to read what I have written, and certainly

I have not stopped to choose my words. I have wanted to put down some account of the girl as though I were in some way wresting something from the wreckage of the storm. The wind is still high, and the air is still full of grit and blown leaves. It feels as though it could never set fine again, and yet probably tomorrow will dawn blue and calm and blank as though none of this had ever happened.

The night before the storm was a night of dead calm. I sat on my verandah and watched the flashes of summer lightning playing across the sky, but they were harmless flashes and there was not a rumble of thunder nor a drop of rain. I was not expecting Ala. I dined with Harker and the American bachelors and left early, in order to sit on the verandah. I went to bed at the usual time and slept fast. When I woke at six o'clock the sky seemed laden and overcast, while the heat was already overpowering, with a curious metallic smell in the air. Very shortly afterwards the wind began to blow steadily from one quarter. From my house I could see that no craft had ventured out of the harbour, and they were huddling together like birds seeking shelter, each one trying to be the centre of the flock. The mat sails had already been lowered, and the bare masts of the junks rocked up, down, round, up, down, round, as the water of the Inner Harbour began to take on a curious swell. The trees in the gardens of Macao bent, then leaned, then began a wild threshing which showered leaves, berries and small debris over the house. Augustine came running upstairs with the boys following him, to direct the closing of the shutters. By now I knew the signs, and I raised no protest when he reduced the painting room to a stifling black hole. It was a scene of silent, harassed activity. The only person who took no part in it was Puss. She slept on in her almirah, with her offspring rolled against her flanks. One by one the servants carried in the heavy pots of plants from the verandah, straddling under the weight. The boys' faces were a curious green colour, and they looked very frightened. I have never seen a Chinese look so before.

By the time all was made fast the tension in the air was so high that I felt an explosion was imminent, and went on to the verandah for a last glimpse of Macao. I could see little, however. The wind was strong, so strong that it would have knocked me over, solid as I am, had I not kept fast hold, and it was blowing continuously, not in gusts as before. A series of unbroken small waves raced over the surface of the bay so rapidly that one would have said the whole mass of water was on the move. So far there had been no rain, but as I turned to go back into the house, a torrent of heavy drops fell from the sky like hailstones. Another few seconds, and the wind and rain together were hurling themselves at the closed shutters of the house.

The hours which followed were as long as any I have known. Weathering this storm was like standing a siege. The violence of the wind threatened to break first one shutter loose, then as we ran to attend to that, another began to come away. Had more than one gone at the same time, I am sure the wind would have torn the house apart, and scattered its contents to the four corners of the earth. Rain spurted through every crack and ran over the floors, which were soon awash. We pushed the water downstairs with brooms. My painting room, crowded with canvases in all stages of completion, was my first concern. My bedroom I abandoned to take its chance. The soaked and draggled net hung over the dismantled bed, and rainwater splashed over the planks, and the wind continued to blow—Heavens, how it blew! Although it was midday, the sky was as black as lead, and the house was in darkness. For once Augustine was unable to provide food: I told him to bring whatever was in the house and he finally produced a bowl of cold rice which I ate up, unpalatable though it was. We remained in this condition, penned up in the house and consumed with anxiety, until the middle of the afternoon. Then the wind began to drop and I remarked to Augustine that the storm was passing. He shook his head.

'My no think so. This is a very big wind. Many houses fall down.'

I did not contradict him, but the wind seemed to be beyond doubt abating. I was so sure of it that I was about to open the shutters to get a breath of air—for the house was stifling —when Augustine seized my arm, saying:

'By and by plenty more wind, more rain.'

He was right. The wind began to tear against the house again, but this time it was coming from the mainland direction, not from the sea. The hills did not protect us at all, as I would have expected: rather, they seemed to funnel the wind in great shrieking gusts. I have never heard such a noise as the storm made at its height. It was like the roaring of a wild animal, or a gigantic waterfall. It was impossible to open a crack, yet with everything locked and barred the wind was forcing its way in, and curtains and hangings were swaying and dancing. The whole house streamed with water —not an inch was dry. Then above the fury of the storm I heard a dull crash. Later I found that one of the larger pots, too heavy to be brought inside, had been lifted by the wind and thrown bodily down the hill. I thought then that the whole house must be lost, and ourselves with it. If one of the massive roof tiles had shifted, the wind would have stripped the remainder and then gutted the house. I saw everything lost, all gone, the paintings in the studio which represented months of work, and in the agony of the moment I seized my sketchbooks and piled them into the cupboard with Puss, as the safest place in the house.

The storm did not get any worse. It continued to blow, unabated, until it seemed incredible that structures made of brick and tile by human hands could stand before it. With a tremendous rending crash the tree in my neighbours' garden fell, fortunately missing us but bringing God knows what destruction with it. I wondered what all the chattering little women and their attendant amahs were doing. Probably they were huddling somewhere in the cellars, beating on gongs, knocking their heads on the floor and burning paper. I felt thirsty and called for some tea, but no one answered me. My servants were in the cellars, too. When a Chinaman is too distracted to boil tea, he is in a very bad way indeed. For myself, incredible though it may seem, I laid myself down on the sodden bamboo mat on my bed, and while the wind continued to howl like a fury and the shutters banged in concert and the water dripped on my face, I actually went to sleep.

When I woke, it was evening and the storm had abated considerably. Augustine was in the next room, moving about with a feeble light, picking up first one thing and then another from the sodden debris on the floor. I told him to desist from these useless labours and to bring me food. There was no reason I could see why a fire should not be lighted and a proper meal cooked. Meanwhile I cautiously opened a shutter—I had got into the habit of thinking of the wind as some wild beast which might leap into the room through any opening—and stepped outside. The air with which I filled my lungs was heavy and unhealthy, and I could see the bay angrily running with dark water. The quiet was almost uncanny to ears which had been assaulted all day by the noise of the storm. I saw the door of the cupboard open slightly, and Puss padded silently forth and joined me on the verandah. The fact that this was now a pool of water somewhat disconcerted her, and she sniffed with suspicion at the raffle of sodden leaves and broken branches which littered it. Then finding the driest spot she could, she sat down in her usual attitude, head craned very slightly forward between the columns of the balustrade, and took in the scene with eyes and ears. Having ascertained that her familiar surroundings remained more or less intact, she came back into the room and wound herself round my legs, with tail erect.

When the meal came, I fed her too, and was amused as usual when she left the table as soon as she had bolted her portion to nourish her well-grown and always vociferous family. She did it with such an air of reluctance, as if she yielded to the demands of duty much against her will, but once she had settled to the washing and feeding of her kittens, what a purring arose to heaven! As for me, once I had eaten there was nothing to do but go to bed. I pulled the driest covering I could find over myself, let down the wet bed-curtains, and sought for sleep.

I woke up again in the early morning, while it was still dark, and immediately a horrible feeling of fear gripped me. I put out my hand for reassurance, but the place beside me was empty. It must have been just before dawn: no birds were yet astir. It was only the waking of a few seconds, and then I dropped back into sleep, but confused figures and visions haunted me till daylight came, and I was able to go out and see what the great storm had done to Macao.

It was a fantastic sight. The lane outside my house which had the previous day been lined with neat garden walls and shadowed by stately trees, was choked with all kinds of rubbish. Broken roof tiles in heaps, bricks and plaster, and torn-off branches, all these were lying in a bed of leaves through which protruded strange derelict objects. I had a terrible shock to see lying half under a broken tree trunk a draggled, grey-striped animal which for one second I took for Puss. It was not my cat, however, but another, poor creature, lying with its head crushed. As I passed it, the back legs seemed to quiver and I looked away. Close by lay a Chinese cotton jacket, and a bamboo basket. The carrying pole was lying farther down the lane.

I made my way along with difficulty and extreme caution, fearing that at any moment one of the shaky plaster walls might fall down on top of me. I reached the end of the lane, and found myself looking straight into the gardens of a mansion occupied by the Company's chief tea inspector. This so startled me, as I had never before had a sight of them from this particular spot, that it was some minutes before I realised the cause. Some intervening Chinese houses had totally collapsed. Nothing remained but ruins of tiles, mud bricks and fragments of wood. Moved by curiosity, I went to look closer. The remnants had already disintegrated under the downpour and it was hard to discern any traces of the former occupants, except that I saw a few pieces of sodden cloth, of a dark-red colour patterned with flowers, which might have been part of a child's dress—at least, I have seen Chinese children wearing similar stuff. I shuddered to think how many human beings inhabit these Chinese hovels. It is true that the removal of these miserable dwellings could only enhance the appearance of this quarter of the town, but what a terrible calamity! I wished to make my way down to the Praia Grande, to see the state of things on the sea front, but a picket of Portuguese black soldiers, creatures whose appearance terrifies the Chinese far more than their soldierly qualities, came round the corner with a swarthy officer at their head. Whether they were looting, or preventing it, I did not wait to inquire: I judged it expedient to return in case my own motives should be misunderstood. In the grounds of the mansion now laid open to view I could see the gardeners and servants busily removing wrecked pots, sweeping up debris and restoring order generally. It struck me that these operations should be going on at home and that I ought to superintend at least the salvaging of my studio.

When I entered the house again I found it full of the smell of broken, rotting vegetation, mingled with the reek of damp plaster and rank earth. The acrid smell of charcoal came up from below stairs, where Augustine had lit a fire in a brazier and was drying my clothing together with his own. All around there was a heavy silence. The usual noises were absent, the clacking of clogs on the pavement, the shouting of pedlars passing up and down the lane, the cheerful clatter of my own household and my neighbours'! Even the great temple gong had not been heard since the storm began to blow. Perhaps the Goddess was too busy looking after her votaries to listen to it. Below me, in the ruined garden, I could see my cat prowling. Crouching low to the ground, she made her way in and out of the tangle of broken

82

branches and smashed earthenware which had produced a little jungle on her doorstep.

As for me, I set to upstairs. I laboured away for about an hour and a half, at the end of which time I was covered with sweat and in a state of exhaustion. Then Augustine came in to announce with a long face that there was no food and no wood to cook with and I must go out to dine. This was not his fault. He had tried to go out to the market, but had been turned back. By order of the mandarin the shops were closed to foreigners.

'Is there no rice left?' I asked.

'Only servants' rice. No good for master to eat.'

Well, servants' rice would do for the cats, and I left instructions for them to be fed, while I debated with myself where I should do best. My nearest neighbour was an eccentric gentleman who had no set hours for meals, while the stately mansion I had walked past that morning was too large and grand, and one of the few houses where I did not care to drop in without warning. Bowie was probably no better off than myself. It would have to be the American Company's house, and I set off, taking with me such eatables as I could find in the house and persuade Augustine to yield up.

When I reached the house after many scrambles and detours, I found a tremendous scene of energy reigning. With Mrs Fay herself presiding and issuing a hundred instructions to her major-domo, every member of the household was busy scrubbing, scouring and sweeping. The wind had ripped away the shutters of Mr Fay's dressing room, but a carpenter had been summoned and was already at work on repairing them. The ceiling had fallen in the dining-room—but the servants had already cleaned that up. Mrs Fay was in her element and thoroughly enjoying herself. Under her direction two of the bachelors were replacing the furniture of the drawing-room. The only unoccupied person was Mr Harker, who, trading no doubt on his status as an ex-invalid, was sitting on one of the sofas making suggestions as to how things could be further improved.

83

Other refugees arrived, bearing like myself contributions to the kitchen, and when we went in to dinner it was found that Mrs Fay's cook had contrived a capital meal. Of course, the cutting off of provisions to foreigners is a favourite device when the mandarins wish to remind them who are the masters of Macao. The procedure is always the same. The tradespeople are ordered to close their shops, which they do, excusing themselves on the ground that the crops have failed, or the chickens or ducks or whatever it is have died of the plague. Two days later, when the mandarins have received a suitable 'present', the bazaar is once more full of food and business as lively as ever. One of the gentlemen said that on this occasion the mandarins feared disorders, once the extent of the disaster became known, hence the edict about provisions. The foreigners must keep out of sight and make no demands for the present, until the people had been fed. The Portuguese troops had been ordered out to deal with Chinese looters who might make for foreign houses.

While Mrs Fay was inquiring anxiously if there were any danger to be apprehended from the population, I felt at that moment something like a physical blow in my vitals which turned my stomach into a lump of lead, and my limbs into ice. Idiot that I was, I had spent a day and a night cowering in my stone house, and had not thought of the girl Ala. Where had she been while the storm raged? She would have taken her boat, as soon as she saw the signs of what was to come, to the shelter of the Inner Harbour, the traditional place of safety—so long as the wind was blowing from the sea. But Harker, who had weathered the storm in the bachelors' house on the Praia Manduco, told us what happened when the storm centre passed over and the wind began to blow from the other quarter. The serried ranks of sampans and egg-boats packed as tightly as roosting birds in the Inner Harbour began to heave at their moorings, then to break loose, and finally were piled on each other as they were driven ashore by gigantic waves. Some had been blown across the width of the Praia into the bazaar, where dozens of flimsy houses had collapsed. He described the battered wreckage of junks and sampans tossing at the water's edge and the dead things tangled in the wreckage—dead chickens, cats and dogs, all of them from the sunken junks—and the human corpses floating in the harbour. Some of the bodies, he said, were dismembered, and torn-off limbs were to be seen floating on their own. The boat people were wailing the corpses on the shore.

My own imagination added to what Harker left out, or what he could not have known. I knew what strength there was, for instance, in those childishly slender wrists: she would have held on with desperation to whatever seemed to offer security, until the arms were torn from their sockets. Harker had described the body of a headless woman with a rattan hat still suspended by a cord from the bleeding neck. How could that body be identified and accorded the gong-drumming, the paper-burning and the proper ceremonial that old custom and decency demanded for a denizen of the Central Flowery Kingdom joining the ancestors?

I never had any doubt from that moment that Ala had perished in the disaster: I was spared the tortures of hope to be plunged at one stroke into the depths of complete despair. I felt myself a stone guest at the feast at that instant when I realised that I had lost the only human being I had the right to love. Ala might have been standing in the room beside me, so clearly could I see her little bare feet and the turn of her ankle before it was concealed by her wide blue trouser, the charming costume of the boat girl which she would shed with such infinite grace and unconcern.

Gradually I recovered myself; I took leave of my hostess, and left the house. I would have made for the Inner Harbour to see for myself, but Harker dissuaded me. As soon as I reached home, I took a light and went into the painting-room. The first thing which met my eyes was a half-finished painting, used to stuff a crack in the shutters, and overlooked. I examined it—it was quite ruined, damaged beyond repair. It was a product of one of my most happy imaginings, an

85

Indian landscape with a temple by the river which I had been working up from one of my old Indian sketch-books, an evocation of the golden light of Bengal, now gone, wiped out by a blind blast from the sky. I could not restrain my grief any longer—I was alone, and made no effort to hold back my tears. I groaned in my misery, I beat my head with my fists and I believe I would have beaten it against the wall, had not exhaustion suddenly overcome me. I fell into my chair on the verandah and surrendered myself to it, hoping to postpone the hour when I should have to pick up the nightmare of existence again and begin the labour of putting my life and my work together. Beauty visits us and is lost, visions flit before our eyes and are gone, but the landlord demands his rent and the cook his pay.

Ah, that girl, that girl! I ask myself, did I love her? I do not know, I only know that something about her which could have been her skin, the colour of a flower, her mouth with almost no savour, her too-black hair, her complete lack of ardour and response as I have come to expect it from women, yet the manner in which she made submission itself an art and accomplishment, had an insidious charm which, had our commerce continued, would I know now have tied me to her for ever afterwards—to her or to another woman of her race. Now I can understand at last the passions of my gross and mundane friends and the complete absorption with their ageing Indian or Chinese concubines. A woman who can make herself as memorable as this to a man will never be cast off: as he ages, the more indispensable will her attentions be.

It occurred to me to wonder whether I had any expectations of a child by Ala. For quite a number of years when I was young I held the view that mixed unions were not fruitful, on the principle that such a mating was against nature, and although valid for pleasure, nature would withhold progeny and the founding of a family. In after years I observed that practice did not square with my theory, for there have been many notable examples.

The next morning, the town appeared to be restored to normal. Augustine prepared to go to the market: I ordered him to inquire for the girl. For myself, as soon as I had dressed and swallowed a mouthful, I ran to the shores of the Inner Harbour. Here all seemed the same to my eye. The sea-going junks and the tanka-boats were tied up in their accustomed places. Yet it was not the same. The men and women aboard their craft stared at me with hard and sunken faces. Their black clothes had an air of mourning. A queer silence brooded over the water. The chickens and dogs, usually so vociferous, were silent. Had they all been lost? The mass of boats still clung together for protection like a swarm of bees with only a little activity on the outside of the mass when an occasional boat shot clear of its fellows, discharged an errand, and then returned as rapidly as possible to its old place. The blazing sun made it difficult for me to pick out individual faces. Several times I strained my eyes to follow the progress of one of the little egg-boats with feverish anticipation, only to fall into the depths of disappointment the next minute. The swinging plaits, the motion of the body bending to the single oar, even the line of the head, would be the same as Ala's: but the faces when I saw them were sallow, toothy masks. I walked up and down the Praia searching feverishly until the notice which I was attracting convinced me that it was necessary to draw off. I returned home, but could not rest or work.

Augustine came back, but had no news of her.

I fretted the rest of the day away in the stifling painting room, trying to finish off a small picture of the harbour. It was no use. In the evening I would have welcomed any company and would have gone out to supper, but could not bring myself to leave the house. I thought that Ala might have come there, to find me gone and the house closed. Of course she did not come.

Next morning I thought of something to do. I went down to the quay where the egg-boats and sampans congregate, and told the rower of one to take me to Green Island. The faces of the boat people were, I thought, already more cheerful, as if the disaster were already fading from their short memories. Truly, life comes and goes easily in the East. We sculled to the island, and I left the boat woman at the ruined jetty of the Jesuits and walked round the path by the banana grove to the little beach with the boat-dwelling on the shore.

The upturned boat and the hut built among its ribs, they were gone. There was not a sign, not a trace of what had been, only some broken pots and crocks half buried in the sand. The wind and the sea had carried away everything that made a home for perhaps a dozen people, one of them Ala. Where had the old women and the children gone? There was nothing left of them there. The leaves had been stripped from the trees in the banana grove, and the broken stems were lying along the ground. The sea slapped sullenly against the rocks as if ashamed of what it had done. Yet I could not tear myself away from the desolation. I sat there gazing at the empty beach until I feared that my means of return might be lost if the boat woman lost patience and departed. No, when I rounded the point I saw she was still there, crouching on her haunches in the bottom of her boat. No sign of feeling showed in her yellow, withdrawn face as she watched me return. I stepped into the boat, and she set it in the direction of the shore.

As we approached the quayside I saw a European standing there, waiting. It was Harker, and I knew he was waiting for me. I was very glad to see him. As I stepped on shore my limbs began to tremble, and I would have fallen without his aid. He would have accompanied me home, but I urged him to depart. Why should I inflict on another the spectacle of a ludicrous grief? I should have been less unhappy if I could have worked, but the feverish energy which has so often enabled me to turn pent-up emotion to creative effort failed me at this time. I could do nothing but ramble from room to room of a house which had never before seemed so empty and so desolate. Ala was dead: I was left with the gap to fill again.

Part Three

CHAPTER 10

The passing of summer in this place carries away a whole existence with it. I woke up chilly during the night, and pulled on another cover. The season of rebirth is coming, November, December, the blue, windless, *cool* months of the year. Impossible not to revive, and to look forward. Actually, I am better. If I did not know by now how to weather these physical and nervous crises I should, I am convinced, be on my way to the Company's graveyard. As it is, I knew when I got up that I was on the road to recovery. The balance of my body was restored. I have no complaints to make of my body, it has served me very well, it functions perfectly so long as I use it with a due regard for common sense. When my mind is calmer I must make some arrangement, Augustine can find me a woman, it doesn't matter very greatly who. I looked at myself in the looking-glass which reflected the same image as it has done for as long as I can remember. I have always been red-faced, and no climate that I have lived in has ever been able to change my complexion.

Apparently I was missed while I was in purdah. There were several notes, which I had not opened, including one from Mrs Fay. She hoped I had not overlooked the card of invitation to dinner which she had sent me, as it was the last occasion on which she and Mr Fay would entertain before he left for Canton: her daughter and niece were looking forward to making my acquaintance. Heavens, the daughter and niece! The two long-awaited young ladies must have arrived, and I missed this event.

I missed Soldier, on my usual walk. I like to think that he is not dead. I wonder what became of him. Could it be that on account of his imposing appearance he was kept alive, and handed over as a tribute to the mandarin of Casa Branca? Perhaps he now sits on a silken cushion in a Chinese hall hung with lanterns and golden inscriptions. Harker could translate them for me.

I would almost get another dog now, but I do not think that Puss would accept it, and I cannot drive her away from her home.

On the way home a Chinese girl was walking before me in the street; at first sight her hair and something about her walk struck me as familiar. I quickened my pace, but it was not Ala.

When I got in, I found there were other letters, including one from Calcutta, from Mrs Chinnery. I felt so strong that I did not put off the ordeal, as I usually do, but opened it at once. Heaven knows what I expected to find, but nothing as bad as this.

Briefly, Mrs Chinnery informed me that my son Edward has been in trouble over money. There are debts (followed a list) amounting to a sizeable sum. Only the influence of my son-in-law had prevented him, wrote Mrs Chinnery, from suffering the due processes of law. But the money had to be found. My son-in-law was not in a position to help further, etc., etc. In short, Edward was my son, and it was time I faced my responsibilities in *that* respect, at least.

Once again to find myself faced with responsibilities! Yet I find it difficult to think too hardly of the boy. It is painful, I know, to be without money when one is young. I myself have never suffered from any inability to make money: if only I could prevent it from going out again as soon as or before it is earned, I should have no worries. But I have my work. Edward has no particular bent, his talents have never showed themselves. In putting him into a counting-house I knew that I was introducing him to a life which I could never have endured, but there seemed a hope that if he did not enlarge his brain, he might at least amass a respectable fortune. But evidently he had rebelled. Mrs C's letter gave little information about the events (why did Edward not write to me himself?), but she said plainly enough that if matters

90

were not made good, there was no possibility of Edward remaining in India. He would have to join me in Macao, where he could no doubt be found employment.

Found employment! when every possible opening in a respectable firm is eagerly snapped up by relations of the present members. There is no course but to send the money. But how? The only money I have I earn by my work, by seizing and transferring on to canvas the roadstead of Macao, the Nine Pins and the Asses' Ears, the flood of brilliant light over the white-walled convents and pillared mansions of the town, and there is never enough. True, I don't owe money here as I did in Calcutta, but that is only because my expenses are small. Mrs Chinnery herself is the biggest drain on my finances. It is true that a certain amount went on Ala. The little wretch was fond of silver dollars. Where is it now, I wonder, her little store, which she was laboriously accumulating, so she told me, in order that she might one day buy a stone house in the village and have security? Probably at the bottom of the Inner Harbour. Part of her fortune she carried always on her person in the shape of gold rings and pins. I hope that she has those still. I could not bear to think of the ornaments which she fought for so fiercely in life, pilfered from her body. I do not know if the other boat people would do that—it might be 'bad joss'—but there are plenty of other ruffians who would not hesitate for a moment. I would rather think that her body has been claimed by the sea which has swallowed up so many without a sign. Every day millions are born in this country, every day millions die. Life is full of violence which passes unnoticed under the blazing sky. Only the hawks which wheel in the eye of the sun see all which happens below, and they are too indifferent to swoop to each new piece of carrion. Ala has vanished without a trace, and nothing remains to remind me of our short passage of pleasure but a handful of drawings which show her small head with the black hair drawn back smoothly from her forehead (she had the round forehead of a baby). The only sketch I made of her naked she found and tore to

91

pieces. Nakedness appalls the Chinese, although they are as concupiscent as any other Oriental people. I have caught the servants peering at some of my paintings in fascination and horror, and of course they think the low necks of the foreign ladies unspeakably immoral.

Just then one of my Chinese servants sidled in to the room behind me, the latest joined, Aloo by name. Neat and sturdy, as unapproachable as the Chinese tongue, I had never exchanged more than a few words with him, but now he volunteered information.

'Master, velly solly, one thing makee master much trub (i.e. trouble in their curious jargon).'

'Well, what is it, Aloo?'

'One piecee small cat just now makee die.'

Seeing I did not understand him, Aloo pointed to the verandah and pantomimed.

'He makee fall. Small cat just now bottom-side. Master come look-see.'

I followed him downstairs to the garden where on the flagstones I found one of the kittens, undoubtedly dead. In spite of Aloo's 'he' it was the female, the thin, gossamer-light, round-eyed female. Aloo picked up the body almost contemptuously. No doubt it was too small to make a meal even for a frugal Chinese. I knew I never would get the truth, but nevertheless I put the question.

'What fashion this cat makee die? How did he fall down?'

Aloo embarked upon an explanation illustrated with gestures.

'All time three piecee cat sit topside (pointing up at the verandah) look-see, look-see birdee fly. He make this fashion ——' and Aloo demonstrated the ridiculous gesture I have often seen, of Puss quivering with excitement, balancing on her hind legs on the balustrade of the verandah, boxing the empty air for a bird or a butterfly which has sailed overhead, miles out of her reach—'and he fall down bottom-side.'

It could be true. I have seen Puss do this many a time, but always recovering herself at the last minute from overbalancing completely and falling on to the stone flags below. Poor 'small cat' had not been so lucky, or so skilful. That enticing bird or butterfly was her last. I hoped it was the true explanation. There was another, less attractive one, which was that Puss, unwilling to tolerate competition, had pushed her offspring down herself. If so, it would be my fault, for having let myself become so distracted by other things as to neglect her. And now there was this fresh trouble!

I congratulated Aloo on his English, and asked him if he intends to become a steward in a big house. He replied that when he has learned enough of the language, he is going to enter his uncle's business, dealing with foreigners.

After this I went out on to the southern verandah again, and raised the bamboo blind. The picture lay before me, full of brilliant light, with the convents, the many-pillared white houses and the crumbling churches of Macao. If I were to live to be a hundred, there is more than enough in the few square miles of this place to last my time.

Ideas: portrait of a merchant (foreign) in a *Chinese* interior. Teakwood throne, lanterns, moon gate, lacquer tea stands, bric-à-brac, etc. There are some who could carry off the part to perfection.

The small children, invariably girls, who run about carrying another child almost as large as themselves in a cotton square on their backs. The heads wobble as if on stalks. Necks are always so innocent. The hair of the children is cropped across the nape of the neck and in a fringe on the forehead. Some of the young women have a hair-style in which the hair is gathered in a flat knot at the back of the head and an ornamental pin is fastened through it. The old women wear respectable black bonnets and scanty buns. Their necks resemble those of old tortoises.

A pig underneath a plantain tree.

I spent most of the day of Mrs Fay's dinner-party working on an Indian country scene, painted from recollection and from sketches in my old scrap-books. It was turning out well, and it gave me enormous pleasure to rediscover those scenes which made so much impression on my mind when I was a young man. The light in Bengal is gayer and the air more balmy than anything China can offer. The ruins of the temples are bathed in a romantic reverie which it would be hard to conjure up round a squat little Chinese joss-house, built out of brick and tile with a demon or two sitting on the crooked roof. There is no antiquity, so far as I can tell, in the whole province of Canton, no minarets of departed conquerors, no broken triumphal arches rearing themselves out of the clutches of the throttling jungle. In fact, there is no jungle, they cultivate cabbages everywhere here. Everything you see is every day, every building is transitory. If it fell down, the inhabitants could put up another one identical overnight. The Portuguese churches of Macao are the most venerable buildings for hundreds, if not thousands, of miles. It gave me so much pleasure to work that I was reluctant to tear myself away when the hour came—even to meet young ladies.

To my surprise, both were equally charming. I do not know why, but I had expected Mrs Fay's daughter to be a child barely out of the schoolroom, and the niece to be something in the nature of a nursery governess. Miss Fay turned out, however, to be a well-grown young lady of eighteen to twenty, with very winning manners, while Miss Winters, the niece, was not so very much older—I put her at about five and twenty—and while soberer and quieter than her cousin has all the makings of a handsome woman. I say has the makings, for so far Miss Winters has not learned to make the best of what nature has bestowed on her, and her expression was sometimes withdrawn, and at others almost forbidding. But she obviously has a lively intelligence, and a capacity for observation. I caught her once or twice studying the company at table with an attention which she did her best to disguise as soon as she saw my eye was upon her. Indeed, there was a somewhat odd assortment of guests on the male side, for many of the gentlemen have already gone up to Canton for the winter season, and their guests with them. Mr Bell and Mr Bowie, with other ancient mariners, had been dragged from their fastnesses to attend, Bowie as usual delighted by sociability and fuss, but talking exclusively of Bengal and the old days in Calcutta, which cannot have interested the young ladies and certainly not Miss Winters, who was anxious to find out all about Macao. Bell, who could have told her a great deal, was at the other end of the table, but Bowie, grown somewhat jolly with the American Company's claret, interrupted his flow of Indian reminiscences to say to Miss Winters:

'If you want to know what Macao is like, Miss Winters, you must be sure to visit my friend Mr Chinnery in his studio. There you will find it all ready for easy perusal. He has books and books of drawings which will show you everything there is to be seen in Macao, pigs, beggars, the lot. I know he makes these sketches to please himself, but I dare say he will show them to please a young lady, which is a thing we do not often see in these parts.'

In fact, I make these sketches to please possible customers as much as for myself, and it is never my practice to refuse to show my work, so I urged the young ladies to do me the honour of paying me a visit. Mrs Fay accepted on their behalf.

I in turn studied the young ladies a little further (of course, every other man at the table was doing the same thing). Miss Fay has plenty of youthful gaiety and good nature, and also looks which will appeal to many. Miss Winters will not be universally appreciated: her beauty is too severe, and what is worse, her intelligence too obvious. But to my mind, she is the more interesting of the two.

Mrs Haverill was also one of the party. She was looking tired (had Captain Galbraith, now gone up to Canton, anything to do with this?) and so not at her best, but even so, she stood up well to the competition of the new arrivals. They looked almost too red and white in colour beside her. She was wearing a gown cut a good deal lower than the two misses could venture on, but she outshone them principally by the charming grace of her movements (each turn of her head and neck spoke volumes), but also in her spontaneous interest and desire to please, which is the quality men esteem most greatly in a woman.

Mrs Haverill turned to me, when we found ourselves together, and said that she had not seen me for a long time and had heard that I was unwell. Was I now fully recovered?

I replied that I had been prostrated ever since the great storm by a nervous shock which I had received, but I was now on the way back to my normal health.

Mrs Haverill turned her beautiful eyes on me and said in her soft voice that she was glad to hear that I had escaped from the tempest without physical injury, but that sometimes a mental blow could do more harm than bodily ills.

I was sorely tempted to tell her the truth—if we had been alone I am sure I should have done so—but that moment Mr Bowie, who had heard some of our conversation, said loudly to the table that he knew there was a packet of letters from Calcutta arrived for me in the last ship, and he hoped the news of our friends there was not so bad as to prostrate me.

'Mrs Chinnery is alive and well,' I said, 'but were I to hear to the contrary that would not, to tell the truth, make me take to my bed.'

'Ah, we know that Mrs Chinnery has made you take to your heels before now,' was Bowie's rejoinder.

I detected a puzzled look on the faces of the two young ladies, who immediately afterwards composed themselves into the prim images of those who have heard nothing. I have known Bowie too long to be offended at anything he can say, but this inopportune reminder of Mrs C, and in particular of her last letter, spoilt the rest of the evening for me. Otherwise it would have been an agreeable evening. We dined well, and the drinking was moderated in deference to the new arrivals. Afterwards we played various games, in the course of which Mr Bowie became quite young again, and at a decorous hour the party broke up and chairs were called for. I was carried off, the bearers making their usual grumbling at having to carry a man of my size. They dumped me down in their usual unceremonious way at the door of my house, I very soon fell into bed and pitched headlong into sleep. Such was my return to society.

Miss Fay and Miss Winter came to my studio a day or so after this event, and I afterwards escorted them to Mr Bell's garden. The end of October is coming on to the best time of the year, the beautiful winter season of Macao when the sun is as hot as summer's in the walled gardens, the sky is more blue than any Italian sky ever was, but the air is dry and cool and the nights chilly enough to make one think of fires and blankets. The garden was at its best, and the girls were enchanted by everything, the white houses, the sights seen en route, the Chinese pedlars and onlookers, now slightly more clothed than in the summer season, and even by the Macanese senhoras passing by hung with stuffy draperies, escorted by one black slave in front and another in the rear holding up a sunshade. In the studio the girls pored over my sketch-books and were delighted when they could pick out something which they recognised—their own house, the church at the end of my lane, Mr Bell's gardener at work among his plants with his pigtail carefully coiled round his head. Miss Fay swore that she has seen my favourite pig in the bazaar and that she could pick out my cow from the little group in the Company's grounds which supplies their morning milk.

My cats came in for their share of admiration, although I had to admit that Puss is rapidly losing her domesticated qualities as her duties towards the surviving member of her family become more and more negligible, and she is taking to an outside life again. She is out practically every night now, and the small hours are once more disturbed by those piercing and savage screams which are the only clue I have to her nocturnal life. By contrast her surviving kitten grows every day more fat, friendly and confident. He is a tom and therefore lacks the brain and I think even some of the finer instincts of his mother. His good nature is infinite, but unlike her, he has very little sense of dignity. Born heaven knows where, but brought up since birth in a cupboard in my painting-room, this house is his world. So far he has hardly ever visited the garden, and seems perfectly happy to stay where he can keep me in sight. He will lie all day while I am working and watch me, occasionally putting out a paw in a lazy fashion to intercept my hand—but when Puss leaps through the balustrade into the verandah, as sleek and tigerish as ever she was, he rushes to her and makes a clumsy butt at her flanks. Sometimes she tolerates him, more often she deals him out a buffet. Mother and son wash each other's faces, however, with every sign of mutual affection and pleasure.

CHAPTER 11

Less than a week later, I was on the water, en route for Canton. The reasons for my so suddenly closing shop in Macao can be easily stated: money, and Mrs Chinnery.

Another letter arrived from Mrs C. Although it did not add very much to what she had previously told me, it put me in a thorough panic. However, there are very few predicaments to which cash is not the answer, and I had no doubt that if I could remit, Mrs C's present problems, and Edward's, would be on the way to solution. But money was in short supply in Macao. The winter season was just opening in Canton, most of the gentlemen had already gone up there, and further visitors would be expected as the season's ships came in to Whampoa. It was a case of chasing business rather than waiting for customers, while if that woman took it into her head . . . but enough of that!

Another consideration which prompted me to go up to

Canton was the ever-present necessity of keeping my eye on the activities of my colleague and former pupil, Lam Qua, now practising as a portrait painter in that city. I never trust a Chinaman who has picked up Western tricks, and he learned enough from me to be able to turn out competent little pieces which have a spurious interest about them through having been painted by a Chinaman, much as though they had been executed by a monkey. So, confiding the house and cats to Augustine, who swore to preserve them during my absence, I decided on instant departure. As for Mr Barretto, his rent could wait—there were other, more pressing calls on my purse.

We sailed from Macao in the morning, by way of the Inner Passage. Although the main annual exodus had already taken place, I managed to get a place sharing an 'inside fast boat' with one of the Company's writers, a most advantageous arrangement for me, as the Company having hired the boat for their servant, my expenses were limited to my share of the commissariat, and the inevitable 'cumshaw' to the head boatman at the journey's end. As I watched Macao fading in the distance behind us, suddenly so small, our sadly shrunken universe, I was almost sorry to be leaving at the most delicious time of the year, when the trees are covered with bright scarlet flowers decking bare branches, faint blue smoke drifts up from the harbour, and dry leaves tickle their way along the Praia Grande. But ahead lay Canton, the great city, work, and riches. Even to the European confined to the Factories, the contact is stimulating. The wide river, jam-packed with native craft of all sizes, the ships of all nations lying in Whampoa Reach, the enormous humming, buzzing city confined within its walls and gates like a hill of ants in which there seems to be scarcely room enough for all the inhabitants to find foothold so that they live packed on each other's backs—all this is a far cry from little Macao.

By noon we had reached the first customs house where a pass was required, and at three in the afternoon we were still tied up there, waiting for it. We had stumbled upon the name day of the most respected god they have in those parts. From the village came the most infernal banging of gongs and drums and exploding of firecrackers. Processions were coming and going in all directions, while our compradore hunted for the official who should have been in the customs house, but of course was not, to obtain the necessary permission to proceed. Just opposite us was a small creek leading off the main stream, and over the creek was one of those hump-backed Chinese bridges. Across the bridge, in both directions, passed a stream of people, each one bent on his own affairs but following on the heels of the one before like a stream of ants. Peasants in their big wicker hats carried loads slung on poles, vegetables, buckets of fish, bundles of live chickens tied together by the legs, and even a pig crammed into a wicker basket, carried by two men with the pole between them. There were women and children, some in their working clothes, but many of them dressed in their best, the children's heads crowned with red caps with animals' masks embroidered on them. From time to time would pass a chair with some official carried in dignified seclusion within, and official runners going in front of the bearers to clear a passage. All these people jostled each other with vigour but without animosity. In this part of the world life consists of giving and receiving buffets: there are too many human beings crammed on to each yard of earth for them to be over-nice about contact with their fellows.

The creek itself was a solid mass of sampans, most of them piled high with loads of reeds and vegetables, looking as if the vessels themselves were thatched. It would have been possible to walk across from one to the other as easily as by the bridge. At the waterside lay the village, on the other side of the creek was a slight rise in the ground which usually betokens a joss-house, and beyond that the ricefields stretched away in a green chessboard to the very foot of the bare mountains.

I could have gone on watching the scene with pleasure but for the appalling, nauseous smell which reached out to us even though we were some distance from the shore. I knew also, that should we go up to the edge of one of those idyllic-looking green fields, we would be attacked at once by hordes of enormous mosquitoes which rise off the water-logged paddy in clouds and settle on the nearest foreigner. Meanwhile, my companion fretted and fumed at the delay, pacing up and down the confined space, getting hotter and hotter, declaring that it was an insult, unparalleled, etc., etc., impossible to do business wih such barbarous people, high time the Navy showed them, and so forth: so it was with relief that we saw a sampan putting out from shore with our trusty messenger in it, waving the precious pass, covered with red 'chops' as if a legion of demented red spiders had been crawling over it.

For the rest of that day, and two more days, we threaded our way through the labyrinth of creeks. Once the journey was under way, my regret at leaving Macao vanished, and I gave myself up to the pleasures of an idle existence. There were shoals of native craft to watch, including the duckboats which lower a gangplank in the morning to allow the quacking regiments aboard to march to the paddy fields, from which they return, obedient to the duck-herd's signal, at night. Plenty of other craft were making their way upstream, but we overhauled them with ease. A couple of Chinese man-of-war junks were sighted, splendid with painted armament, but I believe entirely rotten within. I am given to understand that the corruption in the Imperial Navy's supply department outshines any examples which we can furnish in the West. And as well as all this, I had the most entertaining book to read, which had been lent to me by the Librarian of the British Library at Macao, being the adventures of Captain Dillon, who got on the track of Capt. La Perouse after all French attempts to trace what had happened to the *Boussole* and the *Astrolabe* had failed. (Mr Bell as a young man saw these ships when they refitted in Macao roads in 1787: then they sailed for Manila, and all trace of them was lost for thirty years.) Captain Dillon found indisputable proof that the two vessels had been wrecked on the reef of Vanikoro Island in the South Seas. The ships were completely broken up, but by treating the natives with consideration Captain Dillon got them to bring in scraps of metal which they had hoarded; among these was a silver sword-guard, which put him on the right track.

He says that the pigs of the South Sea islands are the size of cats, and they are black, with red eyes. I should like to see them.

The third morning out, we made Old Duck Fort. That usually means Canton before nightfall. Later we passed the orange grove, another well-known landmark, still going at a fine rate, with the water purling at the boat's sides, the Chinese crew moving with alacrity about their business, shifting the huge mainsail or taking a turn with the oars, and the cooks busying themselves over the fire they had made in the stern. By this time, I was as keen as my companion to reach our journey's end. The trouble with idleness is that it leaves the mind too active—and when my mind wanders, it invariably flies to money, and my other difficulties. For the thousandth time I see my life as it should have been. Had I insisted on taking my birthright and staying in the family business, I should probably have been a nabob by now. Why did I not turn my capacities—I think I have capacities—to the creation of money instead of pictures? Then I could long ago have returned to England, bought an estate and entered Parliament, as many men less able than myself have done, instead of eking out a living painting merchants and their simpering wives, condemned to drag out my days in a Turkish bath which would have killed another man long before this. Above all, I could have had a home.

I am never tired of the company of women, or of watching their ways. How much I admire their dress and all the little refinements which accompany it! They start with such advantages that only a fool could fail to make some play with them. Rosa, for instance, was not really beautiful (except for her eyes and her teeth), but she was a truly feminine woman.

102

She affected many petticoats, more indeed than the mode prescribed, and the allure with which she quitted them one after the other was truly indescribable. In every detail of their daily life, women have little refinements which give the performance of living some charm and purpose. I am in constant fear that living alone as I do, I am getting to live like a brute, like other Europeans in the East, who without their own womenkind become coarse and slack, negligent in their dress and careless of their habits. Drinking becomes their recreation, and native women their solace. I don't fear the mental consequences of solitude in the same way. They call me an eccentric now, they have always done so, and if that means that I have ideas in my head which others have not, am I any the worse off for that? But how gladly could I cherish and admire a woman. I can't change my ugly face, but anything that I could do, I would. Shift my shirt thrice daily, bathe myself in 'smellum-water', hold the looking-glass for her, hook her gown, make every kind of a fool of myself. The thought of my comfortless, untidy house, and my threadbare belongings depresses me beyond measure. Impossible to go on living like this! I was never meant for such a life.

I was distracted from these thoughts by a tiresome present problem—the commissariat expenses of the trip. It is customary to share these, and I was ready to pay up my share. But I was *not* prepared to pay for the inordinate quantities of pale ale, claret, etc., which my companion had seen fit to order. I saw no reason why he could not dispose of what he had not himself consumed to the steward at the Factory. And as if that were not enough annoyance, my servant discovered that some rogue had last night stolen two of my good neck-cloths from beside my bunk, probably by fishing through the barred cabin windows with a long bamboo. I wondered what the thief could then be doing with them: he must be exhibiting them in his village as examples of the comic attire worn by foreign devils.

This servant, by the way, as well as the boatmen, was

horrified at my sitting in the hot sun: they consider that exposure to the full rays dries up the vital juices of the body. This is a topic of great concern to all Chinese, more so perhaps than to any other oriental people, as they set such store by posterity. The vital juices can be replenished, it appears, by consuming a variety of rich and costly foods on which the wealthier classes spend enormous sums in search of rejuvenation. Not all of this is nonsense, but I suspect that a good many of these precious substances can do no more good than a plain rice pudding. However, rich men may spend their money as they like.

CHAPTER 12

The glow of innumerable lanterns and candles, the lights of the great city, could be seen late in the evening reflected in the sky ahead of us, but we were not after all to reach our destination that day. The movement of boats on the river is forbidden after certain hours within the city limits. We had to tie up for the night and make the final stage in the morning. A glorious morning: it is fine to make Jackass Point in the evening when there is a lantern on every sampan on the river, and the Factories themselves are a twinkling mass of lights, but it is beautiful to glide up the river in the first light of morning before even the boat-dwellers themselves are astir. Our back way brought us into the river at Canton itself. Ten miles farther downstream at Whampoa anchorage, the foreign ships from all over the world are lying out in mid-stream, looking like birds about to take off in flight, while tied up by both banks are the large Chinese seagoing junks which range from the Spice Islands to the Persian Gulf. Gaudily decorated and lacking paint, lacking cordage and sadly in need of scrubbing, I wonder how many centuries of use they and their like have seen? Now their numbers are dwindling year by year.

As we approached our destination, the river began to come

to life. Small boats rushed to and fro like water beetles on the surface of a pond. The occupants shouted at our boatmen, and the boatmen shouted back. The sail gave way to paddles, and we forced a way in towards the shore at Jackass Point, through the dense mass of boats pressing along the bank right up to the Factories. There is no polite giving way here —it is each man for himself. The faint column of blue smoke which rose straight into the air from each boat showed that the inhabitants were boiling their morning rice, and they were all the more wrathful at being disturbed. High words rose. The air was still chill, although there was no breeze, only a faint movement of the upper air which caused the columns of smoke to waver slightly, before they were lost in the sky. At the interruption of our passage faces turned our way, old faces, young faces, toothless faces, faces under wicker hats, the round faces of children. They all uttered the same short unflattering observation about foreign devils, and continued to do whatever they were doing before. At last we were alongside, a gang-plank was rigged up, and we were ashore in Canton! No one was expecting us at that hour, there was no one to help with the baggage. Eventually some shivering coolies were rounded up and induced to sling our belongings on their carrying poles, the file of bearers set off towards the big doors of the Factory on the opposite side of the Square, and we followed behind. Half-way across the space lay the corpse of some small animal. The coolies with their bare feet avoided it. The same old pile of refuse still dominated one corner of the foreigners' only authorised promenade, with the usual beggars asleep (or possibly some of them were dead) upon it. It was too early in the morning for them to take any professional interest in us. Not even a cooked food stall was open. The Factory was still locked, barred and bolted, everybody asleep. At last we succeeded in rousing the doorman, and he fetched the steward.

The room he took me to was small and somewhat gloomy, as it looked into an inner courtyard. Its principal item of furniture was a huge looking-glass which age and climate together had not treated very kindly. Still, nothing could damp my spirits. I was intoxicated with being once more in the great city of Canton. I could hardly wait to renew acquaintance with Hog Lane and Old China Street. A bath, breakfast, and then to see old friends!

My first call was at the Chow-Chow Hong (i.e. the Miscellaneous Factory), to see my old friend Hurjeebhoy Rustomjee. This Factory contains a wonderful selection of natives from all parts of India. There are Malwarees, Persians, Moors, Jats and Parsees. The rich smells of Calcutta, Bombay and Madras overlay and swamp the punier odours of China. In every corner of the rambling, untidy Factory each man lights his fire and cooks food according to his creed. The pungent smells of lacquer and of sandalwood compete with the cooking, and everywhere is the insidious musty smell of opium.

I found Hurjeebhoy to be prospering, with a room to himself containing two enormous chests, on one of which he sleeps and on the other he does business. He never ceased to tell me how bad business was, but that is old habit. The 'squeeze' payable to Chinese officials is the chief matter of his complaint, he told me that they are putting it up year by year as the orders from Peking about opium become more and more peremptory. Nevertheless, profits seem to keep pace, as the Viceroy of Canton has just built himself another palace out of his share of the proceeds of the opium trade! Callers began to congregate outside the open door, and although my old friend still had plenty to tell, I did not want to lose business for him, so took my leave. It was not a convenient hour to call at the Suy Hong (otherwise Swedish Factory, now principally taken over by the Americans) in the hope of seeing Mr Harker, as I knew they would be up to their eyes in work, so I resolved to pay a courtesy call on my old pupil and present rival Lam Qua, the 'Handsome Face Painter', in China Street.

Lam Qua's house is like all the other houses in this street, a two-storey building of unpretentious appearance, with a shop on the ground floor, open fronted and closed at night with wooden shutters. Here Lam Qua runs a sort of curio shop: in addition to the main stock of rice-paper pictures, there are soap-stone carvings, 'jade' figurines, and other pieces of rubbish likely to appeal to the taste of visitors. The staircase, really a ladder, mounts steeply to the first floor, where there is a real workshop in operation. Ten to a dozen Chinese work away as hard as they can producing pictures on rice paper of junks, sampans, hump-back bridges, pagodas, and every object which they think sufficiently picturesque to attract the attention of a foreigner. Fortunately these 'assistants' have not progressed beyond the native style of painting: if Lam Qua were to succeed in imparting to them the elements of Western draughtsmanship, I might as well shut up shop myself altogether. Their productions are largely bought up by the officers of the American ships, whose passion for sightseeing causes great amusement. The story is that the same pagoda appears in all the pictures, variously labelled 'Thousand-Goddess Pagoda', 'East Gate Pagoda'; 'West Gate Pagoda', and so on. Where amongst all this hugger-mugger Lam Qua keeps his family (for this is his residence as well as his shop) is a mystery. Probably they are all employed in the business, and sleep on their working tables at night in the usual Chinese fashion.

One more ladder to climb, and I found myself in the artist's studio, a sort of penthouse. What a to-do! It was pleasant to be greeted once more as a master, pressed to take the best seat, and offered food and refreshment. But it was not pleasant to see on the easel the portrait of a European gentleman who passed through Macao not six weeks ago without offering me his custom, not to mention nice little paintings of the creeks, old houses, etc., all competently executed, which I have since found out by discreet inquiry elsewhere, Lam Qua is selling at a price which I would not accept for one leaf from my sketch-book. I have no objection to his painting sailors and boat's crews for twenty dollars a head, as I heard he was doing, but these new activities are getting more serious. Of course, it is my fault, for taking him as a pupil in the first place.

He asked me if I was in Canton for business, or pleasure. I replied Pleasure. That was perfectly sincere, for work has always been my greatest pleasure. I realise how much I owe to heaven, to have been allowed to devote my life to the occupation which pleases me most. My troubles are nothing, compared with this.

I parted from Lam Qua quite cordially, but there is no real confidence between us. Although he is the only man I can talk to about my problems of work in several thousand miles, I cannot open my mind to him as I would to one of my own race, were he my worst rival. Apart from the occasional amateur who has taken it into his head to visit China, I have had no one to talk to, about painting, since I left India. I have had to work it all out for myself.

The following morning, Harker came in to see me with a most astonishing piece of news, namely that Mrs Fay, Miss Fay and Miss Winters were on their way up to Canton and expected to arrive on the next day but one.

For ladies to visit Canton is almost unheard of, it is contrary to all old custom, and is in fact a direct infringement of the Imperial regulations governing the Factories. What the Viceroy and the mandarins, not to mention the Hong merchants (who are supposed to be sureties for the foreigners' good behaviour) will do about it baffles anticipation. It is typical of the spirit of the American ladies to attempt this escapade, although it is true that they are not the first ones to do so. Earlier this year, some of the wives of the Factory came up from Macao as a sort of *tentative*, but when preliminary grumblings were heard from the authorities, they made themselves scarce after a very few days, returned to Macao, and did not press the matter to an issue which would have decided once and for all the effectiveness of this particular regulation. There may, of course, be a purpose behind this escapade. Mr Fay's firm is the leading American house in Canton, and like the independent English firms, it resents strongly the East India Company's predominance in the China trade, and what they consider to be the subservience of the Company to the Chinese government's rules and regulations. Bringing their women here, in the face of Celestial officialdom, is a gesture of American independence. The Company's charter—which to their eyes represents monopoly in its most pernicious form—is shortly about to expire, and the 'outside merchants' are getting ready to take over. Meanwhile the grandeur and the style kept up in the Factory still overawes its younger competitors, and they resent it a little. My own feelings are divided: I can get on very well with the new men, but I feel myself to be a part of the old order (which I, too, rebelled against in my time). To return to the ladies, many of the old gentlemen in the Factories, who have not set eyes on a European woman for many a long year, will be as horrified at the news as the mandarins, but they at least will have to pretend to be civil. There are only two days in which to make preparations for these auspicious arrivals, and Suy Hong must be undergoing a most tremendous dusting and cleaning in order to receive them.

In the meantime, I received the most interesting commission, to paint the old father of one of the Hong merchants. I was conveyed that same day to an immense villa set by the side of a creek, in an inner court of which the old gentleman was lurking like a wizened old spider. In spite of many dissimilarities, the experience carried me back to my early days in India, when I painted the portraits of numerous native princes. There was the same mingling of squalor and grandeur as I had known before, the walls richly inlaid, the floors of marble and none too clean, the same pungent human odours arising from odd corners. The owner of the palace may be dressed in cloth of gold or the richest Chinese brocade, but round him mills an endless number of servants, each one acting with artless unconcern, scratching himself heartily as fancy takes him, spitting where he likes, and in the case of the Chinese, cleaning his teeth in the ornamental fishponds. Ala used to scratch, too, with all the concentrated attention her young body could bring to bear on the act. Even Puss could not rival her. The old Chinese gentleman and I exchanged bows, while an 'interpreter' supplied civilities in copious quantity. I wished that Harker could have come with me. Occasionally some gorgeously apparelled females flitted into view at the entrance to the court where we sat, and having stared their fill at me, staggered—for they were all small-footed—away. They hid their faces very inadequately by holding up their sleeves in front of them, and managed to cast some fairly inviting glances at the foreign devil. I thought from their number and their youth that they must be the wives of the sons of the house, but Harker informed me later that the youngest and prettiest of them all was in fact a concubine of the old gentleman's. Old age has its compensations in this country!

The ladies have come! They are here! What a lark, as Harker would say.

They arrived at midday, at a time when the Square was well filled with a motley collection of Chinese, countrymen gaping at the outsides of the foreign factories, hawkers, criers of various goods and services, and beggars, with an odd ship's crew thrown in for good measure. Chairs being forbidden here to foreigners, the ladies had to walk across the Square from the landing place to Suy Hong where they are lodged, but their disembarkation caused nothing but the most reverential astonishment. Of course, their sex was probably a mystery to the Chinese, the confusion as to who wears the skirts and who wears the trousers here being so great and their custom being so diametrically opposed to ours. The ladies' bonnets however, were objects of awe.

The ladies retired at once to rest from the fatigues of the journey, so we had to wait to the next day to pay our respects. I attended the levee, for I can hardly call it anything else, at Suy Hong. Cards were being carried in every minute, and some extraordinary old characters made their appearance whom nobody had ever seen before. One or two of them were wearing garments of the preceding century, and we concluded that they must have appeared from the recesses of the French and Spanish Factories. Miss Winters gallantly essayed a conversation in French with one of them, and he was astounded to learn from her that France was once more a monarchy. Apparently he did not know anything at all about the downfall of Bonaparte, and quite clearly did not believe that Miss Winters was telling him the truth. She asked him if he liked China, to which he replied that the people had a certain sensibility, but their wine was undrinkable.

Miss Winters looked more animated than I have seen her before, and it suited her. Mrs Fay would have benefited from rouge, and clearly had not recovered from the exertions of the journey. Miss Fay was in her usual good spirits. The daughter has charm in plenty, but the niece has character, enough at any rate to make her fairly unhappy. Her expression in repose is calm, almost cold, but she is clearly a girl ripe for adventure and will seize the opportunity with both hands when it arrives. She notices everything about her and knows nothing of herself, which is a dangerous combination.

A day or so later the Company gave a great dinner for the ladies. Their visit seemed set fair for triumph, as no reprisals had yet been threatened by the authorities. I found myself seated two places away from Miss Fay and was lucky to be so close to one of the centres of attraction, as apart from the three guests of honour, the company was, of course, exclusively male. The French and Spanish antiquities had not been invited, so that we were able to converse in one language only. Miss Fay was full of her adventures. That afternoon she, her mother and her cousin, escorted by several American gentlemen, had attempted to go shopping in Old China Street, but such a press of people gathered in the twinkling of an eye that they had to retreat again.

The two girls were subjected to the covert ogling which the presence of a marriageable woman of his own race provokes from the Canton or Calcutta bachelor; as if the wares

111

were put up before him, and he had only to state his preference and make his offer. Miss Fay was chatting away in her vivacious manner and did not notice anything untoward, but Miss Winters was plainly conscious of the insolence in her neighbours' looks and was nearly put out of countenance. What made my blood boil, though, was to see the Chinese servants standing behind the women, running their eyes over their necks and shoulders in the most barefaced manner and under pretence of serving them, leaning against the backs of the ladies' chairs and trailing the sleeves of their dirty Chinese gowns against the silk and muslin dresses. This should have been stopped.

The dinner itself was sumptuous, no fault could possibly be found with it. The whole company removed together to the drawing-room after, but all that happened was that the ladies were left together at one end of the room while the gentlemen congregated at the other, not taking the least notice of them but busily talking of their own affairs. Mrs Fay and her daughter chatted determinedly and pointed out to each other the beauties of the apartment where we were, but I saw Miss Winters let her glance run over the crowd of males —mine was the only eye she caught. I felt the embarrassment of her situation. Why I did not go to her side I do not know. I suppose it was cowardice that held me back: and I stayed where I was. Not surprisingly, the evening began to flag, and the ladies retired early to the Suy Hong. It was a fine sight to see the procession of lanterns escorting them bobbing its way across the Square.

I returned to my own apartment, where I was overcome with a sense of oppression. Even in December when the days are bright and short and the nights cool and windless, the air is never as clear here at nights as it is at Macao. By this I mean that there is not the same freshness as there is by the sea, where the ever-moving current of air draws the bamboo blinds out from the windows and releases them again, and pours its gentle steamy breath into the white houses and verandahs of Macao. My room is on an inner court. I have

112

no view except of the room opposite, I can only see the city and the river if I go outdoors, but I am conscious that the air which flows to my window carries with it the exhalations of a thousand other human beings, the breath of toilers in rice fields and workshops, sampans and manufactories. The nights at Canton are dead still, although the great city stirs from time to time in its sleep, and sounds which would be lost by day carry distinctly from one quarter to another. Traffic on the river is mostly still, although there are craft whose business it is to work under cover of darkness, and from time to time small screened lights slip quickly down the lines of sampans tied up together like birds in formation. But how quiet is the air! Not a movement, even on the water where the current pours on endlessly to the sea. Only when the morning mists gather does some vague movement of air spring up and carry the sounds of daybreak. The summer here would be torture indeed. I have never been in Canton in the hot weather save in '25, when I was so glad to find myself out of my troubles in India that any other alternative would have seemed cool by comparison. But even my Parsee friends admit that in July the Chow-Chow Hong is 'velly warm'.

Physical discomfort is one thing, though. It can be—here it has to be—endured. But what returned to depress me more than the constriction of my surroundings was the sense of terrible inadequacy, of shame for a life wasted, which I thought I had overcome in Macao. I found myself thinking back to thirty years ago, when I first came out to the East. How happy I was in those days, and how unhappy: now I suspect that the years have dulled the capacity for both happiness and unhappiness. My hand has, I think, grown defter over the years, and my knowledge of my art has increased: I can paint better now than when I was twenty. But does that compensate for the inability to *feel* as I did then, and to experience the alternate onslaughts of delight and despair which used to visit me in those days? I doubt it. Have I also lost my capacity to love, I anxiously wonder. When I was young I fell frequently in love; which state, if reciprocated, could raise me to the heights of happiness, or when rejected, cast me into the lowest depths of despair. Has this deserted me, too? The beauty of women still delights my senses, although the compulsion is not as strong as it was, and although I am an ugly fellow, I know how to please women. But where is love? Rosa was the last human being I could truly say I loved. My little Chinese girl I wanted to love but could not—an extraordinary predicament for myself. Although I realise now how furiously I squandered my energies when I was young, throwing them away first on this one and then on that, taking satisfaction where I found it and giving, I fear, all too little in return, still, I find myself regretting the man I once was.

I found myself so homesick for India that I went round the next day to Chow-Chow Hong, and took a cup of tea with my Parsee friend. I found him worrying about the marriages of his daughters: he was proposing to send for his family to come to Macao from India. The real trouble is that he does not trust his brother, who is in charge of the Calcutta end of the business, and also of Hurjeebhoy's family. If the daughters marry in India, he is afraid that they will marry good-for-nothings who have to be supported at the expense of the business, while if he brings them out here and arranges the marriages from Macao, he will at least get some work out of his sons-in-law.

I pointed out the disadvantages of this plan. If Hurjeebhoy brings his women here, he cannot have them in Canton, so he will have to arrange accommodation for them in Macao, which will cost money. Then if the sons-in-law of his selection turn out useless when they arrive here, he will have them on his back for the rest of his life with no hope of getting rid of them. I feel he would be better advised to keep his burdens at a distance.

'You are always right, you are a wise man,' said Hurjeebhoy, but I knew what was in his mind. He, like most of us, is sick of living without a woman of his own race, and wants his fat old wife to cook his meals and create the familiar atmosphere of home for him.

I should like to make an album of the lowly trades of Canton. The other day I watched coolies packing porcelain, fine cups and bowls, for shipment. They used fine grass only, which they wound so cunningly round the articles, welding them into a sort of pyramid, that you could have dropped a parcel of twenty tea bowls on the tiled floor without cracking one. An old clerk sat at a table and made out an inventory in time with them as they worked. He wore a dark blue silk gown reaching to his ankles, and from his chin sprang a scanty growth of white hairs, which he had conscientiously trained to their fullest length. The variety of hawkers is a constant delight, and I particularly like a man who often hangs about the Factories and chats with the servants, the feather duster man. His dusters are the cheapest merchandise possible, but each one is a work of art, with the feathers arranged in rich gradations of colour. Some even have the feathers so arranged as to make a face. When I see him with his dusters, I remember how Puss when younger was convinced that the article was alive, and would 'kill' it again and again, until there were no more feathers left for her to get her claws into, and Augustine had to buy another feather duster.

I also like to watch the carpenters working in their street, just behind the Factories. To our eyes, they hold their tools in the most inept fashion, gouging towards themselves where we would work away, and they appear to be in constant danger of planing off their own toes, with which they hold the work steady, but their faces are rapt with concentration as a good craftsman's should be, and their naked shoulders shine with sweat, while the object takes shape under their hands.

But just now I have commissions for portraits, and cannot do what I like. The devil of it is money, money, always money. I would work to please myself—who would paint a man when he could paint a woman, or a tree?—but merchants have money, and I need it.

I *must* work harder. How much is boiling in my mind: how little I have achieved. At the moment I am hard at it—yet there is something else which is eluding me, a face half formed in my mind, a face which if only I could capture it would open to me a world of beauty, sights and sounds beyond anything which I have yet experienced. How it will come about, I do not know, but I feel that something is about to happen which will alter, once more, the course of my life.

CHAPTER 14

Christmas has come and gone, the last toast has been drunk. It was duly feasted, although Christmas without the presence of women and children is a sorry thing. The foreigners' rituals were performed, to the great delight of our Chinese servants. They have no idea at all what this particular celebration betokens, except that it means holidays, banqueting and presents, all of which are thoroughly congenial to them. The Factory offered the usual magnificent banquet to the other English and American gentlemen in Canton.

There were no women because the ladies returned to Macao a day or two before, having lasted just over a week. By the end of that time the Hong merchants were at their wits' end to cope with the flood of instructions which they were receiving from higher authority, requiring them to get rid of the foreign devil females without delay; trade was beginning to suffer, and what was nearly as serious, a strike of private servants throughout the Factories was threatened for the next week. So Mr Fay yielded, he really had no alternative, and sent his women away. The inmates of the Factories went en masse to see the ladies off from Jackass Point, so that it was more like a triumphal departure than an expulsion.

Hundreds of Chinese who had not hitherto had the opportunity of seeing them evidently tried to take this last-minute chance of doing so, and it was extremely difficult to force a passage for them through the crowd. There was no incivility, though.

No sooner did the season of obligatory good will pass than a host of petty annoyances descended. This is the inevitable result of confinement in a small circle, where small irritations spring up originating in the various peculiarities of the members of our community. That tiresome matter of the expenses on my journey up was resurrected. I *will not* pay any more. Then a further incident occurred.

A person whom I like least among my fellow-inmates, a humourless, self-opinionated gentleman of some estimation in his own eyes, wandered into my room when I was painting and chanced to pick up Captain Dillon's book on the travels of La Perouse. He made no comment at the time, but having stayed for a while to watch me, went away. Judge of my surprise when later in the day I received a pompous communication from him in writing, expressed to be in his capacity as Chairman of the Committee of the British Library at Macao (the first I knew of it), drawing my attention to the fact that the rules of the Library forbid books to be removed without the express authority of the Committee, and requesting that 'no further infraction of the Rules' should occur. My blood boiled on reading this piece of impertinence. To begin with, I think I am entitled to believe that if Mr da Silva, the duly appointed Librarian, permits a book to be removed for private perusal, he is not promoting an 'infraction of the Rules', but acting with the authority, express or implicit, of the Committee. And if he were in fact to be infringing the rules, who would be to blame—he, or I? I have no doubt as to the answer. Moreover this deliberately offensive letter was delivered to me open and unsealed, not by one of the Chinese servants which abound in this place, but by the steward, who almost certainly took the opportunity of reading it. I knew it would be round the Factories by next day that

117

I had made away with the book! I showed the letter to Harker, and others of my friends. They were sympathetic, but pointed out that this man, if he is Chairman as he claims to be, had authority to write as he did, and as the whole situation is undoubtedly due to a misunderstanding, it would be wisest to do nothing and let the matter be forgotten. The trouble is that I can't forget so easily, although I have had to endure many such insults in my time.

All this, of course, makes a hopeless atmosphere for work: endless bickering, distasteful company. The place like a tomb, no air, no view, nothing. One might as well be in prison. Eyes bad—always a danger signal. Clients clamouring on all sides, but it is no good showing the donkey the stick without the carrot.

I was nearly at the end of my tether when, thank God, it was arranged. I managed to find, or my friends found, a sick American missionary who was going down to Macao to die. I persuaded my hosts that I could not get any work finished except in my own studio, and made my preparations for departure. My state of distress was then such that I would have done anything to get away, even to taking a chop-boat by myself, although this would have meant saying good-bye to my profits from the weeks of work in Canton. As it was, I travelled for nothing, in my capacity as sick-berth attendant.

Luckily we did not encounter any bad weather or other alarms on the journey, as the reverend gentleman, my companion, was not in a state to stand any shocks. When he was first carried on board, I thought he looked too ill to live. The first day and night he lay on the sleeping bench like a corpse, while his servant and I took turn and turn about to watch him. After the first twenty-four hours, to my great relief, he showed signs of rallying somewhat. I think the fresh air and the escape from confinement in Canton must have helped to reduce the fever. As soon as he recovered his senses I read my companion's Bible aloud to him, at his request, for long stretches, which seemed to give him great relief. By the third day the patient's faith had prevailed, and Mr Tucker was so much better that he was able to get up and sit in a chair on deck. By the fourth day, he was regretting the time he had lost from his pastoral labours. Quite a few of the Americans are addicted to missionizing, and a certain amount of hymn singing comes from that side of Suy Hong which has come to be known as 'Sion's Corner', but one would indeed have to be young and energetic to envisage making any impression on the countless millions of Chinese, who already have a system of observances which suits them very well. If there is a Supreme Being for the Chinese, the Emperor represents him on earth, and it is not difficult to show respect to an emperor who could have your head cut off tomorrow. Otherwise the domestic gods of the Chinese seem to be jolly, familiar fellows, presiding over the field and the kitchen, and easily kept in good humour with a pinch of incense and a red candle or two. The fishermen with their patron goddess trust to her merciful and benign influence: nothing like the horrible excesses of Indian superstition enters into their lives. Although missionaries speak to the contrary, it seems to me that their views spring more from unwillingness to admit that men can be happy, sober and industrious under a system totally devoid of all religious inspiration, than from a sincere conviction. Because the Emperor is the apex of such system of state religion as exists, he becomes automatically, in the eyes of these men of God, the worst kind of false idol. Personally, from what I have seen in India (and Ireland), I hold that there is no more heavy load for a simple, uneducated people than an oppressive weight of religion. They die because they will not drink water that has not been consecrated, or they die because they drink water which, although sacred, is polluted with filth. Their minds probably do not comprehend the spiritual significance of their beliefs, but their daily lives are cramped and hampered by all the outward observances with which they have to comply, usually at considerable cost to themselves and benefit to the priests.

However, I kept all these opinions to myself, and as a result Mr Tucker and I got on very well together. I spent much of the journey in the administration of medicines and bed-side vigils, and was rewarded when my companion, who had been carried on board in extremis, was able to go ashore in a chair when we landed in Macao. I saw him carried off to Mrs Fay's house, where he was to be nursed by the ladies, and made my way to mine.

I nearly wept to see my own home again! All those within came running to welcome me, Augustine, Aloo, the cook and the rest. Only my little cat skulked somewhere in the garden and would not come in. Her fat and stupid son had forgotten me, but was easily won back with a little coaxing, and a few titbits. He looked well, so evidently Augustine had been looking after him properly. My things were unpacked, and soon the studio looked as if I had never been away.

At two o'clock in the morning I was awakened by a familiar sound—an imperious summons from a demanding little animal outside the shutters. I got out of bed and opened them a crack. She brushed through the gap and wound herself, purring, or rather roaring, round my bare legs, and in her pleasure at seeing me, distributing over me a great quantity of wet from her coat (I could hear the raindrops softly settling on the earth outside). We went back to bed together, and she settled herself in her favourite position at the back of my knees, thus making it impossible for me to turn over. I put a hand down to stroke her, and I felt her fine soft fur, her pricking whiskers—and could it be her belly was a little swollen? When I touched her, she replied by giving a drowsy purr of contentment, and to that sound I fell asleep again.

How mysterious the world is at six o'clock. This is when she woke me by fidgeting round, wanting to go out again. A grey swirl of mist invaded the room when I opened the shutters, and I could see that the thickness of the night had given place to the half-light of dawn, with its silences and muffled noises. My neighbours' house over the wall was as silent as the grave. It was too early for any sound from the harbour. The only bird which had the temerity to try out its voice was shocked into silence again. Puss walked leisurely to the window, sniffed the air for a second, and melted into the garden.

I had meant to set to work immediately, but once I was dressed old habit reasserted itself, and I could not resist making a tour of familiar places. The Praia Grande, the steep track to the top of Penha Hill, round the hermitage, then the descent to the Inner Harbour. My picturesque point of the shore with its rocks and temple trees, all was unchanged, and there were the usual sampans lying just off the shore while their owners busied themselves on board. There were none of the hostile gestures and shouts of Canton. The sampan people shrug their shoulders at the bugles from the forts, and the black soldiers in gaudy uniforms escorting the Governor of Macao on his useless occasions. When the mandarin procession from Casa Branca signals its arrival, and the barrier gates swing open to admit it into the city, they tremble before authority with much bowing and mock humility, but not even the long arm of the mandarin can pursue the boat-people into the hundred and one little creeks which only they know. It seems to me that they are the freest of all dwellers in this celestial empire, and perhaps that is why they tolerate foreigners who have made some venture to get here and who put up some resistance to the empire which treats these people as outcasts and yet forbids them to leave its shores.

As I was passing it, I called in at Mrs Fay's house to inquire after the health of Mr Tucker. I was shown into the drawing-room where the ladies were. Mrs Fay seemed to be much stouter than I remembered her, but this was probably due to the enormous number of capes, frills and shawls which she was wearing. The girls were also muffled up, and they were complaining of the cold and of the lack of heating arrangements just as loudly as they had previously complained of the heat. We talked a little of everything, and nothing—that is, we all talked but Miss Winters. She has the art of making silence interesting, that girl, but I would have liked to hear her open her lips. In fact, I would like to know more of her.

121

I made a detour on the way to pass by Bell's Lane. To my surprise, the great mansion was shuttered and desolate. Mr Bell was not in residence, and his people could give me no idea of when I should find him at home. I walked through the garden. The pots of plants were blooming and the birds in the aviary looked well cared for, but these are tasks which can safely be left to a Chinese, and I noticed other signs of the master's absence. The garden was filled with a tribe of children who had their origin in the porter's lodge, a sort of cavern in the wall. Washing was hanging up on bamboo poles. Had I possessed a single word in common with him, I would have made some inquiry of the gate-keeper, but we had no means of communication. I went on to see Alexander Bowie, who said that he had not seen Mr Bell since before Christmas, and supposed him to be in his usual difficulty.

On my return, I shut myself up in the painting-room and set to work like a fanatic. Both cats sat on the other side of the door and *roared* at me to open it, but for once, I took no notice. There are these days, wonderful days, when eye and hand and mind are in accord, the hours pass in a flash, all fatigue is forgotten. I sweat, I pace back and forth, I finish with my eyes worn out, my pulse irregular, myself in a state of collapse from nervous exhaustion, but the results are worth it. The painting is there, it remains, it is lasting. It is worth some expenditure of self to capture a vision of the mind. I have to fight, literally fight, to seize and pin down on canvas the image which is there behind my eye. I lost count of what day it was. I only knew that foreigners' New Year had passed, and Chinese New Year not yet come.

I emerged from the bout dog-tired, shaking all over with exhaustion, and with cold. There is no way of lighting a fire in this house. Only one room boasts a chimney-piece (a sumptuous marble affair which must have come out in ballast from Portugal or Italy) but there is no chimney! What I need is a Chinese padded coat to keep out the cold, such as all the respectable men I see in the street are wearing, but I am too fat to find one ready-made, and it is not a good time to approach the tailor. I have had to open a box and get out an old English coat which I have not worn for many a season. Neither Puss nor Tom likes the cold at all! A truce has been declared between them, and Puss now spends most of her time in the house. Usually they are to be found at opposite ends of my bed, well rolled in under the covers.

The other night I dreamed of a fire. I was sitting beside it, in London. I knew at once that I was in London, where I have not been for thirty years, by the hideous din from the street, the noise and dirt everywhere, the mud—and the cold! I was about to set out for the Royal Academy, to see my own pictures on exhibition, when I woke and found myself in China. Probably in London they think of me as dead, or some traveller's tale. I must send something really big, to show them that I am not only very much alive, but very much to be reckoned with.

Work suffered a dramatic interruption when Mr Bowie came rushing in to tell me that the body of Mr Bell has been found, buried in the sand of Cacilha Bay, a favourite summer bathing beach. The body was in a perfect state of preservation, and there was no saying how long it had been there. Nobody, as Bowie reminded me, has seen Mr Bell since before Christmas. All inquiries at his house received the same reply, that he had 'gone to the country', and of course it was strongly suspected that he was once more on the run from his creditors. He was certainly not at Canton, however.

Rumours are already flying round about the manner of his death, according to Bowie. From the circumstance that the old gentleman had been found under the sand, it seems likely that there were those that had put him there. Robbers are always roaming the island: yet who would bother to strike down the old man for the sake of the little which he might have on his person? It was being suggested that one of his Chinese creditors, made desperate by repeated evasions, had determined to have his revenge, if not his money, and had hired an assassin to perform the deed. This is possible, in Macao, and would have been a favoured solution, were it not for the fact that Dr Anderson has examined the body, and was absolutely unable to determine the cause of death. There were positively no marks of violence. Yet another theory is that Mr Bell had sickened and died in the village house to which he had fled, and his hosts, afraid of what might happen to themselves, had taken this way of disposing of the embarrassing corpse.

The possibility of robbery was the one which the Portuguese authorities were pursuing, and they were endeavouring to discover the truth from the informers in their employ —in fact, setting a thief to catch a thief. Whether this will yield any results is doubtful.

Later that day Bowie and other gentlemen went out to meet the body when it was brought in, at the San Antonio Gate. It was to be laid in the mortuary chapel of the E.I. Company until such time as the Portuguese officials would allow the burial to take place. Usually hasty interments are the order of the day here, and in this we are doing no more than bowing to the exigencies of the climate, but Dr Anderson has said that the body has been so perfectly preserved by soaking in salt and sand that it has in fact undergone some sort of pickling process. According to Bowie, Bell has darkened somewhat in colour, but otherwise looks much the same. The body was discovered by boys digging in the sand for bait.

Poor Bell! What an end. It is a strange story, although not as strange as some of the histories Bowie and I can remember. Now everyone wonders what will happen to the mansion, the garden, the aviary and the bird of paradise. Bowie says the creditors would like to seize everything, but Mr Bell's former partner, a Portuguese of Macao, claims that the house and contents are his. The white mansion will become a dirty tenement, I suppose, and the glories of Bell's Lane will be forgotten as though they had never been.

Part Four

CHAPTER 15

I began to paint Miss Fay's portrait (no mention having been made of the niece's) to the accompaniment of a mounting fusillade of firecrackers. Chinese New Year was in full swing. There was no change in the weather except for the worse. The damp chill of the unheated house penetrated into my bones. For once there were no flowers in the pots on the verandah, although I knew that downstairs in the warmth of the kitchen quarters the gardener had been lavishing his care on the little flowering trees which he was getting ready to greet the new year and the official opening of spring. Watching the damp marks creeping up the walls of the house, the plaster peeling off in dirty flakes, and the mist congealing on the branches of the trees outside the window, it was difficult to think that spring would ever come. Augustine had dotted braziers here and there in an attempt to make the studio bearable for the young ladies. For Miss Winters, not Mrs Fay, accompanied her cousin to the sitting, and while I painted that pretty, vivacious young girl, I was conscious all the time of the very different beauty of the young woman who sat in a corner of the room, quietly turning the pages of the sketch-book which I had given her to pass the time. Miss Winters has a beauty which touches me, too fine perhaps to be noted by the crowd, which makes it the more precious to those who do discern and admire it. Perhaps there is too much intelligence in her face to appeal to the average man, but no man would, I imagine, find fault with her figure. Long neck, perhaps a shade too long, fine shoulders, bosom well marked, waist slim. The ankles might belong to a Greek goddess. Feet narrow and high arched, rather long. Eyes;

grey. Complexion; fine. Hair—how can I describe it? To say that Miss Winters has light brown hair is exact, but fails to convey the whole truth. When the light falls on it, her hair has a golden burnish, and when the light shines through it, it has the paleness of ash, but yet were I making an inventory of Miss Winters' features, I should have to list it as brown. Miss Winters' hair is severely dressed, according to the present fashion, it is drawn back from her ears and knotted behind her head, but no doubt it will soon be frizzed over her eyes like a lap-dog, if the women have their way.

How young that face is, and yet so wise! I have become used to the Chinese faces which I see on every side, the opaque skin, the features set in a mask which gives nothing away, the unvarying blackness of the eyes and hair. I had nearly forgotten the play of expression and meaning on the features of a European woman, and the way the blood pulses visibly beneath the transparent skin. Miss Winters' skin is as yet untouched by the suns of the East, yet it has not the unreal pallor of women who spend their lives resting behind closed shutters. That may come later, but just now she is blooming. What is there in Macao to interest a girl like this? A few temples and curiosities, and during most of the year, nothing but a handful of worn-out men, drained by the sun of health and life.

Miss Winters was wearing a blue gown with tight sleeves. There was a little band of blue flowers round her hair. The gown was cut high to the neck but it disclosed every line of her figure. This, I suppose, is the art of the dressmaker. There was a line of small buttons from neck to waist, which ran between her breasts. Whether they serve any functional purpose I do not know, but the mere sight of that row of buttons is enough to conjure up the delight of slowly unfastening them, one by one. Contrast the idiocy of the Chinese woman's gown, which fastens up the side!

No Chinese can be relied on while the New Year lasts. This was demonstrated when the two girls came to go, and only one chair was to be found. The bearers of the other had decamped, chair and all. What was to be done? I suggested that Miss Fay should ride in the chair, and asked Miss Winters if she would be prepared to walk, with my escort. She replied, at any other time, certainly, but she was terrified of firecrackers, a fresh explosion of which occurred just at that moment. It was finally settled that Miss Fay should return home first, and then send the chair back for Miss Winters.

So we went back again to the painting-room where Miss Winters looked at some more sketches and said with her sparkling eyes turned to me that she had always dreamed of seeing India. Oh, it all welled up in me then and came rushing out—the sights and sounds which I knew so well and remembered with daily pangs, the hot streets of Calcutta burdened with a mass of humanity, the hushed quiet of the jungle broken only by the screech of vivid birds, the broken pinnacles of the ruined palaces rising here and there from among the piled-up masses of green, the smell of the dusty country roads in the evening light, and above all, the colours threaded through it all, the colours of skin and of clothes, as garish as the sun and as pungent as the smells of India.

'But you could not go there,' I said. 'India is not a place for women.'

Miss Winters fired up at once, as I might have expected.

'Why not?' she said. 'I am sure an intelligent woman would enjoy everything you have described.'

Poor child, she has no idea, no idea at all what life in India is like for a European woman. Take an interest in things Indian? It would be unheard of, and therefore wrong! And she has no idea of the climate, she has only experienced the winter in Macao. Why, they die like flies, the young and pretty girls who come out to Madras and to Calcutta to be married. They die, or they return to England, ten years later, pale trembling wrecks of themselves, much as the men will return (if they are lucky) in twenty years' time, having outlived two or even three wives, but having made much, much money.

I am so chronically short of paper that I have used my old sketch-books again, and in the spaces between my old Indian sketches appear figures of Chinamen, sampans, pigs and goats. It was one of these later drawings which caught Miss Winters' attention. When I asked her what she was looking at, she pointed to a little sketch of a Chinaman, an old man, squatting on the ground with his pole beside him, tranquilly smoking his pipe. It was a funny enough wizened-up old face like the head of an old monkey, but the drawing had caught the air of simple contentment which enveloped the old coolie.

'I like that drawing very much. He has a good face,' she said. 'I have noticed something about these drawings, Mr Chinnery. Please tell me if I am right. When you draw Chinese, they are people, they spring to life immediately, whether they are bargaining in the market, or rowing a boat, or just sitting by the roadside. I feel that I have seen just that mother, or that hawker. But your Indians never seem to me to have the same reality. They are beautiful figures, draped like classical statues and assuming classical attitudes, yet I feel that you were not interested in them as people, only as figures in a landscape.'

'You are quite right,' I exclaimed. 'When I lived in India, I was fascinated by the country. The figures were incidental to it. The picture as a whole was what interested me. The people in my landscapes were shy, fleeting, beautiful. They had an existence as short as butterflies, during which they brought colour into the world. That was how I saw them.'

'How is it different in Macao?' asked Miss Winters.

'There are no landscapes here,' I replied. 'One hill, a couple of forts, a handful of churches and houses, one bay. I have had to turn my attention to smaller things, to what you see here, hawkers, pigs and coolies.'

'There must have been all those in India. What then is the difference?'

'The people here are solid,' I replied, after a moment's reflection.

Yes, solid, ugly, sometimes malformed from the coolie's

carrying pole, or the endless swing to the oar, or the perpetual labour of the ricefields. They do not sway along the roads in bright fluttering garments, with a flower tucked behind the ear; they wear sober black or blue except on holidays, when the stiff red silks of decorous rejoicing come out of their boxes. Their voices are loud and raucous, not high and giggling, and the smell of the cooked cabbage which they love so much turns my stomach, whereas the spices of India were pleasant to my nose. Yes, they are solid. They have peopled the land, whereas the millions of India drift across the earth's surface, scratching with their feeble strength, lighting their handfuls of twigs for the evening meal, and lying down to die with the classical drapings of antiquity drawn tightly over their heads.

When Miss Winters had gone, leaving me alone in my dingy, untidy house, smelling of damp, cats and neglect, among my faded belongings, I could not help remembering other contrasts. When I was in Calcutta, I was the most favoured English artist in India, and the highest paid. Not only did they flock to me for their portraits, for which I never charged less than two hundred and fifty rupees, but they wanted my company all the rest of the time. You could not see the chimney piece for the cards of invitation, Lord this presents his compliments, Lady that desires Mr Chinnery's company, etc., etc. This place is not my destiny! I was not born into the world to finish my days among the damps and miasmas of a Portuguese native settlement on the edge of nowhere. Above all, there is no one here to talk to, no one to open my heart to, all the objects of my love, hope and trust have been snatched from me one by one. Where is my son, where are the women I have loved? This is why I cling to my memories of India with all its ingratitude, its puffed-up officials with their petty pride and their callous hearts. It was the country where I spent the early days of my manhood, when a smile or a frown could make summer or winter for me. There I was alive, I had noble emotions, I raged or I loved. India held bitter sorrows for me, but I did great things there. Oh, that girl Ala, if she had not been so hard-hearted, how I could have loved her, and what a fool she would have made of me!

CHAPTER 16

Menu for a New Year's dinner:

  MUTTON (real mutton, shipped on the hoof from Nanking), augumented by

  BIRD'S NEST SOUP (an over-rated dish, to my mind)

  FISH from local waters, cooked with ginger

  A HONAN CAPON, boiled, with oyster sauce

  A WILD GOOSE ('fly goose')

  CURRIED MACAO OYSTERS (very good) with Bombay ducks

  FRUIT (lychees, dates, Chinese oranges, etc.). And a

  CHESHIRE CHEESE

I was reading again Harker's account of a celebration which he and others in the American Factory had organised at Canton, when I received a very welcome invitation from Mrs Fay to dine at the Praia Manduco. (Ever since the Chinese New Year began, I have been treated to a series of execrable meals: evidently my kitchen is temporarily in the hands of the gardener.) I accepted with alacrity, knowing that an excellent dinner, even if not quite up to Canton standards, would be put on the table. I was not disappointed. The meal was first-class. One or two ancient gentlemen had been exhumed to reinforce the Reverend Mr Tucker and myself, but as each of these recluses is at daggers drawn with the others (some of these feuds stretch so far back in time that their origins are all but forgotten), and most of them had got out of the habit of society, it fell to me as usual to sustain the conversation. I amused the ladies by recounting how I had sold a picture recently to a ship's captain who wanted a souvenir to take home with him. He was looking for something picturesque, with a flavour of Cathay. Scene after scene, in fact all my available stock, was examined and rejected as being too ordinary. Groups of pigtailed coolies squatting round an eating-stall in the market, rice bowls held under their chins with one hand, chopsticks in the other: two old Chinese grandmothers with babies slung on their backs, gambling by the side of the ancient temple steps: a tanka-boat family eating by the light of a lantern slung on an oar—all these were found wanting as being far too familiar. My captain could not understand why I should take the trouble to paint such humdrum stuff, the kind of things one would see every day. Finally, having ransacked the painting-room from top to bottom, we came upon something to his taste, a charming little scene, and a lovely piece of painting, although I doubted if he would appreciate that. It really broke my heart to sell it—a ruined temple glimmering white above the trees, with the water lapping at its foot. My sea captain was enraptured by this, he must have it, it put him immediately in mind of that stretch coming up to Folly Fort! It was the Pearl River to the life. I drove a hard bargain, for I really did not want to let that picture go: I hate to sell my favourite creations, each one a little bit of myself. The more reluctant I showed myself, the more he pressed me. Finally I yielded and a price was agreed. I took the dollars: he took the picture. He did not ask me, and I did not tell him, that that temple was in India, on the banks of the Hooghly. True, it was painted in Macao from one of my old sketches, but that was as near as it came to the Pearl River. I have long ago learned that the customer sees what he wants to see, and that it is unkind as well as unwise to disillusion him.

My worries I kept to myself. Ships can bring competitors as well as clients. Making the run out to Canton is becoming a popular trip for the itinerant artist who has reached India, and the visiting brethren do not allow their talents to be stifled by any lack of imagination. Invented Chinese scenes, characters reproduced upside down, the most ludicrous

131

confusion of dress and figure, and the thing is given the true touch of Cathay by being seen through a lattice-work reminiscent of a medieval instrument of torture. This is what they take back to London to flood the market. I cannot compete in producing such abominations as junks sailing backwards, and boat girls *rowing* in the European style instead of facing forwards and leaning on the oar. I paint the figures I see, some of them gnarled with age and work, and most of them redolent of garlic and cabbage, and if the public at home does not like it, there are plenty of others to supply their tastes.

Later Miss Winters asked me if I continued to send pictures to London for exhibition. I told her Yes, that I was preparing a scene on Green Island, a ruined boat-dwelling and a fisher family, but the picture was not yet finished (I did not tell her that the canvas was turned to the wall of my painting-room and that anguish still came into my heart at the thought of it). Mrs Fay, catching at a few words of our conversation, asked me if I would show the young ladies and Mr Tucker this pretty little island, its ancient ruins and so forth. I shuddered inwardly. The recollection of my last visit to the island is still with me, the tangled wreckage along the fringe of the shore, the devastated plantations and the empty beach. However many times I go there, that is what I shall always see, although new settlements of squatters will have sprung up and the industrious peasants will have replaced the uprooted fruit trees with cabbage plants. In the few weeks which have elapsed since the storm struck us, hundreds of thousands of new lives will have come into being, in huts and upturned boats, in mud houses in the villages and on board junks at sea, all of them lives without purpose and without meaning—almost without dignity. Reason tells me that there are hundreds of Alas to be found along the Praia Grande every day: but even so, I will not go to Green Island.

Instead, I proposed the Ama temple which was accepted by all, although not without demur by the Reverend Mr

Tucker, who is chary of idol temples (as if a bit of red paper ever hurt anyone!) So an expedition has been arranged.

Two cats sitting on the verandah, between the pots of pink and white camellias which have made their appearance to celebrate the coming of the New Year. Both are washing themselves. Up and down go their heads in unison, nodding like mandarins. Puss's bulk is beginning to incommode her somewhat, but in spite of her matronly appearance, her expression never changes from that of the little wild creature she was when she first came to this house. I wonder who has fathered her next brood, and what assortment of tails and colours I will shortly be presented with. They are not likely to be the offspring of a bamboo broom. (The Chinese have a belief that if a cat cannot find a mate, she rubs a bamboo broom across her back and becomes pregnant. They also say that a cat's nose is always cold except for one day in the year, when it becomes warm.)

The hour of the evening rice. The smell of the hundreds of cooking fires which rise all over Macao. The smell, and the sudden quiet. We are castaways, thrown up on our island, surrounded by the sea, and the weeping mist.

The day of the expedition to the Ama temple dawned fair enough, although not very clear. Fog lay in the streets and on the harbour in the early morning, a fog pierced only now and then by sharp sounds. A burst of firecrackers sounded off as a junk left the Inner Harbour, a voice shouted in Chinese from my servants' quarters, and a dog set to barking behind the wall of my neighbours' house. I had ample time to stroll from my house to the Praia Manduco, so I made a detour by the cathedral and through the bazaar, in order to see what life was stirring there. I found the street of the carpenters up, and hard at work. There was a tremendous noise and chatter in this group of shops, all alongside each other, plying the same trade, and all turning out chairs and tables in the same shapes as the carpenters have always made them, high, square, and uneasy, with sometimes a slab of marble let into the chair seat, to provide the final touch of discomfort. The next street is the boxmakers'. Here they sit crouched in their tiny workrooms which are no better than boxes themselves, fragrant with wood chips, lacquer, cooking oil and a hundred other things (the mixture is not unpleasant), turning out objects costing a few cash which are marvels of labour and ingenuity. Families work together, each member taking on a stage of the work proportionate to his age and skill. The old men fascinate me beyond everything else: their faces are hollowed like bones picked clean, they crouch monkey-like on the workbench and hardly lift an eye to anything else. Occasionally a strange passer-by will attract the quick, bright tortoise look, but usually the foreigner is ignored. These tiny brick and tile shops hang like swallows' nests along the side of a Portuguese church with dirty marble steps and ornate railings. Saint whoever it is, for I can't for the life of me remember which, faces what would have been quite a noble square had the builder's original intentions been carried out. But as it is, one side is missing, and a Chinese bazaar fills the gap, and over all the place are the ragtag and bobtail of the market, hawking their goods, begging, chaffering, shouting and spitting. The pavements are littered with refuse of a character which must remain nameless, and the walls of the church support squatters' shacks where they are not used for putting up long strips of Chinese characters. Here and there a knot of coolies crouch on the ground, playing an interminable gambling game with small stones.

Making my way through this, I reached Mrs Fay's house, where I found my companions in readiness. We climbed aboard, the chairs (we had to take chairs, for the young ladies, of course, could not be expected to walk through the streets) were hoisted up, and we set off. Our procession made little or no impression on the inhabitants of the forest of junks which dipped and bobbed at the water's edge. The loungers on the quayside, cleared incontinently from our path by the shouts of the bearers, gathered up their counters or their pipes and retreated a few yards to squat on another dusty patch of road and resume their occupations. The houses after a little tailed off, the godowns became meaner and the plaster shabbier, and the smell of rotting fish wafting from the place where the fishermen lay their catch in the sun to dry more violently assailed our noses. The ladies took out their handkerchiefs with cries of dismay. The little straw huts of fishermen appeared between the rocks on the shore, and their netlines stretched out into the placid waters of the Inner Harbour. Small sandy beaches looked inviting, until one saw the litter which was washing to and fro at the water's edge. Then we rounded a corner of the road, and before us were the untidy roofs of the Ama temple, our destination, and the ancient trees which surround it.

The bearers halted in their tracks and looked round inquiringly. I directed them to go a little up the hill behind the temple. At a green and grassy spot the ladies alighted, shaking out their crumpled skirts and exclaiming at the beauty of the view. Below us, we could see the black-trousered fishermen making their bows on the steps of the temple, which even from this distance, looked much in need of sweeping. Many of the women had babies strapped to their backs. Their devotions completed, the worshippers sat about on the steps and refreshed themselves from the cooked-food stalls in the neighbourhood. Occasionally a little eddy of blue smoke issued from the portals of the temple itself. Mr Tucker was not anxious to venture nearer, but whether this reluctance was due to a natural dislike of heathen idols or to a hygienic distrust of the far from clean surroundings, I could not tell. However, the young ladies were eager to get closer and peer at the tinsel splendours within, so we cautiously approached and mounted the steps.

The conversations around were broken off short as the Chinese watched our progress, but they evinced no hostility to us.

There was, in fact, nothing to see when the open doors of the temple were reached, only a murky interior where stood the paraphernalia of Chinese worship, oddly shaped vases ranged on a table black with age and grease. The image of the Ama goddess herself could hardly be seen in the gloom. There were the usual red paper and gilt offerings which the Chinese are so fond of. A toothless old priest in a dirty robe appeared, but as we had no language in common, he could tell us nothing of interest. Quite a number of people were inside the temple, but they did not seem to resent our presence in any degree, and after a few minutes we gave the old man some coins and quietly withdrew. The most interesting feature of the temple to me was the strange curved roofline with the heraldic beasts perched upon it, seen at close quarters.

We retraced our steps to the chairs, and the question was what to do then. Nobody wanted to go home. I suggested mounting to the top of the hill to see the view. This was agreed to, and we set off, Miss Fay, Miss Winters and myself walking, Mr Tucker riding, and the empty chairs following behind. The path led in a figure-of-eight round the steep hillside: Mr Tucker shouted to his bearers to go more slowly and they responded by quickening their pace, frightening him so that he nearly jumped out. We plunged into a drift of mist which had caught in a cleft of the hill, and out again, then after a steep last lap up the slope we emerged panting on to the top of the hill, where the clouds obligingly parted to show us the Outer Harbour beneath us, the promenade of the Praia Grande curved round it like a bow, and the palatial residences of the merchants strung along the bow at intervals like pearls on a rope. Nobody was on the top of the hill but a goat-herd who scrambled to his feet at our approach and ran after his charges as fast as his legs would carry him. They, afflicted with the unconquerable

136

curiosity of their kind, turned to examine us before skipping nimbly out of reach.

I do not know of any other view in the world like that from Penha Hill. As you stand facing out to sea, the Nine Pins fade into the limitless distance of sea and sky. Nearer at hand, the Outer Harbour is spread out for inspection: the shapes of the encroaching sand banks can be clearly seen under the water. Turn yourself to face the other way, and you are looking into China, separated only by the strip of the Inner Harbour, always clamorous and busy. On the other side of it are the great bare hills of Canton, where the Inner Passage winds between their fastnesses. Turn to the north, and the Peninsula of Macao—all three miles of it—is laid before you, till it dwindles into the tiny neck of land with a barrier across it, which divides Portuguese territory from China. Bazaars, churches, convents and opium dens all look as clean and tidy from this vantage point as a painted city.

I found Miss Winters next to me as we stood there.

'It looks so small, and yet a world in itself,' she said. 'How long have you lived here, Mr Chinnery?'

'Five years,' I replied.

'Five years,' she echoed. 'I have only been here three months, and yet I feel that I know it all, as if it were my own little country. Do you not find that it cramps you, after five years?'

'Yes, and no. I agree that it is a very small space, but in many ways there is enough here for a painter.'

'I have heard the Harbour compared with the bay of Naples, but as I have never been to Italy, I do not know if it is a true comparison. They say that when you have travelled a great deal, all places begin to resemble each other. Do you find that, Mr Chinnery?'

'No, it has never been my experience, and to tell the truth, I suspect that most people who say it merely want to show off how widely travelled they are—unless they were born without eyes, that is.'

Miss Winters was silent for a moment, and I wondered if

137

she had taken my words as a rebuke, which was certainly not my intention. Then she asked:

'What is India like?'

What is India like! All to be answered in a couple of sentences. Visions rose in front of my eyes and vanished again when I tried to collect my thoughts and give the essence of twenty-five coloured years in a single phrase. At last I said:

'I cannot tell you what India is like, Miss Winters, for when I first lived in India I was a young man, and young men are not interested in their surroundings, they are interested only in themselves. The countryside is something they pass through at full gallop. The river is simply an obstacle which separates them from where they want to be. That house is where a particular woman lives, and all other houses are without any interest to them.'

'That may be true of most young men, Mr Chinnery, but I doubt whether it is true of an artist, and you have painted beautiful pictures of India—I have seen some of them.'

'Most of the pictures I painted in India were done for money, and consisted of what I saw in front of me. The Indian pictures which you have seen were painted since I came to Macao, and began to see India with my mind. That is, since I ceased to be young.'

'How old does a man have to be before he ceases to be young, speaking from the point of view of an artist?' inquired Miss Winters.

'They always say,' was my reply, 'that a man has ceased to be young when he no longer looks at pretty girls. But that time has not yet come in my case.'

Most girls would have taken that as their cue to giggle or simper, but Miss Winters did neither. She smiled a little to herself, and looked out to sea. She had taken off her bonnet, and the breeze whipped her cheeks and hair.

'I think my cousin wishes to go,' she said, and indeed the other two were calling to us that the mist was rising again, and that it was useless to stay. Miss Fay and Mr Tucker were already getting into their chairs as we walked down towards them. The moment had to be seized.

'If you really wish to know what India is like, then come to my studio, and I will show you my sketches—if you would like to see them. They will convey more to you than I could possibly describe.'

'I would very much like to see them. I will ask my cousin——'

I interrupted her.

'I do not think India interests Miss Fay at all. Would not your aunt let you come by yourself? I am a very safe character.'

The girl stands a full head above me, and I am old and fat and ugly, as well as short. I meant all this. In view of our disparity, any hopes on my part would be ridiculous. Yet I made the first move, once more risking a woman's scorn by offering her something which she could so easily refuse. Yet Miss Winters did not refuse; she murmured:

'I will ask her.'

Quite dazed by my audacity, I helped Miss Winters into her chair which fell in behind the other two. I watched the bearers jog off down the hill with my own empty chair following behind.

She is beautiful, she has intelligence, and I could love her. I think she is kind, she is calm, she moves like a goddess, and I could worship her for all these things. Life is poetry, life is beauty. The clouds, the mountains, the mists, the sea, how I glory in them. All these thoughts raced through my mind: all my solitary wanderings were forgotten. Below me, on the winding road, a sedan chair was carrying away a being who could bring light into my world. At that moment, as if it were an omen, a little peephole of a window opened in the mist through which I saw the islands far, far out to sea, like fingers of rock pointing up into a blue sky. Then I ran down the hill by the steepest way into the town. The streets to my eyes were marble and gold: I hurried to my house like a man possessed, but possessed by joy. When the Chinese in the streets saw me pass, their faces grinned from ear to ear, but I did not care if all the Chinamen grinned at me from Macao to Tartary! I reached my house in a sweat—a shout to Augustine, quick, a green tub full of cool water, and fresh clothes. I saw myself in the looking-glass as I pulled on my shirt. Well, I am short, I am ugly, nothing can change that, and women have mocked me in my time, but I do not think Miss Winters will mock. She has too fine a spirit for that.

She says she wishes to know more about India—that is, she wishes to know about my life in India. She is coming to this house. If only it could be today, yet I cannot hope that it will be so soon. It may be tomorrow. Let it be tomorrow! Oh, this suspense. I am too old to find myself waiting like this for a girl again.

CHAPTER 17

She came the next day. I asked how she had obtained permission. It was simply by telling Mrs Fay that I had invited Miss Fay and herself to come and look at my Indian sketch-books. As I had anticipated, Miss Fay had been disinclined to come, and Mrs Fay, after rebuking her daughter for taking the invitation so lightly, had said that Miss Winters at least had better go, so as not to appear uncivil. Mrs Fay was too busy with household matters to accompany her, and apparently saw no necessity. I did not know whether to be flattered or the reverse at this reliance on my age and respectability, but I blessed anything which allowed me to have Miss Winters to myself for an hour.

She was not embarrassed. Perhaps New England manners are more free and easy than ours are. She wore a white gown with grey stripes which gave the effect of silver. When she took off her bonnet I saw the dazzling clarity of her skin, like that of a child. A determined chin, small mouth, round cheeks from which the East had not had time to take the pink and white. I could not tell the colour of her eyes—eyes such as can change their colour at will. When I first saw Miss Winters, I thought they were blue, but on looking longer I perceived that they were grey.

We talked a little and I showed her the sketch-books. Miss Winters made percipient, sensible observations (there is nothing I hate more than stupid compliments and empty comments from those who cannot really think of anything to say) but I hardly heard a word. She looked so charming! The hour was up all too soon, she rose to go, and I escorted her downstairs to her chair. Before she was carried off, she gave me a message from Mrs Fay, inviting me to supper that same evening.

Of course, I accepted. I counted the hours which separated me from seeing Miss Winters again. Hopeless to settle to any work. In the afternoon I went out for another walk, and instead of my hilltop, I deliberately chose the most populous part of Macao, the bazaars and the waterfront. There is a delicious pleasure in wandering thus among a crowd of people all intent on their own occupations. They were eating, sleeping, sitting, chaffering or gambling, and I strolled in their midst, apparently idle. But I was so happy that even the beggars could not annoy me. I stopped at a shop in the bazaar where ivory trinkets were displayed, and the proprietor, who knew me, ran forward to welcome me inside. There was an ivory ball in the shop, pierced with openings, which contained another ivory ball, which contained another, and that one another, and so on. All these diminishing spheres revolved independently inside each other. The whole toy was finished off with a tassel of red silk. Trashy oriental work, you might say, and yet the whole thing demonstrated such hours of patient labour and such centuries of skill that I found myself looking at it with something like reverence. Alas, the price was far beyond my means and we parted, the shopkeeper and I, with expressions of mutual esteem, but no business done.

As he bowed me out of the shop a woman held out her

hand, a beggar-woman of indeterminate age, dressed in rusty black, her hair in wild elf locks around her face. On her back, slung in a coloured handkerchief, was a child, asleep or dead. It resembled nothing more than a packet, with its arms and legs spread-eagled at the corners, and its head lolling helplessly on the neck. The child's scalp was covered with the virulent sores which most of the bazaar children have. I don't usually give to beggars, but the day being different from all other days, I fumbled for a coin. To my astonishment the crone pocketed it with a look of beaming good will on her face and called out something which I took to be a blessing on my head before shuffling off, clip-clop, in her wooden sandals. The child on her back lolled its scabby head in my direction, and I saw that it was peacefully asleep, and also smiling.

I took it for an omen. Let the day be remembered as a happy day, the day when I was blessed by a beggar-woman for the first time in my life.

When I got into my house again, I went out on to the verandah and looked down into the garden. I could hear a woman's voice which seemed to be coming from my servants' quarters, but it did not sound like a Chinese woman's voice. A man answered her, in a voice which I recognised as Augustine's, so I took it that they were speaking Portuguese. The woman's tones were low and caressing, and for the time it occurred to me that Portuguese could be a pleasing language. I strained my neck in an effort to see who was there, but the couple were standing immediately below me and out of my range of sight. Then I had to retreat hastily as they came into view in the garden and both glanced up in my direction, the woman adjusting the black shawl over her head. Now that I could see her face, I made out that she was comely, although not in her first youth. I think she was aware of my presence, for she stood there for a full minute before covering herself with her draperies and sliding once more out of sight. A few minutes later I heard the outer door being opened and then re-barred, and Augustine's voice sounded on the stairway.

I later asked Augustine who his visitor was, and he answered that it was his cousin who had come to see him, a 'Macao lady'.

Having the whole afternoon to prepare, I as usual left my dressing until too late, and having only stayed to see the cats' evening rice brought up, I hurried off to my own supper with Mrs Fay—and Miss Winters.

She wore a dark grey gown, the bodice fitting snugly, likewise the tops of the sleeves, then came various little rouleaux of material which were gathered in finally by a ribbon at the wrists. The effect was Quakerish, but highly becoming. (What would she look like dressed for a ball!) I nearly burst with exultation when I caught her eye. It was a good thing that I am an old hand at dissembling: that is to say, I have learned to dissemble, for it was never in my nature. When I was a young man in Madras and Calcutta I felt violently, I loved passionately, and I did not care who knew it. But it was pointed out to me that my natural behaviour was 'dragging the lady's reputation in the gutter', and I soon found that it made me an object of general dislike to most of the other men, who, being incapable themselves of anything but the most cynical and degrading liaisons, united to condemn any of their fellows whose emotions were young, and honourable. I learned then to sit in the same room as a woman I passionately adored and to exchange polite commonplaces with her, address her as Mrs . . . and Ma'am, and never by one blink of an eyelid disclose the fact that I had left her side at six o'clock that same morning. Women, of course, need no schooling. Artifice is second nature to them. Anyhow, my early lessons stood me in good stead that evening. I told my anecdotes, kept the table in a roar, paid special attention to Mrs Fay and Mrs Haverill—and obtained a rendezvous with Miss Winters for the next day at the Camöens grotto, a most public, non-compromising place of resort.

We met there. She was punctual, I was early. I saw at once when she arrived that she was troubled in her mind, and it seemed that she was displeased with me. I asked her straight away

'Why are you angry with me this morning? What have I done to annoy you? I have never said one word to you which could give you pain.'

Miss Winters hesitated before replying, and when her reply came it was only one word.

'No.'

'Then what have I done, and where? It could only have been at your aunt's house, that I earned your displeasure.'

She looked away from me.

'You did nothing. It was something you said last night. Oh, not to me, you were talking to my aunt. You were speaking of Mrs Chinnery.'

I remembered well enough what I had said: item one, that Mrs Chinnery was the ugliest woman in the world, item two, why otherwise should I have been running away from her for twenty-five years. I have said the same thing on numerous other occasions. There is nothing the company enjoy more than hearing a man make a joke against himself.

'You knew that I am married, though, did you not.'

'Yes, I know that, but it was hateful to hear you speak of Mrs Chinnery in that way.'

'Why?' I asked, although I already knew the answer.

'Because she is your wife, and you must have cared for her once. You may have your reasons for not living with her, but to hold a woman up to ridicule is surely odious. It sounded—so unlike you.'

I did not answer. I was asking myself, how did I come to utter those words? Did I believe them myself? There was a time when Mrs Chinnery was beautiful to me, and I am not the man to consider a woman's looks gone because she has borne two children. What happened? However many times I ask myself this question, I can never supply the answer. Better to let it go, to accept it as a fact of life, like old age, baldness, sorrow, happiness, toothache.

144

Miss Winters evidently took my silence for contrition, for she went on, rather nervously:

'She is, after all, the mother of your children.'

'Of some of my children, you mean. You seem to know a good deal about my affairs, Miss Winters.'

She flushed, but replied steadily enough. 'It is difficult not to know, when the people I live with—my aunt, and Mrs Haverill, and even Mr Tucker—do nothing but gossip all day long about other people and their affairs.'

We were some distance from our meeting place, and were walking in the direction of the famous grotto.

'Then you know all the worst there is to be known about me. ('More, I expect,' she murmured with a smile.) You know that I married a woman when we were both young, that I lived with her for two years, and have lived apart from her for many more. Please don't quarrel with me—there is no need to quarrel about things like that. I asked you to come here to tell you how much I admire you.'

I saw the pink flush which rose and faded away in her cheeks.

'Why?' she asked, in the voice of an angel.

'Because you are young, and beautiful, and good.'

'You do not know that: you know nothing about me at all. We are complete strangers to one another, and you should not be talking to me in this way.'

'Strangers?' We had reached the steps leading up to the grotto, and I was one step ahead, forcing her to stop and look up at me. 'How can you use that word when you know as well as I do that it is untrue? I have been waiting all my life for you. It is impossible for us to be strangers. If you mean what you say, there is no truth in the world.'

I did not wait for an answer, but led her up the steps to the so-called grotto where stood a bust of the poet, Camöens.

'Is that all there is to see?' she asked. 'I thought the temple you took us to was much more interesting.'

'It is just a place to visit. I only suggested it because your

145

aunt might want to know where we were. I really wanted to see you, and you only.'

She turned away, and sat down on a stone bench which stood there. Panic for a moment came over me.

'You do not find me ridiculous?'

She was playing with a leaf, and her bonnet hid her face.

'Why should I find you ridiculous?'

'Because I am old and fat and ugly, and you are young and beautiful.'

She looked up, and I saw that she was smiling.

'I do not find you old, or fat, or ugly.'

'Heavens, ma'am, I have never had any illusions about my looks. You need not flatter me.'

'Your looks are yourself.' Still that angel's voice, now rather faint and low. My knees were suddenly afflicted with shaking. I sat down beside her on the bench. She drew her skirt aside to make room for me, and a fold of her dress fell on my knee, light and warm. I seized her hand in both of mine, and kissed it fervently. She left it in mine for a minute before drawing it away.

'I think I can hear someone coming.'

'We shall say that I am teaching you sketching.'

She laughed outright. For two pins I would have kissed her then, but I judged her bonnet to be too deep. Besides, there *were* people coming, a Macanese lady and gentleman. They approached the grotto, the lady leaning on her escort's arm, and they examined the bust. I fancy they were as little pleased to see us as I was at their untimely arrival. They read out to each other the stanzas carved on the plinth and departed again at a snail's pace, casting backward glances to where we occupied the bench which was, I suspect, their destination.

It was maddening to be subjected to these interruptions, but Miss Winters refused to come back to my house, saying that it was already too late, and she must return home. I could not bear to let her go without knowing when I should

146

see her again. In desperation I suggested that I should take her and her cousin the next day to see the Barrier pagoda. If she liked temples, that might please her.

The pagoda was never visited by the young ladies and myself, however, for when the time came the rain sluiced down unceasingly. The clouds descended so low over the harbour that they almost touched the masts of the vessels pitching uneasily at anchor. I fretted and chafed, going every five minutes to the window to look out, but it was all to no avail. The rain continued to fall, purposefully. Tom watched me reproachfully. Clearly my restlessness was offensive to him, for after a little while he jumped down from my writing-table where he had been sitting, and padded off downstairs in search of better company. He refused to come back for all my calling and coaxing. I had dinner alone, and was bored with my own company. It was still raining after, but I could not breathe in the house and had to go out. Immediately my steps led me to the Praia Manduco, and *her* house. The rain chose at that moment to dwindle and stop, and all round from gardens and yards rose the sour, exhilarating smell which rain leaves in its train. The leaves hung down stiffly from the trees as though flattened by the weight of water. Most of the downpour, rejected by the shallow soil of Macao, was running down to the sea by gutters and gullies. The streets were deserted, although I know that when the sun emerged once more with a glare the wet stones would begin to steam, and the Chinese would erupt in their hundreds in the empty squares. The only human figure to be seen besides myself was a coolie wearing a cartwheel hat and a cloak made of palm leaves. His trousers were rolled up above his skinny shanks. He gave me an unfriendly look, and disappeared into a side alley.

The front of Mrs Fay's house was shuttered, and the rain dripped from the verandahs. I saw it from the corner: I did not care to go too near and be caught gaping like a young man at his girl's window, but I thought I could hear a faint tinkle of music as Miss Fay or Miss Winters performed in the drawing-room on the instrument which, despite all their efforts, was never quite in tune.

On my return to the house I was buttonholed by Augustine, with a long face, asking for money to pay bills. Had I not been transported by happiness, I would have been seriously alarmed. My creditors as usual are making themselves heard on every side. (As soon as one is paid off, another regularly takes his place.) According to Augustine, we are in debt to the butcher, the grocer, the fish hawker, the water carrier, and the tailor. Meanwhile, there was no wood for the kitchen fire. All this was incomprehensible to me, seeing that I had dined at home less than half a dozen times in the last month, and then off the most meagre messes. I pointed this out to Augustine, but as usual he had an answer.

'Cats just now eat plenty meat. Every day they eat meat. And drink plenty milk.'

There never was an argument about household expenses when this matter of the cats' food was not brought up. But I had more to think about than Augustine's troubles. When I could get rid of him I sat down to write a letter to Miss Winters. To Charlotte. Charlotte. Never before was there a Charlotte in my life, I could reassure her on this. I could see one thing quite clearly, which was that this girl held my life in her hands. For her—with her—I would do anything. When she saw this as clearly as I did, life would begin for her as a woman—and what a dance she would lead me.

Puss was lying at my side, too heavy and languid to move. She (and fat Tom) are the only creatures I have in the world to tend. It is that which makes this gulf, this waste of emptiness in which I spend my days. The world is full of fine and splendid things, we are surrounded by sights and sensations in endless variety which any man, however dull his perceptions, must take delight in. Yet what are these pleasures when there is no other human being with whom to share them? A man like myself can live and move in the world of other men, with traders and merchants, sharing their company, the best of fellows, and yet be the loneliest of beings.

For too many years now I have been perpetually alone. Sometimes what I fear most is to be left for ever *outside*. Now that Charlotte has come, I feel springs unsealed within me which I thought had long ago dried up and gone underground. At last to be able to unburden myself, to let myself flow once more with the stream of life. What joy! And I could worship the being who has come to release me.

All this, and more, I wrote to Miss Winters, confident that she would understand me. She herself was seeking, I knew that. But before I sealed the letter, I hesitated. Was I wrong to unburden myself? Would I frighten her into rebuffing me? Was I turning myself into a figure of fun before a girl of her age? The letter once given, it would be irrevocable, while a little by-play of words and hands in a garden meant nothing at all, she would forget it as easily as I. There were plenty of others, no doubt, the Reverend Mr Tucker included, who had taken Miss Winters on to the verandah at her aunt's entertainments, and held her hand. I reopened the letter, and added to it:

'I am not a fit companion for a girl like yourself, I am only too well conscious of that. You should think well what you are doing before you admit me to your confidences—or listen to me. I have lived so much longer than you, and it would be idle for me to pretend that all those years have been well spent. You may feel that this sets a gulf between us—you with everything in the world to come and I with so much of my life behind me.'

At least I must be honest with her, and also with myself. Deceit would be a crime which I could never free my conscience from.

'I can tell you truthfully that I have never met a woman who moved me in the same way as you move me. It is not only your beauty which I admire, it is yourself, the revelations of your spirit which you have given me, the glimpses which I have been vouchsafed of a better existence than I have ever dreamed of.

'You need not read this letter, but I must write it. You

149

need not even give it one further thought: I promise you faithfully that I will never trouble you with a word or sign which is displeasing to you. But do not despise your most humble and respectful admirer.'

By the time I had finished writing, my course of action was settled. I would give the letter to Charlotte at the first opportunity. After that, fate would decide.

The next day (Sunday) I attended morning service in the Company's chapel in the hope of seeing her. She was there, with her aunt and her cousin. No opportunity, of course, to give her the letter.

On Monday she accompanied Miss Fay to a sitting. It was easy enough to give it to her then. I was going to see her at dinner that same evening. Then I would know.

By evening I was in agony. When I saw her, I did not know what to think. And yet she had had time to get the letter by heart! I could not believe that she had thrown it away, she would not be as unwomanlike as that. I could not get a word with her alone.

On Tuesday I took Miss Winters and Miss Fay to Cacilha's Bay. Charlotte said nothing to the point, but her eyes spoke volumes!

On Wednesday I did not see her all day. Desolation.

On Thursday I went sailing in the harbour with the two girls, in a party. We disembarked at a little island, where I managed ten minutes alone with Charlotte. She promised to come to my house, when she could.

Well, fate did decide. What was bound to happen, happened. I acted as any other man would have done in my place. It would have been beyond the power even of men far better than myself to refuse what was freely offered. By offered, I mean that Charlotte was willing, or at any rate, she was by no means unwilling. To be exact, she allowed matters to reach such a point that it became impossible for

150

either of us to prevent them from proceeding to their natural conclusion—a conclusion which I hope satisfied Miss Winters as much as it apparently surprised her.

Men are brutes when their passions are satisfied and they think of nothing but themselves. It was only after she had gone away that I reflected about an event which might alter the whole course of my life, and had already altered hers. It was only then that I shuddered, thinking of the awful responsibility which I had undertaken towards Miss Winters. Never before, so far as I could remember, had I been the one to change a girl into a woman (except, of course, with the sanction of matrimony).

For that marriage I had little responsibility, and indeed in most of my dealings with women, the ladies have taken a full share of the initiative—up to now. What happened between Miss Winters and myself was entirely spontaneous, and neither of us was responsible more than the other, except that a man must put his inclinations more strongly into action.

Today I took a drove of ladies, including Mrs and Miss Fay and Charlotte to the Barrier Pagoda. I did not even have the opportunity of walking with her, but it was not necessary to speak. I could see that she was happy, and I know that nothing can separate us now.

CHAPTER 18

It is arranged that once a week Charlotte shall come to my house for a painting lesson. At least, that is how it was explained to Mrs Fay, and that good lady seemed perfectly satisfied. I should not have been, were I in her place. These meetings are open: all others are by stealth, stolen time, had with the connivance of Macanese maid-servants and Chinese house-boys. Charlotte herself is a creature absolutely without fear, in the rashest stage of youth which brooks no obstacles, and will dare anything. I myself, although a man in love, am the one who urges caution. Useless: she brushes my words aside, or what is worse, reminds me of my own youthful follies, after which I am powerless to remonstrate further. It is hopeless to tell her that conduct which is tolerated in a man is quite impossible for a woman.

Charlotte having fallen, I should have been the happiest of men. Instead, I am often the reverse. How did I come to inspire this passion in a beautiful and accomplished young woman, I ask myself the question, over and over again. She is so fresh and blooming, this girl of mine, a glimpse of the north and of the climes I left behind so many years ago. When I lay my hand beside hers, mine with short stubby fingers, the skin reddened and coarsened by many years of the sun, and usually stained with paint, I feel my ugliness lying between us like a sword, and have to take her in my arms for reassurance. At other times I have watched her sleeping, and marvelled. Why does she love me? For love me she does, I am nearly sure of that. Is it for the pleasure I give her? If that is all, I shall be undone, for soon she will find another man who knows as much as I, a younger, handsome man, and will bestow her love on him. Or is it because I was the first man who was determined to have her, and pressed his determination to the utmost? This, I think, comes nearer to the truth. Charlotte loved me for having made her what she is, a woman. What creatures they are! We are born to give them pleasure, and they to torment us. I know that my peerless Charlotte, my girl with the grave looks and the calm airs, will use her power like all the rest, once she finds she has it.

Meanwhile, what a new richness in life. Everything about her is a refreshment to me: her beauty, her infatuation with the new ways of love she has just discovered, and her encouragement in my work. She has urged me to complete the picture of the boat girl on the shore which I had abandoned after the death of Ala. She is right to do this: I know it will be good—and marketable. With Charlotte at my side I have settled down to work like a demon, before the weather becomes too hot. My blood is running so hot in my veins that I do not need the warm, rich air, heavy with sharp and spicy smells, to remind me that I am a man, if a middle-aged one, and I can tell that we are in for another sweltering summer. Charlotte, still in her first season in the East, is not conscious of the signs, but as the warmth increases I see a languor and sensuality in her which are far from unbecoming. Who would recognise the calm, almost prim girl, with her composed ways, in the voluptuous woman with her hair hanging about her shoulders, petticoats scattered in a drift on the floor? In her passions and caprices, Charlotte shows herself a true woman.

There are no outward changes in my way of life, it is all normal, so normal that it seems odd to be going about my ordinary occupations with this exhilaration shouting in my heart. There is plenty of work and I am hard at it, with Charlotte sitting for the portrait of Ala, her skirt pinned to simulate Chinese trousers and a dish cover by her side in place of a hat. Never before have the air and light of Macao seemed so beautiful to me.

CHAPTER 19

One evening I left my house and walked along the Praia Grande at the hour when the Portuguese ladies and gentlemen take their evening stroll, savouring the peculiar pleasure of being alone in the midst of a company. The promenade was crowded. Below, on the shore, the Chinamen were tending their fishing nets, indifferent to the chattering groups of Macaïstas, who stood about here and there in the thickening dusk. The men turned round to stare, and the ladies giggled as I made my solitary way round the curve of the bay. I walked past them to the farthest point of the land,

and on to the rocks which run out into the bay, and then down to the sand. It was getting darker, and soon I could barely make out the shapes of the fishermen's huts, and the Portuguese ladies and gentlemen promenading slowly on the road above. As I was standing there, I had the feeling that someone was watching me, and turned round, expecting to see some curious Chinese face, a passing coolie perhaps, who had paused on his way to stare at the foreign devil. But there was no Chinese. Behind and just above on the rocks was a woman, or rather a muffled figure swathed in the outdoor costume of a Macanese woman. She looked down at me as I looked up—our eyes met. Her shawl was thrown back from her head, and her features were clear to me. They were fine features, and although I could not for the life of me remember where, I was certain I had seen this woman before. To my great surprise, she beckoned to me from where she was standing, and pointed back to the road. Well, I am not the man to ignore a woman's bidding, so I ascended the rocks again to where she was waiting for me.

'Who are you, madam, and what do you want of me?' I asked.

She smiled at me but made no answer, and I could tell that she could speak no English. I waited for her to address me in any language, or to make some gesture of explaining herself. But she only pulled up the black shawl which lay on her shoulders to cover her head, and turned to walk up the rocky path. I followed her—naturally I was anxious to see how this would end—and she glanced back to see if I was following. When we were back on the shore she turned round to face me, and pointing to the beach, now almost in darkness, she said in urgent tones, fixing her eyes on me.

'Ladrones! Ladrones!'

Now the word 'ladrones' I do know. It is the name which the Portuguese have given to the group of islands lying out to sea which are the first indication to the navigator that he is approaching the Pearl River, and it means robbers. These islands were in fact infested with pirates until the Portuguese succeeded in exterminating them, and were granted their rights in Macao by the Emperor of China in recognition of their services. It was then I noticed that the groups on the promenade had disappeared, and the place was utterly lonely. Was the woman trying to tell me that there were robbers on the shore, and why this concern for me? It then came to me in a flash where I had seen her before. She was, or at any rate she closely resembled, the Macanese woman I had seen in my garden, the woman Augustine said was his cousin. If it was she, had she followed me to the beach? It was futile to address her in English, but I asked again:

'Madam, will you not tell me at least who you are?'

It was no use, she was turning away, and I reached to take her arm. With a swift movement she evaded me, smiled again, and then holding her black shawl over her head, she walked slowly away, moving with dignity in spite of her lack of height. I should have followed her in my turn, but before I had made up my mind to do so she was gone. The gathering night had swallowed her up, just as a deer melts into the jungle or black cat vanishes in a coal hole. Some way off I could hear the voices of a group of people rapidly receding along the promenade. It was a black, still night. Only a little grey light tinged with pink lingered in the western sky, beyond the hills. There was nothing to be seen but a few lights from the little huts where the fishermen sat watching their lines. I could detect no more danger in the air than the warm sultriness of spring. I am no athlete, but even with my figure I reckon myself to be a match for a Chinese coolie with his clumsy pole. Along by the point, the outline of the Ama temple made a darker bulk in the gathering twilight, and the sound of gongs and cymbals came to me on the still air. The priests, then, had felt the touch of the moving season. I could picture them, the light flickering across their hollowed-out old faces as they thumped and tootled in the temple courtyard, while up above them their fantastic clay beasts crouched on the ridgepole.

Far out in the bay a light sprang up. It may have been a

155

fisherman's fire on one of the dozen little islands of which I do not even know the names, or it may have been a torch lighted on board one of the fishing junks to draw the fish into the nets. It flickered at first, then burned with a steady glow producing a focus of light suspended mysteriously over the water, which threw back oily reflections. It made me realise how dark the night was, and how empty the shore—and that it was near to the hour of the evening meal. I strolled home through the cobbled lanes which rang noisily under my feet. It filled me with pleasure to smell the warm air, and to feel myself so young and vigorous. An occasional Chinese brushed past me, keeping to the wall, while I tramped in the centre of the road. Once past me, they always ran, frightened to death, no doubt, by the apparition of the foreigner. I could hear the cries of the mulatto soldiers as the watch was changed in the Bomparto Fort. The night seemed to hold no danger.

I sat down at home with Tom—Puss was absent—to an excellent meal. After which I took a light and went into the painting-room. I spent a long hour there, turning over canvases, and thinking, and finally left all ready to start next day.

It was work, work, the next day, and the next, and the day after that, in spite of the mounting heat. Every morning when I woke the air was filled with fog, and the damp coolness of the night still lingered in the house. Only too soon the fog banks would roll back, opening up the view like a stage setting, and the streets would fill with jostling life. They hate the cold weather, the Chinese inhabitants of Macao. Their life is lived in the open air, on their junks or in the streets, whether they are sleeping, eating, or tending their children, their teeming life cannot be confined in the little brick boxes, just one room barred off from the street with wooden shutters, which pass for homes. It is a constant surprise how many human beings can emerge from one of these dwellings when the inmates are celebrating a festival, and all of them so immaculately dressed, the old grandmother dignified in black silk, the children decked out like small images. The first hot breaths of summer which fill the jaded European with premonitions of what is to come, are the essence of life to them. Where the rice bowl is seldom over-full, warmth is as good as food, and the coolie in his scanty garments of ragged cotton need not shiver for lack of clothes. Rich or poor, a man is perfectly adequately clothed in his trousers and pigtail.

Delicious as it is to paint, it is more delightful still to be interrupted by Charlotte, my inspiration, and my distraction. My lovely girl, my intrepid conspirator! But one day she arrived distracted, with her thoughts clearly elsewhere, and not long afterwards, she began to cry. I set myself to find out what was the matter (I should have guessed it). Charlotte at last confided that she was in a state of great apprehension, and feared that she was ruined. I asked her how long she had entertained these suspicions, and she replied, for five days!

Well, of course, I made light of her fears (five days!), and sent her away more cheerful than she had come, but my day was ruined. If Charlotte were right, I could not conceive of a more awkward situation. Mrs Fay seemed complaisant or blind enough, but even her blindness would be forced to see before nine months were up, and what then? Such an event would hardly go unnoticed in a place as small as Macao: there were no up-country stations for discreet retirement, and as far as I knew, no orphanages to receive the 'orphan'. I would acknowledge my child any day, but how could that help Charlotte? I still could not marry her.

Before long my agitation grew so great that I wandered out of doors, unable to work and unable to remain inactive at home. In five minutes, I discovered my mistake. The sun was still high overhead, and the streets held all the stifling heat of the day. My ears were assaulted by noises and my nose by smells which the colder weather had for the past months been keeping at bay. The hawkers had retreated into the shadow of the walls, and incurious Chinese faces regarded me from the steps of the churches, where the street idlers had installed themselves. All the streets I took seemed to lead from one bazaar to another. I hurried on, aiming to get into a quarter where I could find shade, or a garden in which I could sit. I did not notice, until the first rain drops splashed me, that the sky had suddenly gone dark, and a spring torrent was imminent, then I began to look around me in earnest for shelter. It was then that a chair carried by bearers came up behind me, and a woman leaned out.

'Mr Chinnery, what on earth are you doing here?'

It was Mrs Haverill, unseen by me, except in the midst of company, for many weeks. I advanced and began to explain myself, when the rain began to come down in earnest, and the bearers showed a distinct disposition to be off. Mrs Haverill was carried away, recommending me to follow her to her house, from whence I could take chair and bearers to mine.

The house was at no distance, and when I reached it, Mrs Haverill received me in the drawing-room. She had not taken off her bonnet and cape. Was she expecting me to take my leave without delay, I thought, but then she invited me to sit down. For want of anything better to say, I asked Mrs Haverill if she was continuing with her sketching. She laughed.

'I decided that I had no talent for it, Mr Chinnery, and never would have. It was you yourself showed me that.'

I protested, and she continued.

'You did not mean to, of course. You were kindness itself towards my bungling efforts. But I had only to contrast my productions with the tiniest scrap of paper on which you had scrawled a few pencil strokes to know that I was wasting my time.'

'I am sorry you have given it up, none the less,' I answered. 'If you had persisted, you would have reached a level of execution which would have given you a great deal of pleasure.'

158

Mrs Haverill simply shook her head, and I became exasperated.

'You were afraid of hard work, like all women.'

'You must have known a very poor set of women, Mr Chinnery. The truth is, women usually work twice as hard as men, only they make less fuss about it.'

'I do not refer to ladies' work in the house or drawing-room, very laudable as it is,' I replied. 'I refer to creative work, to the arts. There is no reason why women should not equal or even surpass men in the artistic sphere. They have the perception and the intellect. The reason why they have not done so is that although they are as clever as monkeys, women are too lazy to exert themselves to rise above the everyday run of humdrum affairs.'

'Ah, you think so?' Mrs Haverill rose, and her colour too. 'What about the Lady Way, for example?'

'Madam, you have the advantage of me. Who was the Lady Way?'

Mrs Haverill was really roused. 'The Lady Way was one of the most famous painters of ancient China, and her work has been copied again and again, ever since.'

'Ah yes, the bamboos-and-moonlight school. Yes, I have seen that picture many times, but I have never known until now that a lady was responsible. That explains it, and incidentally illustrates the truth of what I have just told you.'

I had regained the advantage. Mrs Haverill was nonplussed. Apart from the lady of ancient China (and heaven knows how she ever came to hear of her), she had no other example with which to refute my argument. Dearly as she would have liked to fling in my face the famous women sculptors, painters and composers of ancient and modern times, she could think of none. Nevertheless, she made a good recovery.

'I think you are rather hard on my sex, Mr Chinnery, and I know I could convince you that in some respects your theories are too sweeping. But it will have to wait for another day.'

'Madam, are you sending me away as a punishment?'

'I hear that you are very busy just now, Mr Chinnery, and I must not keep you from your work. Also, you are wet, and I am sure you should change your clothes before you catch cold.'

We were back on our old terms, but with a difference. Mrs Haverill I could see enjoyed dismissing me—so as to save me catching cold. She was in her best looks, flushed, radiant, and in a word, triumphant. I remembered with quite a pang of envy that Captain Galbraith was a much younger man than myself, and that some might have found him handsome.

Shortly afterwards, Charlotte's fears were dispelled: and I found myself strangely disappointed.

It was during this time that I went out to dine with Bowie. His Portuguese woman sat at the table with us, but afterwards he sent her away and spoke plainly to me, or as plainly as he dared, mentioning no names. He clearly judged me to be playing with fire. Ala, in his view, was much more suitable, and he hinted that I would do well to replace her with another water-bird. Later in the evening Bowie told me of some resort he had discovered in the bazaar, and was anxious that we should finish off the evening there. I refused: it was thirty—nearly forty—years too late for that. Or, I thought, looking at my old friend, ten years too soon.

How quiet the night was when I returned to my house. Shop fronts were barred, occasionally the shutters let out the sound of a grumbling sigh as some sleeper turned on his hard bench. The streets, so noisy by day, were silent, and the curious jagged mountains of China looming across the Inner Harbour resembled a landscape on the moon. The moon of heaven swung low in the sky, and the lantern borne before my chair was puny by comparison.

Augustine admitted me after the usual delay, and I stumbled up the stairs. Half-way, I was stopped in my tracks by a strange and terrifying noise overhead. It sounded as if all the crews of all the junks in the harbour were running

160

races in their bare feet round and round my room. No burglar could ever make such a noise, I thought. The only other possibility was a wild animal—but what kind of animal could have got into my house? I knew that from time to time rumour reports that tigers have been seen on the mainland, but why should all the tigers of Canton have swum over to Macao and climbed my stairs?

In the entrance hall was a stout stick. I fetched it, and crept up the stairs again. The Things were still at it, thundering from end to end of the floor. I flung open the door of the painting-room, and in the light of the candle I held four green eyes stared at me, while the thundering came to an abrupt stop. There were Puss and Tom, sitting quietly watching me. It was they who had created this devilish din. I put out my hand in a playful pass towards Puss. She ducked like a flash, evading my grasp, and rushed helter-skelter into the verandah. When I made a move in that direction, she ran at me like lightning, slipping round me before I could catch her, and in a second was in hiding under my bed. Tom entered into the spirit of the game and rushed to secrete himself behind an almirah.

I got them out of my bedroom finally and shut the door, but until I went to sleep I listened to them as they played on in the moonlight.

Part Five

Charlotte is in a state of great distress: she has found that the busks of her stays are going rusty. As stays are not easily come by here, this is a calamity. Now I could have told her long ago that it was useless to come to the East without providing herself with silver busks. Anything else will rust and mark the linen. Ah well, she has learned by experience, but she is very angry at the damage. Mrs Fay and her daughter have suffered in the same way, she tells me. I wondered out loud how Charlotte would manage to pass on my advice to them without giving herself away.

'I shall consult Mrs Haverill when I see her this afternoon,' answered Charlotte, 'and I am sure she will say the same thing. If she does not, I shall suggest it to her.'

'I did not know you were so friendly with Mrs Haverill as to consult her about your stays.'

'Mrs Haverill is always delighted to be consulted about clothes of any description. She is always trying to reform mine and to give me useful hints about what suits me.'

I felt that Mrs Haverill's advice might be worth following, in matters of dress, and thoughtlessly said so. Charlotte was not slow with an answer.

'I agree with you that Mrs Haverill is certainly a good judge of effects. Mrs Fay says that her neckline has gone down by an inch, and her skirts up by the same amount, each year since she has known her.'

This struck me as unjust and untrue, and I said so. Charlotte at once repented.

'I am growing to be as odious as all these other cats here. I won't repeat female gossip again. I know that you hate it.

But sometimes I'm really afraid of China when I see what it can do to people's characters, in such a short time.'

'It is nothing to India,' I replied.

'Perhaps not. Some of the stories you have told me are incredible. But all the same, Macao has a creeping effect on everyone who lives here. They become mean and spiteful and absurdly touchy about little things. Even my aunt gets upset, if she thinks she is not treated with sufficient respect as a Number 1 lady.'

I could not resist saying that Mrs Haverill did not seem to have been affected in this way.

'No, I agree that Mrs Haverill is never spiteful or unkind. She seems to be perfectly content to amuse herself with her clothes and her books and her birds. Perhaps that is the most sensible thing a woman can do. The main reason, I think, why she behaves like a normal natural person is that she is not married.'

That seemed to me an astonishing conclusion, and I said so.

'No, I have thought about this a good deal, and really it is not so strange. Most of the women here are not only defending their own position, but their husband's. In fact their own status depends on his. If the husband gets promotion, his wife goes one place nearer to the head of the table. Mrs Haverill is a widow and no one knows exactly what her husband was, so she has the benefit of the doubt, and if there is an empty place near the top of the table, you can be sure she will get it.'

'Do you think she would like to marry again?' I was curious to hear Charlotte's opinion.

'Not unless it were a very grand match. She does not want to lose her independence without increasing her importance, and at the same time Mrs Haverill has to feel that every man in the room is in love with her. She enjoys the feeling that she could marry any one of them if she wanted to.'

'But so long as she is sure of that, she is not likely to put it to the test?'

'No. And I think she would be very foolish to remarry. She is much better off as she is. I am sure the best thing a woman can do in the East,' said Charlotte, 'is to marry a man who dies and leaves her comfortably off so that she can enjoy herself in her own way. Besides, who is there for Mrs Haverill to marry? Look at the men here—there is so-and-so, and so-and-so——'

Charlotte enumerated rapidly the various members of our society, and delineated their characteristics in no very flattering terms. I was considerably startled at one of the things she said.

'Good heavens, how do you know that?'

'Everybody knows it,' answered Charlotte. 'It was one of the first things I was told when I was invited to a dinner party, a few days after we arrived. But I don't mind how odious the people are—I love this place, because of you. It is so beautiful, now that you have taught me to see it. There are times when I want to jump on board the first ship I see; then I think that you have endured years and years of this sort of life, the gossip, the envy, the pettiness of society, and it has not changed you, so I can put up with it.'

'The society may be petty, but you must keep in with it, in a place like this.'

'How can I do that?' answered Charlotte. 'I do not seem to speak the same language as most of the English people here, or the Americans either, for that matter. I cannot be sincere with them, and they are incapable of sincerity, I think. I find that I have nothing at all to say to them, or they to me. The truth is that I despise them, nearly all.'

She threw back her head, displaying her magnificent long white throat, her eyes flashed, and the colour rose in her cheeks. I sighed, as I realised with the deepest foreboding what had occurred, and that I was mainly responsible for it occurring. A natural rebel had emerged. But what could a woman gain by rebellion? It was a poor prospect for Charlotte if she began by despising the men from among whom she would have to find her future husband. For marry she must. I remembered with alarm what had taken place at the last dinner party I attended at the Company's house. As usual, the conversation turned on the doings of the mandarins. This time, they had forbidden an English gentleman to enlarge his house by throwing out another verandah, and had compelled him to pull down work which had already begun. There was an outcry about this, and most of the table were vehement in their indignation. 'Outrageous!' 'We should stand for it no longer!' etc., etc. Someone—everybody —must go and call on the Portuguese governor and urge him to take action. I cannot imagine anything more repellent to the Portuguese authorities than taking any action which would upset the equipoise, the delicate balance of forces between themselves and the Chinese, nor did I see what any Portuguese governor, however belligerently inclined, could do. True, the Chinese armament is quite laughable, but he swarms in millions on the other side of the barrier, while all the force the Portuguese have here amounts to a few hundred soldiers, mostly black at that, armed with sticks (only the officers have swords). However, I did not point this out to the fire-eaters at the table, and was prudently confining my attention to the curried oysters, when I heard Charlotte's voice uplifted.

'But surely, Mr Bowie, we are in China and we have to respect Chinese laws and regulations. Macao is strictly a part of China, is it not?'

There was a moment of shocked silence before Bowie replied.

'When you have lived a little longer in the East, young lady, you will find that the first essential for a white man is to make himself respected. All these mandarins or what-do-you-call-ems want to do is to give themselves face by humiliating us. That's all there is to these pettifogging regulations, and that's why we mustn't sit down under them.'

In face of practically universal disapproval, Charlotte stuck to her guns.

'I do not see that there is anything wrong with obeying the

165

law in China, as elsewhere. After all, if the foreigners don't like it, they can always go away.'

Bowie snorted and another would-be-tactful gentleman interposed.

'Nobody talks of disobeying any Chinese laws as long as they are reasonable, but we are entitled to expect that the Portuguese shall give us proper protection. Otherwise trade will become impossible.'

Charlotte then remarked that it seemed hardly worth while remaining in Macao in such discomfort in order to trade, when the Chinese did not want to do business with us.

The effect of this heretical remark can be imagined. Bowie turned a deep apoplectic red, her neighbour on Charlotte's other side looked disgusted. As for me, I remained silent, knowing better than to embroil myself. Thirty years ago, I would probably have spoken up just as Charlotte did. Now discretion, and the realisation of the futility of interposing my opinions, kept me silent, but a supporter did rally to Charlotte's side. Mr Harker had just lighted up a Manila cheroot, which he now removed from his mouth.

'Miss Winters certainly has a point there. In a sense I feel we must regard ourselves as paving the way to a better understanding. Even the Chinese will become converted to the blessings of trade in time. Our personal sufferings will benefit posterity, although our friend may have to go without his verandah a little longer.'

'You always see the Chinese side of it, Harker,' grumbled old Bowie. 'This all comes of learning their outlandish language.'

'My Chinese came in quite useful when it was a question of extricating you from your contract with Pan Qua How,' was the answer.

'That's quicksilver, my boy! Never touch quicksilver, that's my advice to you.'

'Thanks, I won't. But I can put you in the way of a little deal in camphor wood, if you are interested. I heard . . .'

They were off. Puffing smoke and talking prices, cargoes

and supercargoes, shroffs and sycee, the dining-room might have been a counting-house. The ladies had withdrawn and were now occupied in the drawing-room tearing reputations to shreds. As soon as we joined them, I looked round for Charlotte, but she was not there. Later I descried her on the verandah, but she did not come in and I could not join her there.

Later, however, she reproached me bitterly for not having supported her on this occasion, when she was only saying what she had heard me say a score of times.

'But not to the faces of those concerned. I know better than to tell a merchant that he is not conferring an inestimable benefit to China by giving the Emperor's subjects a chance to buy his opium. Also, the Company were our hosts.'

Charlotte was petulant.

'That did not mean that you had to sit with the men the whole evening. I cannot believe that you found their conversation interesting. Money, money, money, selling, selling.'

'Oh, my dear,' I answered, 'I have been listening to such conversations since before you were born. I was brought up on them. My father was a merchant—he owned a factory at Cuddalore, not to mention half an agency house at Madras. I know something about these things.'

'What happened to your family business? You have never talked about it.'

'Well, the Madras house failed eventually, and that hit my father, although he made a good deal of money out of it first. The factory is still a going concern. One of my brothers is in it still. The rest of us sold out.'

'Did you ever think of going into the business?'

'I haven't the head for business. My father always used to say "You had best stick to your painting, George, you would ruin us in a year if you were to come into the factory." None of us was any good to him, he said, we were only an expense. There were too many of us, but that was his fault.'

'Were you fond of him—your father?' asked Charlotte, diffidently.

'You could not but be fond of him—he was a jolly old man. He led my mother a dance, though, at times.'

'And were you happy, when you were a child?'

Looking back, yes, I recollect golden days following each other without end, although I suppose there were the inevitable tragedies of childhood too. Still, we seemed to play most of the time, while the storms of life—and financial crises followed each other—passed over our heads. A child should be happy—yet I suspect that Charlotte was not. She never talks about it, just as she never mentions her family, or what her life was before she came to China. Yet she is passionately interested in every detail of mine, in everything except what concerns Mrs Chinnery. Charlotte cannot abide the mention of her. Yet tears were in my darling girl's eyes when I told her about the loss of John, and all my other disappointments. She is all that I have left in the world to love.

I wanted to make a miniature portrait of Charlotte to keep, although I refuse to give her my ugly likeness in return. I have all the gear put away. I got it out and set to work, but it is hopeless. My eyes are far beyond it. If God would give me a new pair of eyes, I would ask for nothing else to the end of my life.

Seen from my window: an ordinary group of every-day life, an old man and a child. The old man is a yellow Chinaman in blue frock and trousers, his face worn down to the bone. But the child he is watching is as fat and round as a puppy. Whether it is his grandson or his son it is impossible to say. If these people can afford it, they take younger and younger women into their households, and they never cease to breed until they are at their last gasp.

If Ala had lived, would she have given me a little George Chinnery with a yellow face and slit eyes, or should we have had a blue-eyed Chinese girl? God is he who knows, as my old Mussulman friends would say.

168

Charlotte and I have had our first quarrel, and she has shown me that she is capable of being as unreasonable as all the other women I have known. The quarrel arose over a matter of no importance at all. Charlotte came across a book of drawings of Ala which I have not shown her and would never have intended to show her. That Charlotte found it at all was due solely to the detestable habit women have of prying into things which do not concern them. I did not want my shelves and cupboards tidied: Charlotte took this duty upon herself, and then took advantage of this self-imposed task to look where she should not.

It was when I told her this, as I was forced to do in self-defence after she had accused me of libertinism and deceit, that I had my first glimpse of Charlotte in a rage. Never tell a woman the truth, it is the most dangerous thing a man can do. Had I been content to bow my head and let the storm pass over, no doubt I should have escaped comparatively unscathed, but it was the injustice of the accusations which forced me to deny them.

I am not a libertine, and a few drawings which may seem improper to a young lady do not make me one. I did not show these drawings to Charlotte, as she has no right to inquire into every act of mine. By the same token, I have never deceived her as to my relations with Ala. I have never entered into them.

All the same, I was frightened by this glimpse of an almost furious pride in Charlotte. The fact that I was not sitting alone in my room, when she arrived in Macao, waiting for her to fall, apparently seemed to her outrageous. The truth is, Charlotte has not enough self-control, and the present situation is imposing a great strain on her nerves, inflamed by the trying climate and also, I gather, by friction with her aunt. I have implored Charlotte to be more accommodating to her aunt's wishes, seeing that she is beholden to her in everything, but Charlotte, by nature self-willed and imperious, does not take kindly to living in a subordinate capacity in the household of another, which is bound to be her fate until she marries and has a household of her own. But today, when once more she complained about her life with the Fays, and I tried to reason with her, her immediate response was to suggest that she should come and live with me.

I was horrified that such an idea should ever have come into her head (forgetting the many, many times it has come into mine as I ranged my empty rooms). I must have sounded angrier than I meant to, for Charlotte lost some of her assurance. Nervously she tried to argue with me, saying that I had lived in the same house with Rosa, and mentioning the names of others she had no business to know anything about. I replied that whatever had been my relations with other women, I had no intention of ruining a young girl of respectable family.

'You forget that I am hardly a young girl.'

'Whatever your age is, the thing is still impossible.'

'We could perhaps marry some day.'

'Thank you, I have kept out of jail so far, I do not want to find myself in a Macanese one, for bigamy.'

'But it was you yourself who said——'

'Said what?' I interrupted her.

'That you did not think your marriage to Mrs Chinnery was valid, here in Macao, and that you only had to prove it.'

'Whatever I said then was nonsense, and you had better forget it.'

I had said it, though, in a mood of madness, when I really thought it might be true. I saw Charlotte's lips quiver, and I knew that in a minute she would begin to cry. Why was I behaving with such senseless cruelty? She was all I had in the world to love, and the only human being who truly cared for me. But I knew that there was no hope for us, and that only separation lay ahead. Charlotte did not see this—she could not see it. That was the difference between her age

170

and mine. She still believed that in this world one only has to take what one wants. I have long since learned better. Useless, though, to reason, for Charlotte's eyes became suffused with tears, a high flush came up in her cheeks, and she burst into sobs, exclaiming between fountains of tears that I did not love her and only wanted to be rid of her. She added that I never gave a thought to what she was risking for my sake.

I *have* thought of this, over and over again, far more often than Charlotte, I fancy. In addition to the ever-present fear of awkward consequences, there is always the chance that Charlotte's stratagems, invented visits to Mrs Haverill, for example, or excursions to one of the ever-diminishing number of picturesque sites in Macao, even her failure to make progress in the art of sketching, may one day be exposed, with results fatal to her reputation. It was a false and unfair accusation, and it hurt me.

All of a sudden, I could not bear to remain in the room with a weeping girl, just as I could not bear to reason any longer with unreasonable youth. I did not pause to reflect, I had my coat on, and seizing my hat I ran down the stairs, ignoring Augustine, who emerged from some retreat, and out into the street. There stood a chair backed into an alleyway, and a set of bearers dozing beside it. They were Charlotte's, though, and I could not take them. I hurried down the lane in the sultry afternoon heat, and on to the Praia. It was the unfashionable hour, nobody was abroad, even the fishermen slept in the mat shelters at the end of the lines of nets. I walked the length of the Praia, hoping to find a breath of wind at the point, and sat down on the granite wall. A bird-seller went by, carrying on a pole his collection of bamboo cages, whose inmates clung in silence to their perches, their bright voices dulled by the outrageous heat: his eyes flickered over me, but he sidled past in silence. Not another soul was about, or would be at that time. I sat and feasted my eyes undisturbed. The sun crept on and the shadows lengthened and changed, the water lay in alternate bands of silver and shade, and out at sea the islands floated just within view where sea and sky become one. I forgot the sweat which trickled down my face, and the wet shirt and coat which clung to me, as I watched the light come and go on one object after another as the sun dropped lower in the sky. Then the shutters began to bang as they were thrown back along the houses in the alleys, and I got up and walked home. As I came within sight of my own door I felt a rush of relief. The chair and bearers were not there. And most illogically, a feeling of great tenderness came over me for Charlotte, so young, unhappy and unreasonable. My conscience pricked me as I climbed the stairs. I suppose I should not have left her alone in the house, though so far as I know neither Augustine nor the servants have ventured any kind of insolence. Upstairs everything was so quiet, so peaceful, that I hurried to my painting-room and forgot everything in the pleasure of work.

I would have made my peace with Charlotte in the course of the next few days, but that Macao has been shaken by one of those events which periodically burst like a thunderclap on the heads of our community and become the sole object of interest until the echoes have died away. The first I heard of it was when, on returning from my morning walk, a gentleman of my acquaintance who was being carried past in a chair called out to me:

'Good morning to you. Have you heard the news about Jack Bowie?'

I answered that I had not, and he continued.

'He attacked a Portuguese gentleman yesterday, in broad daylight, beat him with an umbrella on the Praia Grande.'

'Good God,' I exclaimed, 'whatever for?'

'Nobody knows, it seems to have been some sort of seizure. They say that Bowie acted like a madman, they could hardly drag him away.'

My informant knew no more, and we parted, I to go straight to Bowie's house, but when I came in sight of it, it was barricaded as if to stand a siege. I tried to gain an entrance, but no efforts could obtain an answer. There was nothing for it but to return home, where Augustine supplied further news. I told him that Mr Bowie's house was shut.

'Perhaps Mr Bowie go away until the man is better,' suggested Augustine. 'This man hurt very badly. If he dies, I think Mr Bowie never can come back.'

I did not see how my old friend could have killed a man with an umbrella, even had he wanted to, but Augustine insisted that the victim was badly hurt.

'Mr Bowie old man, but very strong.'

I asked Augustine if he had been told the reason for this attack. Augustine put on an expression of would-be mystery, and succeeded in looking sly.

'People say many things, but I think this Portuguese man is the husband of Mr Bowie's woman.'

'Then why should Mr Bowie attack him?'

'I think this Portuguese man ask Mr Bowie for money. That, or he want to take his wife back. So Mr Bowie get angry and want to kill him.'

Well, I had no doubt that the town was buzzing with rumours, and that this was one of them. Later in the afternoon I went out to try and gather better information. I called at several houses, one after the other, but could get no news beyond what I had already heard. Nobody knew the identity of Bowie's victim or what had become of him except that his friends, after separating him from Bowie, had carried him off in a condition of collapse. Nobody had seen Bowie or could tell me his whereabouts.

Half-way through this morning, however, a message was brought to me that Mr Bowie asked me to visit him at his house. You may guess that I did not waste my time, but set out at once. When I reached his house, it looked as shuttered and deserted as before, but the bearers had apparently been instructed in advance, for they diverged into a little side alley which I had not noticed before, and here they set me down before a small side door. A servant was waiting behind the door, which opened instantly, and I passed through what were evidently a woman's apartments, littered with cushions and small trifles left in disorder as though the occupant had just concealed herself. I found my old friend lying in his usual long chair on the verandah, hookah at his side. His two dogs were comfortably disposed near by, and thumped their tails on the matting at my approach. A Chinese boy was hovering in the background ready to bring whatever was required, and except for the fact that the window shutters were closed and the verandah blinds down at eleven o'clock in the morning, the whole establishment radiated calm and repose. Bowie ordered another chair to be brought up, and as I dropped into it, I exclaimed:

'Well, upon my word, Jack, you are taking life easy for a man who has set the whole town by the heels.'

'I have nothing else to do but take it easy,' grumbled Bowie. 'Officially, I have "gone to the country". But I'm sick of sticking here alone. I was really sorry to have turned you away yesterday, George. I heard you were outside, but I did not dare let you in at the front door. It would have spoilt the effect.'

'Who are you hiding from, Jack? Are you afraid the Portuguese will arrest you?'

'I should like to see them try,' growled Bowie. 'No, it is L—— (he named one of the senior Company men) I won't see.'

'Is he in Macao?'

'He is indeed in Macao. He came down a couple of weeks ago. Yesterday morning he sent me a damned impertinent letter. Where is it now?' Bowie turned over a mass of papers, dog-eared and ringed with the marks of glasses, on the table beside him. 'I remember now, I threw it away.'

'What did he say?'

'A lot of damned nonsense. Said he was sorry to hear of the unfortunate incident—why should he be sorry, blast his eyes? Said that as senior representative of the British community—now what the devil does he mean by that, George; since when was L—— senior representative of the British

174

community, whatever that may mean? If he means the oldest resident, that's you, now that poor Bell has gone, or if not you, then I am.'

I tried to get back to the point.

'What was the purpose of the letter?'

'That's just what I'm telling you. The fellow said that by virtue of his position, or what he thinks is his position, it will devolve on him to present the British case to the Portuguese authorities. Then he asked me for my explanation.' Here Bowie became incoherent with rage. He attempted to heave himself out of his chair, but the effort was too great, and he dropped back again.

'So what did you do?'

'Nothing. Of course I did nothing. I wouldn't even notice a letter like that. Then I got another.'

'What did that say?'

'It said that he was sorry to have had no reply to his first letter, and proposed to call on me to discuss the matter. So I told them to put the shutters up and say I had gone to the country.'

'Well, what is the explanation?'

'Explanation of what?'

'They say you half-killed a man, for no reason.'

Bowie laughed till the tears ran down his face.

'Half-kill him! You don't damage a rascal like that with a couple of taps. Not that I wouldn't have given him more if I had had the chance.'

'Who was he, Jack?'

'A fellow called Jesus da something, da something else— the biggest scoundrel in Macao is what I call him.'

'I have never heard of him. Is he your landlord?'

'I shouldn't be surprised. He must have made enough in his dirty deals to buy up half Macao. He is the one who swindled me over those ten chests of opium in '29.'

'You mean when you got the worst of the bargain for once?'

It is dangerous to chaff Jack Bowie. Bolt upright in his

chair, red with fury, he told me once more at length and in detail the story of this unfortunate consignment of opium. The sound and the fury were terrible. I could see a couple of Chinese servants peeping from the end of the room, half-frightened and half-delighted at the noise, and at one point the dogs got up and started barking. Bowie cursed them into silence and resumed his tale.

'Since then that fellow has kept well out of my way. I haven't set eyes on him. Then on Monday evening, as I was going past that crowd of Portuguese down by the waterfront —usually I don't go that way, I am not anxious to run into any of them—who should I see but this Jesus, and he saw me. You would think that that rascal would hardly have wanted to push himself forward but that is exactly what he did. Took off his hat and grinned as though we were bosom friends. I saw red, George, and that's the fact. I stopped the chair and I got out and said, 'Sir, I don't know who you may be, but you are an infernal scoundrel, sir.' Then as he didn't get out of the way, I gave him a couple of taps with my umbrella to move him.'

'So you never gave him a beating?'

'No, I wish I had, but he got away.'

'Well, they say he is pretty sorry for himself.'

'Nonsense. No such luck.'

Bowie leaned back in his chair and fiddled with his neck-cloth. His face still wore its indomitable expression, but its fatness and redness could not disguise the dropping of the features. The thought flashed through my mind that my old friend, if he continued to drink as he did, was due for a stroke, and I would miss him badly. Bowie glanced up and saw me watching him.

'What are you staring at me for, George? You are not painting me. If I ever want my likeness taken, I'll go to that Chink fellow in Canton. He is cheaper than you, and he makes his customers look better.'

I replied that if that were the state of affairs, I would be taking my leave, as my time was valuable, and customers with less exacting requirements were awaiting me. On my way home I saw a coolie squatting and eating noodles from a bowl, at one of the open-air eating-stalls in the market. With his head thrown back, he was pulling up the long glistening strings between his chopsticks and stuffing them down. I got the impression that the man's guts were being pulled up through his mouth. The church façade behind him was blank, and the iron grille before the doors was closed, as though the gods of the foreigners were indifferent to this strange offering.

To my surprise, and amusement, I found myself receiving a visit that afternoon from L—— himself. This was none other than the individual I had had dealings with in his capacity as Chairman of the Library Committee. I asked him to forgive my continuing to work—I could listen to him just as easily. He looked round him, and took a seat somewhere behind my left elbow. I could see him from the corner of my eye each time I stepped back from the easel. It was the most imposing chair in the room. I expect that was why he chose it. He sat there, a fatly-important man in freshly laundered clothes, endeavouring to assume an air of importance. I said nothing. I went on painting.

'I have come to have a word about this affair of Bowie's.'

I still said nothing, and after waiting a minute L—— continued.

'I know you are a friend of his.'

'Mr L——, sir,' I said, 'would you mind putting your head out of the window, and just look slightly to the right. I want to know if the streamer is flying on the Chinese customs station.'

L—— looked put out, but after some delay complied.

'Yes, it is.'

'Thank you. Just tell me, will you, what colour it is.'

L—— leaned out again, and then brought his head back.

'Well, I would not like to say. It is hard to tell exactly.'

'Thank you,' I said. 'That is exactly what I always find myself. So I shall put it in the colour I feel it should be.'

177

L—— reseated himself. He gave the canvas on which I was working a cursory glance, but he was not interested.

'We were speaking about Bowie. I wish you could persuade him that he is not doing himself or the British community any good by persisting in his present attitude.'

I replied politely that I felt this point of view could best be explained personally by L——, and that Bowie was, in any case, a man singularly difficult to persuade.

'It is not very easy to see him at the moment. That is why I feel that the word of a friend might be opportune.'

I said that I doubted if it was the office of a friend to persuade another to discuss a matter which was obviously repellent to him.

'Oh come, Mr Chinnery, making every allowance for friendship you must admit that Bowie's behaviour was indefensible. He behaved like a madman, and you must see the position he is putting us in with the authorities.'

I said I did not think the Chinese worried much what the various European factions did.

'The Portuguese are the authorities we have to deal with here,' said L——. I hastened to soothe him by telling him I was sure Anglo-Portuguese relations were safe in the hands of the Company and himself.

'If you see Bowie, will you kindly tell him what I have said. If any relations are to be preserved, he must give an explanation.'

'As you say, it is not easy to see Bowie just now, but if the opportunity should arise, I will gladly tell him.'

There was nothing more to say, and L—— left. It was not until I broke off work at dinner-time that I learned from Augustine that Charlotte had come to see me while L—— was there, and had gone away again.

CHAPTER 22

I have received my first letter from Charlotte (strange—I did not even know what her handwriting was like before) and I have it in my hands—the proof positive that Charlotte loves me.

The letter is frantic, miserable and unkind. Charlotte has tried to be cruel to me, and has only succeeded in tormenting herself. She reproaches me for what happened yesterday when, according to her, she was turned away from the house by my servant, on the pretext that I was busy working. If I am tired of her, as appears to be the case, I could at least tell her myself and not send a message by Augustine. There is more of this in the same strain, reproachful, bitter and undignified. Of course, it is all the result of a misunderstanding. Augustine has either been stupid, or quite possibly malicious, or even neither of these things. The mistake may have lain with Charlotte herself, who is not used to pidgin English. But what does it matter? It can all be put right. The main thing is—Charlotte loves me.

It may well be asked, how could I possibly doubt this. Had she not given me proof enough, the highest degree of proof possible?

Till I received that letter I still did not know whether Charlotte loved *me*, or whether, as I suspected to be the case, she had fallen in love with her first lover. I was the man who had introduced her to the delicious excitement of being desired, as well as to pleasures hitherto unknown to her, and her nature had expanded to embrace what was offered to her. In some ways a little arrogant with her success, Charlotte had been inclined at times to treat me as nothing more than the man who entertained her on a bed in a shuttered room during the long steaming monsoon afternoons. But this letter could only have been written by a woman who loved a man.

'I realise that your work is always the first thing in your life, that it comes before me, and I do not grudge it being so'—— were any words so patently untrue? It was sweet to see Charlotte attempting to deceive herself and me. It was a jealous letter, written by a woman who could not bear to have anything come between her and the man she loved. I felt all at once, happy, secure and young, those three states that mean more to us than anything in the world. Not that I have ever wished to be young again, with all that crushing weight of ignorance and inexperience to carry. That is something which we shed by degrees as we struggle on, but we have to accept in its place the knowledge that disappointments, worldly failure, and worst of all, rejected love, can overtake us. To feel young was for me to feel that tomorrow would be better than today, that no serpent would emerge from under a stone and sting unawares, and if a letter came for me, it would contain good news and not bad. That is the joy of life which I suddenly recovered, on reading Charlotte's letter. Money troubles, jealousies and spites, these things cannot be escaped, but they are pinpricks. I am far above them, so long as Charlotte loves me.

If only I could see her, but there was I with the studio filled with clients (it might have been the old days of Calcutta), while Charlotte was in a house filled with prying women's eyes. I dashed off a note which I sent over to her together with a packet of drawings. I dared not write much: I put these sentences on a loose sheet. 'You have entirely mistaken the position, I will explain your error as soon as I see you. Till then—G.C.' She might have to show the parcel. What I had written might just pass as the admonition of a zealous drawing master!

In the course of the afternoon I received the packet back, and between the sheets another letter.

'My aunt is not well. I know I shall not be able to get away from the house during the day. I will meet you at the rocks by the Ama temple in the early morning. Wait for me there at 8 o'clock.'

A hideous imprudence! But I was lost in admiration. I knew I should not be able to dissuade her, either, so I did not try. In any case there was no more time for writing. The sitters withdrew, but on their heels came the gossips, to discuss the Bowie affair, ad infinitum. If a man works at home, they think he is not working in earnest. But I gather opinion is now strongly on Bowie's side. The Company's action in rushing to intervene and 'grovel to the Portuguese' has enraged the independents, with the result that Jack Bowie is becoming the hero of the hour, and I have hopes that a public subscription will be raised to commission me to paint his portrait, umbrella upraised, in the attitude of the vindicator of British rights. If the picture is refused by the Macanese senate as an ornament to the Leal Senado, it could well be hung in the British Library, or even in Dr Anderson's Eye Clinic, to strike terror into those Chinese who recover their vision as a result of attendance there. Bowie has admittedly kept out of range of my brush for twenty-five years, but he would not be able to resist a (free) compliment.

When the last of them left, I went on to the verandah. The wind had changed, for the evening breeze brought with it a sudden penetrating smell of rotting fish from the drying grounds where the catch, fresh from the abounding sea, is left till mature enough for Chinese taste. Idly I noted that the gardener had brought up fresh plants, strong fleshy growths with bright red flowers, springing up in assertive abundance, like the smells, with the heat of coming summer. He had evidently run out of green pots, for every alternate plant was in an ordinary unglazed earthenware container. This is the season of fecundity. When rain falls, it falls torrentially. I watch it advancing across the sea like a curtain being drawn. Islands and mountains vanish behind it, then like a flash it engulfs the town, and Augustine comes running up to close the shutters. As soon as the rainstorm passes the sun bursts out more fiercely than before, and the steam rises from the hot, rank soil. The peasants are working thigh-deep in the mud. What Nature does so easily, I have to struggle to create. Nothing is easy—except my love for Charlotte.

I have been working, when the portraits have left me time,

on an Indian river scene. The time, near dusk, when a great and beneficent peace descends on the world, and the light of India is at its most beautiful. Then gentle dark-eyed women draped in spotless white carry pitchers to and fro with antique gestures. How often have I watched the women of India carry water, particularly those water girls of Madras who look like figures stepped down from a classic frieze. In this country a little clockwork figure of a Chinese man or woman passes by at a staggering run, shouldering a yoke with two buckets suspended from it. The grace, the charm and the pitchers are absent, but five times as much water is carried at once! But to return to the picture, I have captured the temple at the time when the setting sun falls directly upon it. In the foreground is the dark and solemn river, in which white-clad men and women are wading. This old temple on the bend of the river is one of my favourite subjects, but this time, truly, I think it is the best I can do.

I gazed at the picture until I nearly toppled over with sleep, and I decided it was time to go to bed. Puss appeared as soon as I was ready for the night (an unusual event, she has not been back for many days) and jumped on to the bed, to station herself on my feet. She shifted her position, washed herself and purred loudly at intervals during the night, but my dreams were of Charlotte and myself, floating on an Indian river of delight.

I met her at the seashore, as she had bidden me. I was there before the appointed time, but I had hardly reached the rendezvous when I saw her in the distance, making her way on foot along the winding road. She was muffled in a cloak with a scarf over her head. I had come prepared to defend myself, but there was no need for it: when we met, our unspoken words of bitterness died on our lips. Hand in hand, we went down to the rocks, where Charlotte threw off her cloak, exclaiming that she was suffocated. Already the sun was getting hot. She had been walking fast, her skin was pearled with sweat and her colour was high—she could have been a farm girl run out to snatch a few minutes with her lover behind a hedge! We spread her cloak on a little patch of clean sand. I took one hasty look to make sure we could not be seen from the road, that there were no inquisitive Chinese about—but I doubt if Charlotte even thought of this. She was exultant at the success of her escapade. No one came near us, and in a little while, with Charlotte in my arms, I would not have cared if they did. We were both oblivious of the cold, damp sand beneath us, the monotonous beating of the sea receded, and my Indian river had risen up from its mysterious depths and carried us with it, till it receded, to leave us cast up as flotsam on the beach, Charlotte's damp hair clinging like seaweed strands to my cheek.

I should like never to have to sell the Indian temple picture. I should like to keep it for my own pleasure, to show me, when I am old, how well I once could paint, and to remind me, when I am beyond great grief or great happiness, that life was once sparing with neither.

CHAPTER 23

It is more than half-way through May, and the gentlemen are arriving back in boatloads from Canton, with the end of the tea season, bringing with them the news from the Chow-Chow Factory, Hog Lane and all the rest, including the story of the shocking end of Captain Galbraith.

The captain and his companion had been about a month in Canton, handsomely lodged by the Company, and given every opportunity to see the limited sights permitted to foreigners. They were invited to a Chinese dinner at the mansion of one of the Hong merchants, where Galbraith violated decorum and good manners in various ways, notably by making persistent comments on the absence of the ladies of his host's household and asking when they were going to be produced, etc. The following day, he and some others were on the river in one of the Factory's rowing boats, when they came abreast of one of the 'flower boats' anchored there. Galbraith wished to go as close as possible so as to get a good view of the female inmates (who have usually no objection to displaying themselves to the gaze of foreigners), and when the boatmen declined to do so, as it was not considered safe, Galbraith jumped on board the nearest sampan and proceeded to make his way towards the flower boat by crossing from this boat to the next, and so on. His companions were horrified, but could not persuade him to return, and he was seen to reach the side of the flower boat, which stood much higher out of the water than the small craft surrounding it. A crowd of men of the most villainous type, no doubt the keepers of the women, came rushing upon deck, and that was the last anyone saw of Galbraith, for the little rowing boat began herself to attract notice, and it was impossible to linger. Next morning Galbraith's dead body was found cast up on Jackass Point. Whether he had died from drowning or from a blow on the temple, the mark of which was clearly visible, was not established.

His companion, Mr Hardiman, came in to the studio to collect the two portraits, one of himself, the other of Captain Galbraith (both fortunately paid for), which I had agreed to pack in a metal container, and I was sorry to see his state. I was not surprised myself to hear that Galbraith had come to a bad end, but the suddenness of death in the East shocks those who have not had a lifetime to become accustomed to it.

Meanwhile, Mrs Fay continues to be unwell, and Charlotte is tied to the house in constant attendance on her. I can do nothing but think about her, and write letters which I usually end by tearing up again. It is too much of a risk. If I had succeeded in teaching Charlotte shorthand, which I often thought of doing, I could be less guarded in my expressions: but then she would be able to read my diary, and my last reserve of privacy would be taken from me.

It was about this time that Augustine came up to the painting-room where I was working and remained for such a long time fidgeting about that I felt sure he had some troublesome request (almost certainly connected with money) to make. At last I asked him to state his business or depart, as he was in my way, and he then asked me if I would agree to paint a lady, a relative of his.

'A Macanese lady?' I asked.

'Yes, a Macao lady. She is a widow-lady.'

A Macao lady might be any colour under the sun, and the description of her as a widow-lady led me to think that she might be fairly well advanced in years. I asked Augustine if he had told the prospective client what my fees were, and he answered.

'Oh yes, lady can pay, I guarantee that. The lady wants very much to have this picture.'

That settled the matter. I had no excuse to offer for refusing, and any way I would not wish to disoblige Augustine, who is in his own way devoted to my interests. Once I had agreed to execute the portrait Augustine was overjoyed, and as if anxious to press the matter on before I could change my mind, he asked me when the lady could come for the first sitting. As there was no possibility of expecting Charlotte, I appointed the following afternoon.

When the time came, and Augustine ushered into the painting room a black-draped figure, muffled up in the fashion of Macao, I must confess I was curious to see what would emerge. I had got so accustomed to the idea that the sitter would be a grandmother that it was with pleasure and surprise that I saw before me, when she had been divested of her outer wrappings, none other than the 'cousin' who had talked with Augustine in the garden and who had appeared to me, in such a bewildering fashion, on the Praia Grande. She was indeed well worth looking at (although no longer in the first flush of youth). An olive skin, but more Mediterranean than Chinese, pleasantly rounded features, figure ditto, and a splendid pair of eyes which illuminated her whole face. A ready smile, and a general air of competence suggesting the matron. Imperious black brows sweeping across in one straight line could be formidable, were it not for the small, charming, pouting lips—the mouth of a baby. I wonder if Augustine has any more cousins like this!

There could be no difficulty in posing such a statuesque creature, but little progress was made that day, for I had barely got the lady settled when Augustine happening to go into my bedroom, discovered that Puss had given birth to four kittens on my bed, whereupon a scene of total confusion ensued. Puss, the culprit, was the only one who remained quite calm, and she continued tranquilly cleaning and feeding this new brood while Augustine tried to shift the blame for letting her get into the bedroom from himself to one of the Chinese boys. Then he proposed to take the kittens away and murder them. This I could not allow for a moment, although I certainly do not want four more cats in my house and no more, I suspect, does Puss. Augustine insisted, I lost my temper. The two Chinese servants appeared from somewhere as they always do when there is a row, and hung about enjoying the fun. I ordered them off, and told Augustine to bring a box or basket and put the kittens in it. At this point the lady client entered the scene. I do not know what she said to Augustine in what I took to be Portuguese, but he turned to me beaming.

'The lady say, more better keep one piecee small cat. That way, cat b'long happy, master b'long happy, and by and by lady take away small cat.'

I looked at the woman doubtfully. She had risen from her chair and thrown back the black lace shawl which she wore round her shoulders. She smiled and nodded vigorously to me.

'In that case the lady had better choose which one of them she wants to have. Show her the kittens, Augustine.'

This remark was translated to her, and Augustine rendered back her reply.

'Lady say, all same colour, no matter, so long as small cat b'long man cat,' was his version.

This should have made the matter easy, but Augustine and I, two mere males, were quite unable to decide the point of sex, and finally it was the client who, laughing again, made a rapid inspection and selection from the four mouse-like objects tendered to her. Puss was so delighted to get back the one kitten left to her that the stealthy departure of Augusine muffling the cries of the three doomed victims went unnoticed. It was I who suffered in her place.

After this emotional excitement, to go on with the sitting was out of the question. The sitter seemed quite unsurprised. She took her leave and walked to the door with the steady confidence of women who for generations have gone barefooted and carried pitchers on their heads.

Not long after, Harker dropped in, his dogs at his heels. When I heard his light step on the stair, I thought at first it was Charlotte. But I was glad to see him. We went on to the verandah. Under his arm Harker had a long rolled-up object which he placed carefully against a chair before sitting down. For some time no reference was made to it, and I assumed from its shape that it was some purchase of silks which Harker had made in the bazaar. Finally he reached for the packet and began to undo the fastenings.

'I brought this to show to you,' he observed, 'although I know you are no admirer of Chinese art. But I would appreciate your opinion in any case.'

He took off the outer wrappings and unfurled a picture put up on rollers in the usual Chinese way. A loop was attached to the top roller, and Harker hung this over a nail on the wall. The roller at the bottom of the picture held it flat.

'Did you buy it?' I asked.

'No, but I am thinking of doing so,' was the answer. 'I am told that it is a particularly fine specimen of this artist's work.'

I looked at it. The picture, for I suppose I must call it that, was the usual unfinished collection of brush strokes which the Chinese call a landscape, in which hills, rivers, cliffs, waterfalls, rowing-boats with dwarf figures lying in them, and other grotesque figures, are scattered liberally and with a complete disregard for the basic laws of perspective, over a tall narrow expanse of silk or paper. The execution, as in all their productions, was of the sketchiest, and imagination had had to be called in to fill many of the gaps where the artist's inspiration had failed him. Instead of a frame, which would be impracticable in an article made to fold up, the picture was bordered with strips of brocade in a formal flowered pattern which added to the discordant effect.

I gazed at it in a silence which continued until Harker burst out laughing.

'All right, I won't press for an opinion, I can see from your face what it would be.'

'Take the thing out of my sight,' I said. 'Whatever are you going to do with it, if you are fool enough to buy it? Hang it in your office?'

'No, I should send it home to one of my sisters, who draws a little. I think she would like to have a try at copying it.'

'Copy that thing? For Heaven's sake, what for?'

'There is a good deal of interest in these things in America. Native products, traditional art forms, you know, are what the ladies talk about. I am told that the painter of this is renowned for his way of depicting bamboo stems bending in the wind, and is held up as a model to Chinese.'

'I would not advise your sister to take him as a model, however.'

One of the dogs got up and sniffed at the scroll. Harker rolled it up and put it away in its wrappings.

'Seriously, you see no merit in this sort of art?'

'None whatever,' I answered. 'To my mind it is not art at all, just rudimentary scratching, as primitive man might have drawn on the sand. It is the product of a people who don't know how to draw, and will never take the trouble to learn. It is the same thing with their ancestor pictures—they have not progressed beyond a child's vision, partly because they do not want to progress. They are content to copy over and over again, perpetuating the same faults.'

'Possibly a child can see in some things more clearly than an adult.'

'Possibly, but to see without understanding is worse than not to see at all, to my way of thinking.'

Harker stretched out his long limbs more comfortably on the leg rest of the chair and clasped his hands behind his head. The dogs lay on either side of him and panted gently in the heat.

'I wonder how far this barrier can be broken down,' he observed.

'Which particular barrier would you have in mind?'

'The barrier of total non-comprehension between ourselves and the Chinese. It is not only the difference of language, clothes and customs, it goes much further than that. Take art, for instance. What they value as the highest form of man's creation is to your highly trained eye a mass of scrawls, simply beneath contempt, and if you were to show the average Chinaman a Madonna by one of the most famous artists of the West, he would probably not even see that it was a picture of a woman and a child. Yet the eye, the physical organ, is the same in the Chinaman and ourself. What tastes ravishing to the Chinese disgusts us, and vice versa. It is agony for us to endure the other's dinners. Their ears delight in the most appalling and discordant noises you ever heard, and as far as sense of smell is concerned, you would think that a Chinese was born without it, except that he sometimes admires the scent of flowers.'

'Yet you personally like them?'

'Oh yes,' replied Harker. 'I always get on with them very well indeed. They are always so jolly and obliging. Provided you can keep a Chinaman laughing, there is never any trouble.'

Augustine had lowered the bamboo screens on my instructions earlier in the day to keep out the heat and glare. I pulled them up now, and the level rays of the declining sun fell in a long bar of light across the verandah. With little grunts the dogs shifted their positions and lay with their forepaws and noses in it. Puss appeared ghostlike from the bedroom and walked across the back of my chair, eyeing the dogs (who did not see her) with nonchalant contempt before taking up her position on the balustrade. In the courtyard opposite, my invisible neighbours had brought their talking bird out for his airing, judging by the whistles and croaks which greeted our ears. Their little pug set up his frenzied yapping, servants hurried about unseen on clacking clogs and shouted to each other in their broad uncouth tongue. For the hundredth—thousandth—time I went to lean my elbows on the balustrade and look out over the town, the bay and the islands.

'What is life?' asked Harker. 'What we see, or what we are? I have often wanted to know the answer. You are a professional observer, you of all men might be able to tell me.'

'I have lived thirty years in the East,' I answered, 'and I can only tell you what I believe. Each man lives in himself, and what I paint in my studio is reality to me.'

'Well, then, my real life is books and ledgers, tea and opium, bills at sight on London and Calcutta, notes of hand, and how to make ten per cent on the discount. I had better not linger here in this abode of higher thought, but get back among the merchants where I belong.' And Harker departed down the stairs as swiftly as he had come. I heard his young energetic footsteps resounding down the lane, and his voice calling to the dogs.

CHAPTER 24

I have been quite ill for a week with a short sharp attack of fever, which is now on the mend. It was brought about by imprudence. One night of insufferable heat(it felt as though a storm were on the way) I got up from my bed after an hour of fidgeting and turning, set open all the doors and shutters, and produced a fine draught in which I slept. Result—next morning I found myself with a chill and fever. I have had such fevers before, and I know that I can throw them off— if I were not as strong as I am in body (my mind is another matter, any agitation of the nerves can make me quite ill) I should be dead long ago. But illness in this climate is a miserable experience. The effect of the fever is to add to the sultriness of the day another burning heat coming from within. The skin is on fire, and the sense of touch is mysteriously enhanced. I become conscious of every separate layer of clothing, the feel of linen, the feel of flannel against the skin. A stock is impossible, I have to relapse to a neck ribbon, I who hate and loathe sloppy dress, and were it not for the danger of taking a further chill I should paint in shirt sleeves.

I stayed at work as long as possible—in this lightheaded state surprising effects can sometimes be achieved. Then my hand began to shake and I had to give up and lie in a chair on the verandah. The next day I was worse and I did not get up, although my bed rapidly became an instrument of torture. The muslin curtains had to be kept closed in order to defeat the flies which would otherwise have descended in their hordes: likewise I found it impossible to open the shutters to admit fresh air without letting in also the heat and glare. I lay in the half-dark, in an atmosphere which would have been uncomfortable enough in all conscience without the inner heats of fever. Sweat poured from my face and neck on to the pillow, and a damp patch grew where any limb touched the sheet below it. To add to these bodily miseries came mental ones—those agonising thoughts which lie in wait for their moment when the body is subdued into compulsory idleness. The little demons knew they had me at their mercy.

Money, always in the forefront. I am now well on in middle life, I have worked for nearly thirty years and I am as penniless as any young cadet coming to the East for the first time, with this difference, that the cadet has his hopes and his life in front of him while I have had a good slice of mine. There is never enough money, even for my simple needs. True, I think I can now paint better than ever in my life, but what good is that to me if I cannot make a living? I do not know what processes of law debtors are subjected to in Macao, but I suspect the worst. I cannot go through all that again.

If I were well, I could work and throw off such thoughts. After all, Bell bluffed it out for many years in Macao, and when he died he must have owed a fortune all round. And he lived in his pillared mansion right up to the end and nobody thought any the worse of him. Yes, but he was a merchant, a reputable man who had the misfortune to get the worst of a deal, while I—I am an 'artist', that is to say a person whose position in the social structure is questionable and financial standing nil. The system of mutual credit between Englishmen which kept Bell out of actual bankruptcy, paid his servants and provided his table, thus allowing him to devote his life to reminiscences and the improvement of his aviary, will not come into action for me, I am sure of it. With the possible exception of Jack Bowie, the English community here would watch me sink and then congratulate itself, just as it did in Calcutta, on having got away with pictures commissioned and not paid for.

All these thoughts tormented me as I lay on my bed listening like some castaway to the noise of the sea beating on the reef— in my case the noises of the town which are the familiar background to my working days, now strangely remote behind the shutters—and also the thought of my loneliness. Not the loneliness which comes from temporary isolation, or the longing for a mistress too long unseen, but the deep sense that I am not like other men, and that try as I may, I shall never be accepted in their company. Again, if I were well, such thoughts would not have troubled me. I have lived my life so as to extract from it every shade of meaning that I could find—if that meant ignoring or being ignored by some of my countrymen, I have had compensation in the daily richness which has surrounded me. Besides that I have had, and I still have, good friends, the thought of which over the thousands of miles or the scores of years which separate us, should be enough.

That brought my thoughts to women—women, my sorrow, my despair, my inspiration, the only influence which has made the passage through life tolerable for me—and to my worst and most deep-seated fear, that this inspiration should fail me.

The afternoon of that first day I was so much worse that Augustine asked me if he should fetch the English doctor. My immediate answer was No. I did not think, was not in fact capable of thinking, but my instinct was to retreat like an old animal into its lair. I know my own constitution better than any of the doctors. Their advice has never been of any use to me. Doctors killed my son, they killed Rosa and two of her children. They shall not get their hands on me if I can help it.

Next day the fever had mounted higher, and my brain no longer held a coherent thought. The fantasies which flitted before me no longer troubled me, in fact they gave a little distraction to the hours which crawled by in heat and darkness. In the afternoon I fell into a sort of delirium. I could no longer focus my eyes properly, and what seemed to be clouds of vapour constantly formed and reformed at the end of the bed. Augustine was there, certainly, at one stage, and I told him to bring a broom and sweep the mist out as it was stifling me. Then it seemed to me that a woman was there, a woman dressed in black with a little veil on her head, but she too kept vanishing into the air. A pity, as she was handsome, and it seemed to me that I had seen her before. At one time I was conscious that a woman was sitting beside me, and a cool hand which was certainly real enough was laid on my hot forehead. I tried to take the hand in mine, but the woman moved away and although I called to her 'Rosa!' she did not come back but disappeared into the horrible mist. I could hear her moving about the room but she would not come to my bedside. When I called for a drink, it was Augustine who brought it.

After two days of misery, as often happens, the fever slackened abruptly, leaving me haggard, dirty and half-starved, but on the road to recovery. I was struck by the curious silence of my house, used as I am to having each hour of the day stamped with the sound of the appropriate activity—the mopping and sluicing of water over the tiled verandahs in the early morning, Augustine's daily sorties to the market, the visit of the hawker who brings the cats' fish, the pad of bare feet in and out of the rooms as the house is cleaned, clogs below in the courtyard, the crackling of the little fire of leaf stalks and branches on which the gardener boils his tea, the flop of water on tiles again in the evening as the gardener moves with his watering-can along the row of flower-pots. The drops run down the balustrade on to the floor of the verandah, and a little cascade pours out of the drainage hole and over the side of the house, carrying with it mould, broken flowers and struggling ants which usually manage by frantic efforts to extricate themselves from the torrent and climb back into the verandah again. Then loudest of all, the sound of the cats' dinners coming up the stairs, the Chinese boy clashing the plates, and the boisterous response of my two pensioners as they rush to upset him by winding round his legs while he pads across the room to set the dishes in the verandah. But my house seemed so suspiciously quiet as I lay there that I feared I would find the cook vanished, the flowers untended and withering in their pots, and both cats run away in search of food. Finally I struggled out of bed, and into a dressing gown. Of old habit, I went straight to the painting-room, to reassure myself that all was as I had left it. One or two things had been moved, as they always are when I am not in control, but otherwise all was well. Once on my feet, my energy began to return, and I called for my clothes. When these were brought I was struck by their conspicuous neatness—rents seemed to have been mended, and missing buttons replaced.

And a really well-ironed shirt was laid out, for once. It was all very mysterious, but I felt disinclined at that moment to investigate further the cause of this very welcome state of affairs.

I do not know if my recovery has been set back, or if I should claim that I have totally recovered. This afternoon Charlotte came to see me.

I was dozing in a long chair when she arrived, not that I have adopted or ever shall adopt the odious habit of the siesta, but after a morning spent in dragging myself round the painting-room striving after an effect which persistently eluded me, I felt too apathetic to read or write. Thus I did not hear the street door open, and Augustine admitted her. I was roused by light quick steps on the stairs, such as no Chinese ever had. Outside the door they hesitated—she did not know where I was. I called, and Charlotte flew to my side.

'Oh, you poor darling. Oh, my darling, my poor love. Thank God you are better. You have not been taking care of yourself properly. If only I could have been here to look after you. Tell me that you are better—you do not know how much I have suffered at not having been able to come to you. It has been such a long time since we were together. You still look so pale—' and so on and so on, in a babble of woman's nonsense, all the sweeter to me because it fell from the lips of my dignified Charlotte. She herself was blooming. The spell of incarceration with Mrs Fay had done her no harm. She was as fresh as a rose. I feasted my eyes on her until she began to blush and look aside. The verandah was all too public. I took her by the hand and led her into the bedroom, quiet and shuttered.

'You must not tire yourself, you are not nearly well yet: you must not—indeed you must not!' Charlotte went on repeating right up to the last minute when it became obvious that I was not going to heed her admonition, and she continued her faint protestations and her token resistance to the end, thus giving me the pleasure of overcoming them with a token show of force. The struggle was short and sharp, and the victory was mine.

Did any conquering general have a greater triumph? Before me was no sacked city but a lovely woman laid low, reclining languorously among the ruins of her hair and her dress (we had not the time to get rid of this impediment). In that moment I forgot all I had been telling myself for weeks past, that our enforced separation was really all for the best, that we should have to part and that for Charlotte's sake it would be better were the parting to come soon. The sight of Charlotte limp and quiescent, overcome with languor (all but her sparkling eyes) tightened my hand on my preserve, and all my good intentions flew to the winds.

It was a little later that I heard, or thought I heard, someone moving outside the door.

A sudden gust of anger took hold of me, born of my new strength. Some confounded servant or other, I thought, spying on us with his crooked oriental eyes. I got up and went over to the door. There was no one there.

Then I had to get Charlotte away. The statutory hour allotted for her visit was well past, and moreover I was expecting Augustine's cousin to come for a sitting. There is a bitter sweetness in sending away a loved woman, even though desire may be temporarily satisfied, from your side. Charlotte was reluctant to move, unwilling to look at the clock, and clung to me as she had never clung before. When at last she roused herself, she went into a fit of consternation on discovering the state of her gown, and began moaning about gathers, and hems. Well, there was nothing I could do about these matters, although I succeeded in finding some pins with which to repair the worst of the damage. I was becoming increasingly anxious about the imminent arrival of the client—although the heavens would have to fall before an inhabitant of these parts would be punctual. I saw

Charlotte depart with some relief, while hoping profoundly that she would succeed in getting into her aunt's house without that lady seeing her. Her dress might escape notice, her glowing cheeks and starry eyes, never.

The Macanese lady came about half an hour later. The sitting was uneventful. Before she went she put through Augustine a polite inquiry as to my health to which I returned an equally polite formula of thanks.

It was after this that I discovered Tom had been in the bedroom all the time. Well, he is an oriental, but his eyes are not crooked. Moreover, I am pretty certain he was fast asleep.

Part Six

CHAPTER 25

The aftermath of fever left me low in spirits and lacking in invention. One early-morning expedition in particular left the rest of the day spoilt for me. I was returning through a lane near my house, when I saw the body of an animal lying in the gutter. The coat was powdered with dust, but showed in places a familiar reddish-brown colour, and instead of passing by I went to look at it. It was not Soldier—I had to turn the body over with my foot to make sure—but another large dog rather like him, although evidently an old animal. The poor brute must have been starved: there was nothing there but a show of bones held together by the shabby old skin. Quite probably he had been turned off, when old and useless, to fend for himself. As I was turning away from the sight, a woman came at me from out of a side alley, one of the most repulsive-looking beggars I have ever seen, imbecile and barely human, but possessing a terrifying degree of persistence. Usually I can deal with the nuisance, but this witch-woman was something outside my experience. She mopped and mowed, shaking her layers of filthy rags, and darted to and fro in my path, trying to bring me to a halt so that she could display some ghastly deformity, her stock-in-trade. With a show of firmness I finally got clear, but not until I reached my house did I feel safe from pursuit.

One becomes hardened in the East to man's inhumanity to man (and with more difficulty, to man's treatment of the lower animals), but here in Macao we are generally spared the sort of spectacles which daily beset the foreigner in Canton, the petty offender suffering in the cangue, the prison horrors, the opium-dazed wretch being led to the execution ground, and all the minor brutalities of Chinese officialdom. We live under a milder, more languid despotism, and the civic pride of the city fathers would not tolerate the spectacles which teem in the gutters of Canton. I returned dejected by these sights to the studio, to the realities of life and the problems which I had failed to face, the main one—Charlotte.

It was not only that while dragging myself back to health I lacked the impulse to see her and to play the lover's part, I knew that the decision I had come to on my sickbed was the right one—despite my instant lapse from it. No visions of a bright future opened for Charlotte and myself, the only portents were of darkness and disgrace. She had given me so much—how could I ask for more when I had nothing to offer in return. Was it not my duty to take the harder part, to renounce my happiness, and cut myself off from Charlotte's favours?

When I got about again, I avoided those occasions on which I might encounter Charlotte, I eschewed the ladies' entertainments, putting off from day to day the moment of explanation. I don't know what I hoped to gain by delay, whether I thought that my sentiments might in some mysterious manner communicate themselves to Charlotte if I stayed away from her, without further decisions on my part, but I should have foreseen what would happen, that Charlotte would come herself to seek me out, worried by my continued absence, and fearing that I was still sick.

I think she was a little nettled to find that I was perfectly well in body, although low in mind, and I was unreasonably disturbed by her appearing, when I had almost accustomed myself to her absence. It was difficult to talk naturally, and after we had exchanged a few trivial remarks an awkward silence fell between us, which Charlotte broke.

'I don't think it can be good for you to shut yourself up like this now that you are better. Why did you not come to the dinner last night? You were expected—and I was hoping to see you.'

'On the last occasions when I have attended these dinners, it was to find that you were not there.'

'That was when my aunt was ill. Now that she is better, I can go out again.'

'All the same, it is better that we should not see one another too often.'

'Are you ashamed of me?' asked Charlotte, very low. I saw tears come into her eyes. Charlotte never used to weep so easily. 'I do not understand you. I shall never understand you. You say a thing one day, and the next day it might never have been said. You have told me over and over again that our lives lie together and that nothing can separate us. Now you don't want to see me.'

It was the moment to speak up, to tell her everything, all my doubts and torments, and it would be the end. An end to the awful burden of guilt.

Charlotte had walked to the edge of the verandah and was standing in the strong sunlight looking over. It was now or never. Such resilient youth would soon recover from the blow, whereas every day which passed made it more difficult to break off, while bringing the inevitable disaster one day nearer.

'Charlotte, I have something I must say——' I began. But her attention was distracted by something she saw in the garden below; she did not hear me. She turned round to me, and the sun shone through her dress and her hair.

'There is a woman down there in your garden,' she said. 'Who can it be, I wonder, at this time?'

'Probably a relative of one of the servants.'

'It is not a Chinese woman, she looks like a Macanese. Are you expecting a sitter?'

'No, I am expecting nobody, I have no idea who the woman is. What does it matter? Charlotte, please come here.'

She came and sat down beside me, but I could feel that she was both puzzled and resentful. My confidence in the moment began to drain away. If I were to try to tell her now, she would take it all amiss, there would be hysterics, she might even refuse to accept the decision and all these agonies of making up my mind to the step which I knew to be the only right one would go for nothing. It would be better after all to write. That way I could not be interrupted.

When Augustine next came up, after Charlotte had gone, I asked him what his cousin was doing there. I told him the picture had still many things to be done to it, and could not be ready to take away for some days yet. Augustine looked guilty and began to make excuses and to protest about his being very sorry.

'What was she doing here today?'

'She came to see me.'

'What was she doing in the garden, then?'

Augustine became confused, stammered and finally came out with the truth. 'She just now live here.' I could hardly believe my ears.

'She lives in this house?'

'I think the master not mind. I do not want to trouble the master. Only one room. This house plenty big for master.'

Augustine then recounted a long rambling story, all about his and his cousin's domestic affairs, the marriage of a son, disputes over the ownership of a house, impending litigation and so on, the sum total of which added up to this, that his cousin had for the moment nowhere to live, and he had permitted her, without consulting me, to occupy an empty room in the servants' quarters of my house. 'That room long time empty.' I suppose I should have been angry, but it is quite true that this house is large and one occupant more or less makes very little difference. I have never once been into the downstairs rooms which the servants use. I contented myself with telling Augustine that his cousin must leave before Mr Barretto next called, for he would certainly raise the rent, and for the moment thought no more of the matter.

After all, if I had not asked him, I should probably never have known about it!

Old Chinese women. I was watching two of them today, haggling round a barrel of fish. Both respectable old bodies decently dressed in much-washed black cloth. Their necks were like withered old tortoises, their arms and legs like sticks, but their eyes were bright with interest and animation. Black looks when they saw me sketching them, however, and in a few seconds the group had melted away.

Where does the flesh go, which clothed these skeletal figures? To feed the uproarious, demanding younger generations? I hope at least that these give the walking ancestors good black silk suits for feasts and holidays, and number one first-chop coffins, lacquered to the old ladies' choice with comforting emblems of immortality.

I sat opposite Mrs Haverill at a select gathering last night. Charlotte was sitting some places off, and it amused me to have the opportunity of watching both women at the same time. It might be said that Mrs Haverill makes the best of herself, and Charlotte the worst, but that is over-simplifying the case. It would be more true to say that Charlotte has nothing to hide, and disdains artifice, while Mrs Haverill is the embodiment of art. To begin with, the hairdressing of the two women is entirely different. Charlotte does her hair in a style which makes no concession to current fashion. It is drawn straight up from her brow into a knot at the back, as one might see on an antique statue, and the effect is the same. Mrs Haverill wears the current arrangement of curls which is apparently so casual but really most artfully disposed, so as to conceal the hair line, veil the forehead, and distract attention from any weak points. Charlotte keeps always to the same style of dress, admirably well cut and setting off her figure to advantage, but undeniably severe. Mrs Haverill's costume abounds in frills and soft little feminine touches which attract both the eye and the fingers with their delicious allure. Above all, there is the difference in manner. Mrs Haverill can sit between the Reverend Mr Tucker and Jack Bowie, flash her pretty eyes at them in turn, and make each of these worthy gentlemen feel that he is the sole object of her interest, and that the state of the souls of the inhabitants of Canton, and the price they are willing to pay for thrice-smoked opium dross are topics of the most absorbing concern to her. Charlotte talks with animation and intelligence on those subjects which interest her, but when the conversation has not been to her taste I have seen her companion comically chilled by the stony profile presented to him. Of course, Mrs Haverill has had many years of dealing with bores and is a natural coquette into the bargain, but given a thousand years of experience, Charlotte will never be as truly feminine as Mrs H. Well, so much the better. Charlotte is passionate, but discriminating, whereas with women like Mrs Haverill—one never knows.

After dinner I managed to find an empty seat at the lady's side.

'Have you time to accept a commission from me, Mr Chinnery?' she asked.

I replied that nothing could give me greater pleasure than to paint Mrs Haverill. She laughed, and for once looked confused.

'Oh no, it is not I. I do not want a portrait of myself.'

I looked at her inquiringly. (Why give the stock reply if she was not going to be a customer?) Mrs Haverill caught my look.

'I think it will be best if I come to your studio. What hour would be most convenient to you?'

Of course, I said any hour which suited the lady. Finally, we fixed on eleven o'clock the next morning. From somewhere I was conscious of Charlotte's puzzled, resentful glance. She was at the other side of the room, alone. Later in the evening we found ourselves standing together.

'What would you like to do?' I asked her. 'Join your aunt, join the games table, or entertain the Reverend Mr Tucker. All these alternatives are open to you.'

'I would like to be entertained by you,' answered Charlotte.

'Ah, that's not possible—here.'

In the next room Mrs Fay was sitting with her daughter and other ladies. Charlotte made a move in that direction, and I stood back to let her pass.

'Do you love me?' she suddenly asked me, in a low voice.

'Do you doubt it?'

'Sometimes.'

That was the end of our conversation. Charlotte went to join her aunt, and I spent the rest of the evening talking with Bowie and a group of old friends. Meanwhile, my letter to Charlotte lies in the drawer of my writing-table—still unfinished.

Mrs Haverill kept her appointment for the next day. Of course, I had been speculating for quite some time before as to the purpose of this visit. She may have been in earnest, when she talked of a commission. On the other hand, ladies have been known to visit an artist's studio with other things than art in mind, and a sitting can quite easily develop into something more adventurous. At least, that is what many of them hope. Mrs Haverill was shown upstairs by Augustine, visibly admiring. She looked both cool and elegant. After preliminary greetings, she came to the point.

'Mr Chinnery, I know that you made a very fine portrait of the poor, unfortunate Captain Galbraith.'

I assented.

'Mr Hardiman took it home with him, and it must be a great consolation to his afflicted family. But there, I know, another female relation who was greatly attached to the Captain and who would prize some remembrance of him, such as a miniature portrait.'

I said that nothing would be easier, in London, than to have a miniature made from my likeness.

'The difficulty,' said Mrs Haverill, 'is that this particular lady is not at all well circumstanced, and I would particularly like to make this miniature a gift to her.' She looked at me imploringly. 'Can you not help me, Mr Chinnery?'

I said that with the best will in the world, no artist could make a likeness without a sitter, or a picture to copy.

'I have a likeness.'

Mrs Haverill had been holding a packet all this while. She now opened it, and disclosed one of the productions of my Canton rival, in which the 'handsome face' painter had out-done himself. It was an astonishing piece of work. Captain Galbraith had enjoyed a high colour in life, but he blazed forth from the picture like a turkey-cock, resplendent in red and gold. His hair and eyebrows by contrast were as black as night, or as Chinese lacquer. He stood out of the canvas, petrified, like nothing that ever was alive, yet as solid as an animal, fit indeed to be an ancestor. I hoped that Mrs Haverill found the portrait consoling.

'Even with this,' I said, 'I can do nothing. I cannot now paint miniatures. I would do it if I could, but I cannot. Not even for you.'

Mrs Haverill had never sat down. She stood just as she had been when she gave the portrait to me. Now I handed it back to her. She laid it down on the table, where her gloves were. Her whole figure drooped. I could see that she was woefully cast down.

'Not even for me,' she echoed, sadly.

'It is not the will which is lacking, it is these (I pointed to my eyes) which are not fit for service.'

I half-expected to hear her break out into soft remon-strance and assurances that my eyes were as good as those of a boy, that my work was getting better year by year, etc. But she kept her head averted and began to draw on her gloves.

'I am sorry, Mr Chinnery,' she said. 'I have troubled you unnecessarily, and I fear caused you some distress.'

There she was, comforting me for having been unable to assist her to a more worthy remembrance of her Captain than a Chinaman could give her. And to have come to me, of all men! I watched her walk before me to the door. I shall never understand women's fashions. Mrs Haverill and Charlotte wear gowns of approximately the same dimensions: although I *know* what Charlotte's body is like under the folds of stuff, I could *see* every line of Mrs Haverill's through many yards of reasonably opaque material, at each step she took. At the door she turned and thanked me again. Oh heaven, I thought, if only a man could tell what she really means by that melting voice, those eyes which are raised so candidly and yet drop before an answer to the question can be read in them. At ten paces from us there was a bed: the best consolation I knew could be offered there. No one was in the offing, no clients expected, no servants on the stairs. All that was needed was for Mrs Haverill to make one gesture—or simply to stand still. I took the decisive step forward —and then Mrs Haverill uttered, in her pretty, fluttering voice, one of her senseless, social remarks.

'We shall meet, I expect, on Wednesday evening. I shall have the pleasure of seeing you at the Company's house?'

Oh bubble pricked, oh moment gone beyond recall, when all she had to do was to let her eyes and her flushed cheeks and her quickened breathing speak for her! I felt a furious hatred for Mrs Haverill, so wily and yet so transparent, so inviting and so virtuous. Why knock at a door unless you wish to enter? The Captain was the right man for her after all, I thought. After a certain amount of flirtation on the sofa, he would have proceeded straight to his end and she would have enjoyed every minute of it, protesting, token struggles, feeble cries (not loud enough to attract the servants) and all. I made up my mind then and there never to be alone with Mrs Haverill again.

I have seen Augustine's cousin again. She was standing at the end of my garden, carrying on an animated conversation over the wall with one of the invisible occupants of the house next door. The female voices ran on and on not unpleasantly, interrupted at times by trills of laughter. A small green bird has also made its appearance in the lower regions of the house. It occupies a small box-like cage hung on the outside wall, and sings nearly all day in a sweet and piercing voice. When it falls silent, I miss the notes and wonder what is wrong. Going out one day I inspected it more closely. It is nothing to look at, and it immediately fell silent at my approach and began hopping up and down from the floor of the cage to the perch. One would hardly think a creature so unassuming in appearance would be capable of producing such a volume of sound. The only food in the cage was a head of most unappetising-looking seeds, but Augustine assured me that they are the proper thing for such birds to eat. Puss sits on the flagstones below and watches the bird by the hour. In these days she does not go far from home, where her surviving kitten sleeps rolled up like a hedgehog in a box at the back of my cupboard. If I want to summon Puss I only have to pick him out, and his puny screams will fetch her from the farthest corner of the garden.

Although we are near the end of June, the heat is not oppressive. The days would be pleasant, full of work and interest, but—I still have not taken the decisive step. I have abandoned the idea of writing to Charlotte, after tearing up page after page. It would be easier after all to tell her, rather than put it in a letter which might fall into the wrong hands. But I have had no chance to speak to her. She has been strangely elusive: one might almost say that she has been deliberately avoiding me. Yet I must not put off the decision any longer.

It was at this point that I received a visit from Harker, full of a project for participating in the Chinese Dragon Boat Festival which is to be held in a few days' time. This is an annual event in this part of China, and it apparently commemorates some sage of antiquity who drowned himself in consequence of a slight put upon him by the current emperor. The celebration takes the form of boat races! They are held at Canton and at other places on the river, and all the local population turns out to watch. Harker's original proposal was to raise an Anglo-American crew to compete in the event, but it did not arouse much enthusiasm, even among the young bloods of the Canton Rowing Club, most of whom are now down in Macao. They said that they were quite prepared to row a race, but not to paddle, which is the prescribed method of progression for dragon boats, and that furthermore the outcome was doomed, for if the foreigners' boat did happen to win, it would undoubtedly be disqualified as being on the river in defiance of all rules and regulations, old custom, etc. So Harker was now organising a rival regatta in the waters of Macao, the boats of all the companies to compete in sailing and rowing races. Gong beaters are to be hired, and suitable stocks of firecrackers laid in. The Portuguese governor and his lady have graciously consented to attend, and all the taipans and their families will be present. The only stipulation the Portuguese have made is that the regatta shall not be held on the same day as the Chinese festival, to avoid confusing the popular mind, and it has been provisionally fixed for the day after.

Harker went away delighted with the sketch of his two dogs which he had not realised I was making and left me alone to work—and also to my thoughts.

A banana tree.

A goat. Legs folded under it like a collapsed chair.

Two water buffaloes (difficult subjects these, they charge if they catch the scent of a foreigner). Prehistoric monsters, covered with wrinkles of the swamp, mild-eyed monsters living in fields of green paddy and directed by little boys.

A girl stepping out of her petticoat, a ring round her on the ground. A magic ring?

Oh, Charlotte, why are you not here? How can I bear to live without you.

Last night I dreamed about Rosa.

CHAPTER 26

The day of the regatta duly arrived. Stands had been put up
to provide seating accommodation for the important people,
and the sound of hammering had been reverberating along
the Praia. The late-sleeping taipans could not be expected to
rise in the fresh of the morning, so the races were fixed to
start at 5 p.m., when the fierce heat of the sun would be over.
There was to be a rowing event, sailing ditto, and a sampan
race in which the competitors were to be confined to using
a single oar, Chinese-fashion. This idea was nearly dropped
as being too undignified, for usually only native skill will
induce a boat thus propelled to go forward at all. I have seen
young sailors at Whampoa try it for a lark, and they invariably ended by spinning round in a circle. However, we make
fun of the Chinese often enough, as Harker observed: it can
do no harm once in a while to let them get their own back.
The climax was to be a paddling race, in true dragon boat
style.

As the hour approached I went down to the Praia, where
quite a crowd was assembled, including numbers of Portuguese. They must have abridged their siesta by quite two
hours. Some had quite a tail of slaves, and it was comical to
see these togged up in dirty finery. I wondered where Bowie
was, and if he had ventured out.

The ornate seats prepared for the Governor and his lady
were not yet occupied, but the heads of the various companies
were in evidence, and their womenfolk in the latest fashions.
The sun blazed down on the awnings, the limp flags and the
fine dresses, there was a bang from the other end of the
Harbour, and the first race was off. It would be tedious to
describe it, or the others which followed: there were the
usual long intervals in which the competitors were being
rounded up, or made false starts, and in these intervals we
all left our places and wandered about to greet friends.
Before long I caught sight of Charlotte sitting with Mrs Fay,

her daughter and Mr Tucker. I could see, even from a distance, that Charlotte was very pale.

Mrs Fay greeted me with all her usual warmth. There seemed to be nothing wrong in that direction. I shot a look at Charlotte who immediately got up from her seat, saying to her aunt:

'It is terribly hot under the awning. I think I shall walk about a little. Will you come too, Polly?'

Miss Fay declined, saying that she was very well where she was, and that the next race was just about to start.

'Charlotte, take your parasol,' was all Mrs Fay said before she turned back to watching the Harbour where the sailing boats were manœuvring round in small circles. Mr Fay was in command of one of them.

Charlotte walked away. I went after her.

'I must talk to you.'

'Very well.' I could hardly hear her speak. We were standing in the middle of a patch of bare and shadeless ground. Charlotte put up her tiny parasol and held it over her head. She looked ill and tired. Opposite us, leading off the waterfront, was a narrow lane which offered the only privacy. I led Charlotte into the shadow of the high walls. The lane went uphill for fifty yards, then turned a corner, and before us were the railed-off gardens of a convent. A flight of steps led up to a gate in the railings. The gate was locked and barred, but the tall bushes which overhung it cast some shade on the steps. This was the end of the lane proper: a little path continued between the convent railings and the house walls which, if followed, would bring one eventually back to the Praia again.

I spread my handkerchief on the steps—it was the best I could do—and invited Charlotte to sit. She did so, and fell to scratching with the tip of her parasol in the dust. Her manner was so strange and so distracted that I felt alarmed. Now that the moment had come, now that I was standing in front of her, every word which I had rehearsed with so much care left me.

'It is a long time since I have seen you.' These lame words were all that came to my lips.

'Yes, it is,' returned Charlotte.

I bent down and took her hand, intending to kiss it. Immediately she snatched it away and sprang to her feet.

'Charlotte, what is it?' I exclaimed. Her breast was heaving with emotion.

'You said you would like to talk to me,' she said. 'Well, whatever you wish to say—if there can be anything to say—please tell it to me now.'

'In the first place, I want to know why you are behaving in this manner.'

'I don't know what you mean.'

'Oh Charlotte, please be reasonable,' I exclaimed. 'Tell me what is wrong, why you are treating both of us in this way. Whatever it is, tell.'

I would have taken her in my arms, but the pleading, desperate look she gave me made me desist. An idea rushed into my mind.

'Who is it?' I exclaimed. 'One of the young men, I suppose. You need not be afraid to tell me his name. You might have told me earlier. I would not have stood in your way, I assure you.'

Charlotte laughed, a hard bitter laugh.

'It is not I who have someone else.'

'Nor I, either. Charlotte, what do you mean by saying that?' Charlotte's dress was white, the bush above her was dark green and had small red flowers on it with brilliant yellow stamens. Ants were busily running up and down in the cracks of the steps. Bang! went the gun from the harbour.

'What is the use of talking? What good will it do?'

'But I don't even know what you are trying to say. Charlotte, I swear to you that I love nobody but you, there is no other woman in my life. Please sit here, quietly, beside me for a moment. Nobody is coming.'

I still felt I must do it. I prepared to grope my way towards

211

the speeches I had prepared. But Charlotte suddenly flashed into anger. 'How can you tell me such lies?' she exclaimed. 'Oh, I know you have deceived me often before about little things, things which had no importance, and I know that sometimes you were simply forgetful, but I never dreamed that you would be untrue to me in something which mattered so much to us. Even now, when everything is over, you cannot stop lying. You say that I am the only woman in your life, when all the time you have your mistress living in the house.'

'What are you talking about?'

'Oh, stop this pretence,' Charlotte cried, 'I cannot bear it. You talk to me of love, and you tell me that I am the only one who matters, and yet you have your mistress in the house, your Macanese woman.' In a low tone she continued, 'I suppose you have talked to her about me—about us?'

'Who told you that,' I asked, 'about a Macanese woman?'

'Why, everybody knows it.'

'I see.'

She was not sure. I could feel that she was waiting—hoping—for me to deny it. I stayed silent. What purpose would be served by undeceiving her, only to have to tell her in my turn that I was abandoning her, not for another woman, but for an idea which she would never understand. Now that events had been taken out of my hands, I could only let myself be carried with the tide. But it was not the way I had wanted our meeting to go.

'It seems that I have been the last person in all Macao to know about this,' Charlotte went on, 'even though I might have guessed. After all, I saw her with my own eyes, in your garden. But it was not until Mrs Haverill——'

This was too much to be borne. It was intolerable.

'Mrs Haverill! That gossiping woman! That is where you get your information. Well, and if I am what you think, and what the other ladies in your circle think, what has that got to do with you or them? Must I be watched every minute of the day? You spy on me, you leave me no sort of privacy, you pry in my studio, and you come running to tell me what you have heard. Why should I listen to these disgusting stories? I tell you it is not your business. Leave me alone!'

Charlotte recoiled into the shadow of the wall. 'Ah, how cruel you are,' she said, staring at me. 'How I pity all the women you have known. Your wife—Mrs Chinnery—I used to believe all the tales you tell of how she persecuted you, and how wretchedly unhappy she made your marriage. Now I see that it is you who are impossible to live with. Rosa was lucky, I suppose. She died before you had time to find out how miserable you were, and how she had been the ruin of your life.'

'Leave Rosa out of it,' I commanded. 'I won't hear her name on your lips. She was a good woman.'

'A good woman!' She stood before me, tall and beautiful, in her white dress and fashionable bonnet. She was gripping the little parasol with both hands.

'She was my wife in everything but name. She gave me children. While you—you are just a girl who can be had. How do I know what has been going on during all these weeks when you have invented one excuse after another for keeping me away? You say that there is no one else, but why should you expect me to believe you, when you are so willing to think the worst of me?'

Charlotte grew red with anger, then white. She could hardly speak. 'How can you?' she said at last. 'You, of all people, to suggest that I—I suppose you think that something gives you the right to speak to me like this. Let me tell you you are wrong. You own nothing of me. In fact you are nothing to me. I hate you—I hate you as much as all the rest of them here.'

'Very good, madam, I understand you perfectly. You hate me. Now leave me alone. Leave me in peace.'

Charlotte stared at me as if she had seen a snake, until all of a sudden tears began to slide down her cheeks. Then with a kind of gasping sob she snatched up her skirts and fled, not down the lane to the sea, for I barred her way, but along the

213

path beside the railings of the convent garden. I rushed after her, I called 'Charlotte, Charlotte, come back!' but I doubt if she even heard me. The path consisted of slippery, uneven stones on which I slid and stumbled, and when I reached the limit of the convent bounds she was nearly out of sight. I saw her turn into a narrow alley between steep walls, and saw her no more. I clung to the railings until I had recovered my breath. Then I retraced my steps along the path and sat down on the steps where my handkerchief still lay. I replaced it in my pocket, and put my head in my hands.

No one stirred in the lane. It was still intensely hot, so hot that I could not bear the idea of leaving the shade where I was. From time to time a scarlet petal fell on the steps beside me. The seahawks screamed, screamed as they circled relentlessly round overhead. A fusillade of cheers and bursting crackers sounded on the Praia. It could have been barely ten minutes since Charlotte and I left the others, and now she was running for home, making for refuge like a hunted animal which tries to hide from the bright sunlight. I could see her reaching the steps of the Fay's house at last, with panting breath and heart thumping, making for the shadows of the darkened bedroom where she could lock the door behind her. Probably the house would be empty and the servants all down at the waterfront watching the fun. A little breeze got up at this moment and wafted up from the Praia the sound of gongs and drums. Evidently Harker had been as good as his word and had secured the traditional accompaniment to the dragon boat race.

Meanwhile, what was to be done? My first impulse, to go after Charlotte, I had discarded. I could see nothing clearly but this, that I had cut her to the heart—and all for the ignoble pleasure of having the last word. Every way seemed closed to me.

There was nothing for it but to rejoin the others. I got up, and found that I was no longer alone. On the other side of the railings stood the black figure of a nun, watching me. Although I could not see the face shadowed by the deep head-dress, I could feel the inquisition in the look. Did she see me as a possible marauder—despite the locked gate and the high railings—or had she been there the whole time? There we stood with the bars between us: she was a tiny little woman, and an old woman, I fancied. Then quite suddenly she glided off, the only sound the clicking of the string of beads she wore. As she turned I caught a glimpse of her face—it was as yellow as a guinea. One would have said that she was a Chinese.

There was no more waiting in that place. She might come back, and bring others. As I walked down the lane the din from the waterfront reached its height. The ladies in the stands were waving their handkerchiefs in encouragement and the boats were passing the stands, the two in the lead going neck and neck. Harker was paddling in one of them. Mrs Fay was agog with excitement, and could hardly spare an ear for me when I told her that Miss Winters was feeling the heat and had gone back to the house. Mr Tucker, side by side with the pretty Miss Fay, looked twenty years younger. I do not know who won the race, although I must have witnessed the finish. I remember very little else that happened that afternoon. I suppose I cheered with the rest, congratulated the winners, listened to the speeches of the notabilities who presented the prizes, and when it was all over, went home like everybody else. There was a grand dinner in the evening but I did not attend. The only person I wanted to see, and the only person I could be certain of not seeing, was Charlotte.

Next morning I wrote a letter to Charlotte. I poured out my heart to her. I begged her to forgive me for the words I had used at our last meeting, words I had never meant to say. I offered to swear by all I held most dear that there was no other woman in my life. I said nothing about parting. Instead I wrote about my love for her and my confidence in our future. Finally, I implored Charlotte to see me, to appoint a time and a place, anywhere, any time, and I would be there. I gave the letter to Augustine and told him he was to get it

215

to Miss Winters' hand. An hour later he brought the letter back to me and said that missie would not take it.

Many years ago, in India, I was riding a pony which threw me. I cut my right hand deeply on a sharp stone which all but severed an artery. I remember that I got up again on to my feet and gazed at the blood which poured out with every pulsation of the heart, thinking 'I shall lose my hand and then I am finished.' I could see it all quite clearly, the disaster which was bound to follow, ruin for myself, starvation for my wife and children in Ireland, and I was able to contemplate it without emotion, but I lacked the necessary impulse to apply a tourniquet to stop the bleeding. If a friend had not chanced by and taken prompt action, I suppose I might have bled to death on the spot. He was not even a friend, I now recall, merely an acquaintance. He was a captain in an Indian regiment, a taciturn, unlikeable man. His wife subsequently ran away with a brother officer, and he was killed in an insignificant skirmish.

So now I did nothing but let the days go past, unable to think of any step I could take which would break the deadlock—waylay Charlotte on one of her excursions, call at the house and contrive a moment alone with her—while all that the past months had meant to both of us was running out in bitterness and misunderstandings.

Then I heard, I forget who it was came in and told me the news, that there was one last out-of-season ship sailing for Calcutta in the course of the next few days. Normally she did not carry passengers, but there was a certain Mrs Oliver, a Company wife, who had been very ill (I knew that). The doctors thought that the rest of the summer in Macao would finish her, and she was being placed on this ship together with her child as a last desperate expedient. It had been arranged that Charlotte should go with her as a companion, as Mr Oliver could not get leave of absence.

This had been arranged and she had not told me!

I determined to try once more. I wrote on a small piece of

paper 'I have just had the news. I must talk to you. It concerns my life, and yours. I will wait near the temple early tomorrow morning. If you cannot come then, I will wait in the house in the afternoon. I implore you, if you ever cared for me at all, not to refuse.' I folded the paper and put it inside an Indian box which I had in the painting-room, one of those boxes which cannot be opened unless you know the secret, which I had one day shown to Charlotte. I entrusted the box to Augustine and told him he must get it to Miss Winters that day, he was to take no refusal, he must have it laid on her dressing-table or her bed. He said that he understood: what he thought, I do not know.

Next day I went to the temple in the early morning as I said I would, and waited there for an hour: but she did not come.

By the afternoon I had ceased to hope, yet I sat there in my chair, my ears alert for any sound at the door, unable to read, or write, or even to think. At four o'clock she came.

'I tried to get to the temple in the morning but it was impossible, all the others were awake so early,' were her first words.

She was carrying a packet, I didn't know what it was, I laid it down somewhere and took her hand.

'Oh Charlotte, why did you refuse to take my letter?'

She did not cry out in protest, or look bewildered, she simply gazed at me. 'I have not refused to accept a letter from you. I have received no letter. When did you send it to me?'

I told her, adding: 'It must have been a misunderstanding with one of the servants.'

'I cannot understand it at all. Myra, my aunt's maid, is the only one of the servants who can speak English. She is Macanese. Augustine always goes to her. But Myra has been away for the past week—her parents are sick. None of the others has come near me. Then you did write to me?'

I nodded.

'Have you got the letter still? Let me read it now.'

She held out her hand, smiling. The letter was in my

pocket then. I had been carrying it about with me during the past week. But I shook my head. 'It would do no good for you to read it now. I was only trying to explain—and asking you to forgive me for what I said to you.'

'There is no need for you to explain anything to me.'

'And do you forgive me?'

'Yes, if you in turn will forgive me the horrible things I said to you. But I think it is best for me to go away. You were right when you told me to go. You meant that.'

I did not answer. We sat in silence, each one contemplating a future without the other. Finally I roused myself.

'Do you have to go so soon? The ship you are sailing in has no accommodation fit for any woman.'

'It is the only one sailing just now. I don't want to have to wait until the autumn. Besides, I have committed myself now. Mrs Oliver needs me. She cannot travel alone.'

'When you get to Calcutta, Mrs Oliver will go to her parents, I suppose, but what will you do? Will they take you as well?'

'Mrs Haverill has given me a recommendation to some friends of hers. If they do not want a companion or someone to supervise the children, I expect there will be others who will. I can stay with Mrs Oliver until something is arranged.'

'You really mean to go, then.'

Charlotte rose. I did the same. There was nothing more to say, but neither of us could utter the word 'Goodbye'. With a swift movement Charlotte lifted my hand and held it for a moment against her cheek. Then she turned to go. In my turn I possessed the hand which had held mine, I kissed it, I turned it over and kissed the palm, I held on and would not let it go until at last she fairly tore herself away. I heard her footsteps echoing on the stairs. She was gone.

The packet which she had left behind her contained, carefully packed, all the sketch-books which I had at one time or another lent her. They were all in order.

When Mrs Oliver, her child and Miss Winters left Macao

several days later, I was not at the waterside to see them rowed out to the ship. I am sure there was the usual crowd of Europeans on the Praia fluttering their handkerchiefs in farewell and some wiping easy tears, while the little fleet of sailing boats followed the ladies out into the channel where their ship lay, so as to prolong the parting to the bitter end. Fortunately my absence is not likely to have been remarked upon. I am, after all, an eccentric.

At the end my resolution weakened, I could not keep myself from going on to the verandah and watching from there. But the actual embarkation took place at the Inner Harbour which is hidden from my house, and when the boat carrying Charlotte and Mrs Oliver out to join their ship rounded the point and came into my line of vision she came into the full glare of the sun. I was unable with my dazzled eyes to make out which of the two white figures on board, still bravely waving, was Charlotte's.

CHAPTER 27

It is overpoweringly hot. I have no desire to come out of hiding, and no desire for work. I had no idea it was possible to sit idle for so much of the day. Curiously enough, the time does not seem to drag, in fact the evening is upon me before I know where the day has gone to. I have never been torpid like this in my life. I wonder if I am ill, but if it is sickness, it is one I have never experienced before, and I do not know what to do about it. I sleep heavily. The nights are black and thick and hot. The heat is something I have never known before in Macao. Before I go to bed, I watch the lights of the fishing-boats moving out into the bay, over the oily black water. Harker and some of the younger men have been out with them, having persuaded a junk-master to take them. Were I still their age, I should have enjoyed the experience, but I have been too long in the East and these things are spoiled for me. I would rather sit on the verandah, in the dark, letting time pass.

The East has a sovereign pain-killer. You can smell it everywhere, in the mansions of the rich, in the shopkeeper's back room, in the straw huts where the coolies scrape their coppers together for one pipe of dross. Is that the way out? But the habit takes hold, and in spite of everything, I don't want to be impotent before my time.

All of this afternoon there was a piercing wailing which went on and on without cease. It was the sound of some creature in mortal distress. It seemed to come from the other side of my garden wall. Unable to bear it any longer, I went down to investigate and found there in the lane, sprawled on the ground asleep in the shade, a cat seller. It was the captive, the sole occupant of his wicker cage, which was uttering these unearthly cries. The creature was an orange-coloured cat in good condition (these cats are offered as food, and would not of course be saleable if too thin), and it padded round the cage, only stopping at intervals to tear the wickerwork with its claws, and never ceasing to put forth its piercing wail.

The hawker, when I roused him, could not understand me, and I had to summon Augustine who was likewise asleep in his room, and instruct him to buy the cat. The first figure demanded was exorbitant, a foreigner's price, and I very soon got tired of the chaffering and returned into the house, leaving Augustine to drive the best bargain he could. Very soon he came up to me and said he had secured the cat (by weight) for two hundred small cash, and what was he to do with it. I told him to bring it upstairs, which he did. The cat spent the afternoon quite peacefully on the verandah without attempting to escape, but crouching silently and watching with amber eyes. At dusk Puss came in, and Tom emerged from his daytime hiding place. Both sided together, for once, against the newcomer. Fat Tom confined himself to spitting defiance from a distance, but Puss threw herself at the intruder, biting and tearing, and a cloud of fur arose. After a moment's scuffling the combatants fell apart and I was able to pounce on Puss and incarcerate her in the bedroom. Dinner-time came, and I instructed Augustine to bring an extra plate of food, although he protested.

'You give he chow, he never go 'way.'

There was a moment's hesitation, then the food was swallowed with avidity. Afterwards, replete, the new cat stretched himself out again and dozed with half-closed eyes.

Later in the evening, when it was dark, I carried the orange cat down myself, and released him in the lane. He strolled off negligently, pausing now and then to sniff at something or to pull at a blade of grass. Once he came back to look at me, then he wandered down the moonlit lane and out of my sight.

If he gets into the hands of the cat-seller once more, I cannot help it. At least I have done my best for him. Now it is up to him to look after himself.

Coming back into the house, I nearly ran against the Macanese woman in the downstairs passage. She stood back, effacing herself to let me pass. I did not know she was still here, I have not seen her for a long time. It is quite contrary to what I told Augustine and I could insist that she go away, but what would now be the use?

In the night a thunderstorm woke me, and after it had passed I could not sleep again. I got up and sat in a chair, listening to the water running off the tiles. My one light flickered dimly in the corner of the room, surrounded by a little flight of night insects. My thoughts ran on death, and on a strange story which has gone the round of Macao.

About six months after Mr Bell's disappearance, three Chinese fishermen came to his house at dusk and asked to see the steward. They brought with them a small sealed packet, and they told the following story.

The fishermen had their huts and their little patches of paddy on Fishermen's Point by Cacilha Bay (where the body was found in the sand). Six moons ago, a foreign man came to their hut in the evening, when they were eating their rice, and spoke to them in Chinese. He told them that the body of a foreigner was lying on the sands of the bay, and that for their own sakes they should go and bury it lest they should be accused by the mandarin of being responsible. The fishermen replied that being innocent of any wrong, it would be better for them not to meddle with the matter at all and there would be no reason to connect them with it. The foreigner then asked if they were not afraid that the ghost of the dead man left unburied might haunt them. The fishermen answered that they were innocent and they would rely on their own gods to lay the ghost. The stranger then adopted a more menacing tone, and pointed out that if the ghost of the dead man were affronted, their paddy might never bear rice, and their nets would be drawn in empty. At this the fishermen perceived that their arguments could not prevail, and they had no alternative but to do as they were asked, and they got up from their meal to go to the beach. The foreigner restrained them, saying that it would be better to wait until the following morning and go when there was light enough to see to dig the grave deep. He gave them a sealed packet, the very packet they had with them, and departed.

The next morning the fishermen rose at first light and went to the bay. There they saw, at a little distance, the body of a man lying on its back: and when they went closer they saw that it was the foreign man who had visited them the night before. This caused them to be sorely troubled, as they did not know whether their visitor had been a man or a ghost. So they dug a grave in the sand in which they laid the body, covered it up as quickly as possible and returned to their huts, where they let off crackers and burned a red candle to propitiate the departed spirit.

Days passed, and the news spread in the market place that a foreigner was missing and eventually got as far as Fishermen's Point, but naturally the three men kept as quiet as mice, not wishing to bring down trouble on their heads. Then followed the discovery of the body by boys digging in the sands, its resurrection, and reinterment in the Company's burying ground. For six months the fishermen held their peace and kept the packet unopened, but all the while becoming more troubled in their minds. Now they desired to return the packet where it rightly belonged.

The steward opened it. It contained four dollars, each one wrapped in red paper, as is the custom for gifts, or rewards. The fishermen utterly refused to accept the money. Bell's former steward, a man devoted to his master, would not touch it either. In the end it was donated to Doctor Anderson's Public Dispensary.

I remembered discussing the matter with Mr Bowie, with Mr Harker present. Bowie put the whole thing down to hallucination.

Chinese peasants are riddled with superstition, and terrified by ghosts and demons of all kinds. Even so, I thought the story was too substantial to be put down to a hallucination, and said so. It seemed to me more likely that the story was true, and that it was Bell who had visited them.

'If that is so,' said Harker, 'there is one thing which puzzles me. I always understood that the late Mr Bell did not speak a word of Chinese. In fact, he told me so.'

'If that's the only thing which puzzles you,' said Bowie, 'you are of a more credulous turn of mind than I am. Why should Bell, speaking Chinese or not, go to a hut full of fishermen and ask them to bury him when he was still alive, and then go and lie down on the beach and die? And what did he die of, pray tell me? Anderson could find no sign of anything wrong with him.'

'I cannot explain it,' said Harker, 'any more than you can, as I am convinced that Mr Bell in his lifetime could not have uttered a syllable that those men would have understood. I suppose there was no possible doubt about the identity of the body. You gentlemen saw it for yourselves.'

'I did not, but Jack Bowie here did,' I said.

'There could be no doubt about it, no doubt at all,' said

Bowie. 'That was the body of poor Bell and I saw him buried.'

'Perhaps we had better see if he is still there,' I said, 'if he has this gift of dematerialising at will.'

This had scandalised Bowie. With imprecations he declared that he had seen Bell's body decently laid to rest with proper Christian burial and that was the end of it.

'The whole story is moonshine,' he continued to assert. 'Pure heathen superstition from start to finish. As for a few dollars and some bits of red paper, what can you make out from them? There's plenty of red paper in the bazaar.'

This story now kept running through my mind. Less sceptical than Bowie, I never doubted that it was true. As for Bell denying that he spoke Chinese, that did not surprise me. He would have considered such an accomplishment unbecoming, suitable only to junior clerks. What inspired me with pity was that the stiff, withdrawn old man, always as proud as a peacock in spite of his owing money all over Macao, should have come to such an end, begging burial from strangers and then laying himself down to die on the sands of Cacilha Bay. How he must have frightened those poor fishermen, this strange, staring foreign devil, to have forced them to do as he said. I know the Chinese horror of a corpse: no one will touch it, they are afraid of evil spirits or worse still, of the mandarin. It was in the winter, the fishermen would have been wearing their wadded cotton coats when they went out reluctantly to execute their task, the sand would have been cold and heavy to their spades. Perhaps that was why they did not put him very deep. And Bell—what had driven him to turn away from his own kind in the end when he knew, I am convinced, that his death was near? Had his long exile in the East turned his brain, or had he come to realise that he had cast his lot in with the Chinese and had better entrust his bones to them, rather than to the Company? If that was his intention, it has been thwarted, for the Company have him in their graveyard now, and they are going to plant a monument on him to keep him there.

I have often thought about my own end. I have always thought I would like a family deathbed, with rows of kneeling descendants, or failing that, a friend or two to keep me company up to the last minute. Now I know I shall be lucky if I am not alone. Alone. That is the only real death, and I am living it now.

This apathy and idleness could not continue, and sure enough, an explosion came. A client called in to demand the portrait of his wife which he commissioned some months ago. (The sittings were in fact in March.) I had to admit that the picture was unfinished, whereupon the husband became very peremptory indeed and high words would have passed on both sides had I not had many years' experience of humouring difficult clients, and in consequence kept my temper better than he did. But I had to promise to complete the portrait within the week.

To tell the truth, I had forgotten all about the particular commission, I had laid it aside for so long. The sitter is another silly, frilly woman, whose husband dotes on her, and she is bored by him. When I got the canvas out, I was appalled to see how much remained to be done. Still, there was nothing for it and I set to work, fortified with ample supplies of cold tea, determined to carry on until the lady was finished. What a price one pays for a few dollars! The strain of labouring at the unrewarding details of an uncongenial commission, in the height of the summer, nearly finished me. But the husband came and saw, he graciously approved, and he has paid. I have never in my life earned money so hard, and I was not allowed to keep it for long, either. Augustine immediately appropriated the greater part of it to satisfy the butcher, the shoemaker, the tailor and the cats' fish man. Shall I ever be done with this endless scraping!

The episode did me some good, however. I had begun to think that I should never work again. I realised also that it was time for me to go out. I cannot become a recluse without reason, and no reason exists which can be admitted. If an event should not have taken place, the correct rule is to behave as if nothing had happened. That is the view of Augustine, and of my Chinese servants, and it is the view to which society also subscribes, so I have to play my part. And who knows, if I pretend my grief is not there it may die of itself, starved of food, squeezed out of life by iron indifference.

So as soon as I felt well enough to leave the house, I resumed my habit of an early morning walk. On the way back I called at the American bachelors' house, where I found Harker at home, entertaining another somewhat unexpected visitor. Harker is, among other things, a sympathetic if detached observer of missionary endeavour, and has struck up an odd friendship with Father Gonçalves of the College of St Joseph here. The good Fathers run a Chinese printing press in the College—clandestine and illegal, of course, as it is contrary to regulations for a foreigner to print in the Chinese language, or for that matter, to learn it. But the St Joseph's press has been running more or less consistently for the past twenty-five years, as has the Company's. But whereas the Company's press has metal type, St Joseph's use the old Chinese-style wooden blocks, which produce atrocious results but, as the Fathers say, they are movable and can easily be secreted if the Chinese authorities raid the building. The result is that St Joseph's has so far suffered no losses in this way, while the Company has had its entire type confiscated more than once. The drawback of the wooden blocks is that they are dreadfully susceptible to the ravages of termites, and Father Gonçalves was even now in despair. The College was just about to embark on the printing of his Sino-Portuguese Dictionary, on which he has spent many years of his life, when it was found that the white ants had eaten the essential characters overnight.

I said that as the Fathers' labours were like those of the ants, never ending, there should be some fellow feeling between them. In fact, missionaries are the most industrious class of Europeans we have exported to the East, and by far the most dreaded by the Imperial authorities. The weekly newspaper at Canton, heavily financed by the pious American firms in Sion's Corner, trumpets forth the views of the Presbyterian Church on Chinese idolatry and corruption, while the Fathers at Macao retail the lives of the Saints (in 24 volumes) to allcomers. I know a good deal about these matters, for until recently the bulk of the tracts and pamphlets in the Chinese language destined for distribution in the interior had perforce to be produced elsewhere, and a vast amount was printed at Serampur, my place of enforced residence in 1825. There the Mission Press was at it day and night, they were running a vast factory in converts as well as in religious literature. They converted their Indians, trained them, and set them to work turning out vast quantities of paper printed in every language of the East, to facilitate further proselytising. Naked coolies staggered down to the water-front carrying bales of tracts, to be sent down-river and shipped off from Calcutta. Pamphlets printed in Serampur can be found, put to various uses, in fishermen's cabins and peasants' huts from the Great Wall of China to the Spice Islands, and the rejects from the presses filled the demand for wrapping paper in Serampur and for miles around. My cook came back from market with his spices and chilis reposing on the Ten Commandments in Pushtoo or Pali.

I had nothing at all to do in Serampur but go down to meet the daily boat from Calcutta which might bring good news (but more often none), and loiter back through the baking streets, past the water tank, the huge gnarled trees, the women gay as parakeets in brilliant colours, to the bungalow where John would later join me, young and healthy, amused by everything, delighted by a ride across country or a morning idling in the bazaar. Life was cheap, easy and convenient in Serampur, the two of us lived on next to nothing, while down-river my Calcutta creditors were pillaging my studio. At one time I thought indeed that I could have lived happily for ever in Serampur, sketching by the river banks, watching the girls bringing pitchers, and the comings and goings of Indian life.

I was seeing Serampur in my mind's eye as I made my way back through the streets of Macao. I hardly noticed the ungraceful figures in their uniform black or blue clothes which thronged the streets and squares, nor heard their unlovely voices. It was a pleasure when I reached home to get out my sketch-book and live once more by the waters of the Ganges, in scenes peopled by the faces I am used to.

Part Seven

CHAPTER 28

The wind has changed direction. Not that it is any cooler, there is not as yet any drop in the temperature, but the wind is dry. Everything in the soaked and sagging house is drying out, tightening up. Soon cupboard doors and drawers which could not be closed all summer will begin to have yawning cracks in them. The cats feel the change, too. Their hair has become electric, and they are given to sudden moods of frantic energy when they run like crazy creatures in and out of the rooms, and then crouch down under the furniture, watching me with round, bright eyes. The pace of the 'season' is doubly intensified, breakfasts, dinners, parties and excursions are being organised on all sides, for there is less than a month to go before the gentlemen return to Canton.

The last few evenings I have sat in the verandah and watched the dry lightning flickering behind the bare hills of Canton. Thunder rumbles occasionally round the valleys, but there is no rain. The peasants are working in their irrigation channels. I long to get the summer over, but the south-west monsoon dies slowly. Sometimes a warm, clammy breath of it returns, to remind me of a wasted month. Never mind: as I was walking down from Penha Hill I noticed a tree with twisted trunk and leaves just touched with colour which reminded me so powerfully of Bengal that I had to stop and stare. Round the tree grazed three or four scraggy goats, also the exact image of their Indian counterparts. No gloomy black-trousered figure was in sight to remind me where I was, but I looked in vain for the brown-skinned child with liquid eyes whom one would normally find in Bengal, sitting on a rock singing to himself, or peeping plaintively on a little reed pipe. The goats browsed steadily with a tearing sound. As I remained motionless they took no notice of me but for one, the leader of the flock, who positioned himself so as to keep me in view, and from time to time raised his head to stare at me with his yellow eyes, chewing meanwhile on his last mouthful. The scene put me in mind of something glimpsed years ago and not forgotten, and I hurried off home to get out my notebooks. I had to turn back many pages before I found it, but there it was just as I remembered, the tree, the straw hut in the background, the browsing goats and the child in his white clout, nervous of my presence but determined not to desert his precious charges. The sketch was so true that I could smell the scene, as well as see it: the smell of dust from the worn-out soil of India, the smell of smoke from the cooking fires, an occasional dash of violent scent.

In order to see more clearly, I bent back the covers of the book. Something fell out. It was a slip of paper on which I had written a note to Charlotte. Tears came into my eyes as recollection and sensation came rushing back. I had ceased to blame Charlotte for leaving me—these things never happen to us through no fault of our own. I had lost her by my own failures. Now every small thing about the house reminded me of her, even the shelves and cupboards which she had so often tidied, which were now in full confusion again. So often she had pushed the chairs on the verandah into tidy array, pulled the tables up to them, and cleared away the litter of dirty cups and glasses which always seemed to be found there. It used to annoy me when she insisted on doing servants' work, but what would I have given to have her there to do it still! It was delightful to watch her as she moved round on these self-imposed tasks. The hair which she wore drawn up high exposed a neck so innocently bare, so untouched by climate, by worry or by age. Could the necks of those old market women ever have been like it? An immense hatred of the whole Chinese people came over me: a hideous race, ugly in speech, in manners and in dress. Their virtues, if they are virtues, of ant-like industry, respect for the ancestors and observances of ritual cannot compensate in any way for their lack of outward attraction. And among all the women of China only one has ever been kind to me, and she not a girl of the highest virtue. A sudden burst of loud laughter from the courtyard irritated me unbearably— one of the servants was lounging there, carrying on a shouted conversation with another inside the house.

Augustine served me a dinner so horrible, so utterly distasteful, that I told him to take it away. It was a native meal, consisting of a fish which would have been better left where it came from, rice boiled to death in the usual Chinese manner, and some sort of vegetable outwardly resembling cabbage, but with an aroma so nauseating as to be impossible to describe. I told Augustine to bring me something else, but he said there was nothing else in the house, not even eggs. This was the servants' food, he added, as if I could not have guessed it. I could have wept! After forty years at my art, and twenty-five years in the East, to be served my servants' food. I nearly threw the dishes over the verandah, but then I had a better notion and set the whole meal before the cats, who rapidly made a clearance of it with the exception of the nauseous vegetable, and this I regarded as positive proof, if any were required, of its inedibility. Finally I chased Augustine and the empty dishes downstairs, and with a very vacant interior sat down on the verandah to contemplate my Indian scene and consider the possibilities.

Next day I made my peace with Augustine. After all, he serves me faithfully, and it is not his fault that money is short. He appeared to be greatly reassured, and inquired:

'What thing Master like for dinner?'

Now Augustine knows my tastes and my prejudices, and he does not usually bother to ask what I want. But so evident was his desire to please that I answered at once:

'I would like birds'-nest soup, Augustine, followed by ricebirds, beef steaks, and lychees.'

'Rice-birds all fly away,' murmured Augustine, 'and lychees no yet come.' (Lychees, Ala's favourite fruit! Of course they would come in with the turn of the season, then there would be lychees in heaps on the market stalls, lychees to be pulled off the trees by those who could reach them, the red-brown husks would be thrown down everywhere.) 'Beef steak, birds'-nest soup, can do. But all these things very dear. Master have got money?'

I had not, and told him so, saying rice would do.

'No have got money, no can buy rice.'

'Never mind, Augustine,' I said, 'when I have finished this, there will be plenty money.' I indicated my Indian scene, roughed out. Augustine contemplated it without much enthusiasm.

'More better Master paint faces. That way more money.'

This being the state of affairs in the house, to solve the dinner problem I accepted an invitation to the board of the ever-hospitable Company. I tore myself away from my Indian goats and goat-herd and set out on foot, no chair-bearers being available. (More 'mandarin-trouble', I supposed.) I had completed about half the distance to the Company's house, and was about to turn down one of the steeply sloping lanes, when I became aware of a commotion ahead. The lane was blocked by a group of Chinese in some sort of uniform, that is, their tunics were adorned with a character which had I suppose some significance to the Chinese populace, and they were congregated round a stationary sedan chair.

Now I am not one to run my head into trouble: my experience has taught me that it is better to avoid it, in these climates. If the Chinese should turn out to be some official's entourage, it would be wiser to steer clear of them: and I was just about to withdraw quietly and make a detour, when I observed to my horror the door of the sedan open, and a European woman begin to get out. I also saw that the Chinese were endeavouring to prevent her escape by combining to overthrow the chair. The bearers were nowhere to be seen, and had presumably run away.

Well, there was only one thing to do, and that was to go to the assistance of the lady. In the twinkling of an eye I made up my mind, and borrowing the technique of the Chinese 'braves' who go into action uttering loud shouts in inverse proportion to their martial valour, I raised a war yell and hurled myself down the hill into the midst of the mêlée. I had the advantage of impetus, weight and surprise, moreover I had a walking stick with which I dealt indiscriminate whacks at heads and bodies. The Chinese did not pause to discover whether I was one man or several. They fled helter-skelter down the lane, and I was left confronting a badly shaken Mrs Haverill, deathly white and clinging to the side of the sedan for support.

'Come along quickly,' I said, 'in case they should gather reinforcements and return. I shall feel happier when we are in sight of the Company's house.'

Mrs Haverill shook her head. She seemed scarcely capable of speech, and I hoped she was not going to faint.

'No, you go on alone. I must return home. I have had such a shock, I do not feel fit to continue. I must ask you to make my excuses.'

This was annoying, and I hastily reviewed the situation. The Company's house, Mrs Haverill's house and my own were all roughly equidistant from the place where we were. Of the three, my house was possibly the nearest, but if I were to escort Mrs Haverill there until her fright had subsided, I should have had to accompany her home afterwards, and meanwhile, what of the dinner? Equally, I could not leave her where she was, in a state of semi-collapse.

'Then you must allow me to see you home,' I said.

Transferring her from the sedan to my arm for support, I got Mrs Haverill into motion and hurried her as quickly as I could through the back lanes in the direction of her house. Fortunately we met no Chinese on the way, for it was obvious that Mrs Haverill's nerves were thoroughly overstrung, and the sight of a harmless coolie might have aroused great agitation. Once safely inside her drawing-room, Mrs Haverill sank on to the sofa, murmuring, in reply to my expressions of concern:

'I do not know how to thank you sufficiently, Mr Chinnery, for coming to my rescue today. Had it not been for your courage . . . Indeed, I do not know what would have happened, if you had not arrived when you did, and chased those men away.'

'Well, neither do I,' I replied, 'but as nothing happened, you must try and forget about it, although it must have been a very unpleasant experience for a lady.'

Mrs Haverill shuddered and shut her eyes, then opened them again and sat up in indignation.

'To think of such a thing happening in broad daylight. If the Portuguese authorities cannot keep order here, then they should let the British and the Americans do it. All the Portuguese will do now, I suppose, is make a complaint to the Chinese mandarin which will get nowhere.'

'Probably not,' I said, 'particularly as I am tolerably sure that those were the mandarin's men.'

'How can the Portuguese allow it?'

'They have no power to stop it, as the Chinese allege that Macao is a part of China, and that the mandarin is the true authority here.'

Mrs Haverill closed her eyes again.

'Those odious little yellow officials at the Customs House: I shall never forget my first arrival here. But you must not allow me to keep you any longer, Mr Chinnery, from your dinner. Once more, let me thank you most profoundly for what you did today.'

I determined to act on impulse.

'Before I go, Mrs Haverill, may I ask you one question?'

'Of course.' She was all attention.

'Why did you advise Miss Winters to go to Bengal?'

Mrs Haverill opened her eyes very wide.

'But I did nothing of the sort, Mr Chinnery. Miss Winters' decision to accompany Mrs Oliver was entirely her own. It was not my place to advise Miss Winters, nor was I asked to do so.'

'Yet you gave Miss Winters letters of recommendation?'

'That was done at her own request. Miss Winters was concerned that she might not be able to stay long with Mrs Oliver's parents, so I wrote her a letter of introduction to old friends of mine in Calcutta.'

'As a companion?'

'That was at Miss Winters' own suggestion.'

'Good heavens, madam, you apparently know something about India, what sort of life do you think is in store for a girl like Miss Winters who goes there as a companion?'

Mrs Haverill's colour deepened, but she replied calmly:

'I think that Miss Winters was taking a sensible view of her position when she asked me for this introduction, and I do not myself consider that her prospects are as gloomy as you make them out to be. In fact, I think her chances of contracting a suitable marriage are greater in India than they are here.'

'Madam, what can you mean by that? Are there no bachelors here?'

'I mean that the number of young men in Macao is strictly limited, and as Miss Winters certainly did not put herself out to please them, it is small wonder that they became discouraged. In India there is bound to be a wider choice.'

'Is that all you mean?' I demanded. 'I fancy you had it on the tip of your tongue to say that if Miss Winters' reputation in Macao were a little tarnished—by your ladies' gossip, perhaps—she would do better in Bengal.'

Mrs Haverill drew herself up.

'I never listen to gossip, Mr Chinnery, and I do not know what you are talking about.' But her eyes wandered off mine, and I was sure she lied.

'No more do I listen to gossip, Mrs Haverill, not having the entrée to ladies' circles, and if I were to hear any, I would not repeat it. You may rely on me, madam, I am the soul of discretion itself. Some of the more senior ladies may lose their heads a little from time to time, and may even behave rather indiscreetly, but who is going to bring that up against them?' Mrs Haverill flushed a deeper red and turned her head away. 'Certainly not I. I do not set myself up as a judge of the morals of others. I would live and let live. But why then, madam, did you and the rest of them with your gossip drive Miss Winters away from Macao?'

Mrs Haverill gave a faint cry, and sprang to her feet.

'Mr Chinnery, I do not understand what you are talking about, so I do not know how to answer you. You must forgive me, I have had a great shock today, I must ask you to retire.' Mrs Haverill made off in the direction of her boudoir, and I showed myself out into the street. Only when I was outside did the irony of the situation strike me. I had given myself away completely to Mrs Haverill: but she would never be able to disclose it, for fear I might make public her own folly.

I reached the Company's house to find the ladies and gentlemen half-way through dinner. I told my story and found myself the hero of the hour, while Mrs Haverill's absence was universally regretted. The attack on her chair was, however, made very little of. (Had it been the wife of one of the heads of the Factory inside it, how different the story would have been!) It was universally agreed that the mandarin was getting restive on account of the approaching Portuguese carnival, and he had judged it a suitable occasion to assert his own authority by banning foreigners from riding in chairs. This is such a familiar piece of strategy that the feeling was Mrs Haverill had only herself to blame by trying to flout it. I could see that this did not suit those American gentlemen who were present, but being guests at the Company's table, they had to hold their peace. Mrs Fay was more outspoken when I found myself beside her in the drawing-room.

'It is the mercy of Providence, Mr Chinnery, that you arrived when you did, or else what would have happened to Mrs Haverill? Those Chinese might have robbed her, or *anything*. I think it is the greatest shame that the matter is not going to be taken up. The Portuguese should be made to take action. We Americans could look after ourselves, given the chance, but if Mr Fay makes any complaint to the

Portuguese, he is told "We do not know who you are, we only know the Company." Yet after all, we are just as much entitled to protection. The Portuguese authorities here are making all this money out of us, yet they will not lift a finger to protect us.'

I could understand her sentiments, but all the same it was a relief when Miss Fay came up to join her mother, and created a diversion.

'Mr Bowie has been telling me all about Calcutta,' she said. 'It sounds a most splendid place, and I am bursting with impatience to have Charlotte's first impressions. We all thought Macao was grand enough, when we arrived here, but it seems that it is simply nothing compared with Calcutta. All the houses are palaces, and every European goes about with a whole train of servants behind him.'

'Well, you will have some time to wait,' said Mrs Fay, 'before you can hope to hear from Charlotte. The ship can barely have arrived yet. I wonder how that poor Mrs Oliver stood the journey, with a young child, too.'

'Charlotte said she would try to send us a letter by clipper, if one were sailing, then it could be here in three weeks, or even less. Mr Chinnery, did you know that one of the clippers now at Lintin is called "The Cowasjee Family"? I never before heard such a name for a ship. . . .'

Miss Fay rattled on, and I made mechanical replies. I was busy in mental calculations, which were still occupying me when I took my leave. Yes, if she had a reasonably good passage, the old *Stirling Castle* must even now be nearing the mouths of the Hooghly. Very soon Charlotte would be casting her eyes for the first time on the 'City of Palaces', and landing on the very same Bund which I left behind me with such relief six years ago. If little Macao, with its merchants' houses, tile-roofed Chinese bazaars and barley-sugar churches had impressed the two girls, what would Charlotte think of Calcutta, probably the biggest city she had ever seen? I contrasted the dinner I had just left, a gathering of merchants arranged in self-appointed order to constitute a little

237

hierarchy, with the really splendid banquets of Calcutta. Titles, orders, uniforms, hundreds of guests present at a time, vast halls blazing with lights, and such tribes of attendants that your handkerchief was back in your hand before you were conscious of having dropped it. Not that I myself have ever yearned after these magnificent scenes, with all the wearisome bowing and scraping entailed, but I had many good friends in Calcutta I would give much to see again. I would like to pass down the street and see the house in which I had lived with Rosa. I wonder who lives there now. After she died I left it as quickly as possible, I could not bear to remain, but now that time has blunted the edge of that sorrow, I would be happy to go back and live there again. The house would only remind me of earlier, happy days.

CHAPTER 29

Charlotte! Soon she would be landing, completely friendless, in Calcutta where she knew not a soul but Mrs Oliver, who would no doubt escort her, as an act of grace, to one of those assemblies where she would be looked over by such bald and toothless civilians as were on the look-out for a new young arrival to replace wives numbers one and two, succumbed to fever and neglect. They are quite selective, these old gentlemen, nothing but the newest and freshest will do, and if they could empanel a jury of matrons to reassure them on the vital point, no doubt they would do so. What other chance is there, despite Mrs Haverill's facile optimism, for a penniless girl with no family? Charlotte will have to take what she can get, which may be a worn-out man too old to give her children, too old for a husband.

We should have had children. We ought now to have children. I could see that house of mourning repopulated by Charlotte and myself. In five years Calcutta has had time to find out what it lost when it sent me packing. There is still no one there who can compete with me. I can easily build up a connection there again. Then Charlotte and I could marry— I don't exclude that possibility. After all, anything might happen.

These thoughts raced through my head all night, while the summer lightning jumped and quivered across the sky, Tom and the kitten slept rolled together in one basket, and Puss prowled somewhere outside in the garden. Several times I got up and stood at the window to watch, and listen. There was no possibility of sleep until four or five in the morning. Even so, I woke again in a couple of hours, and as soon as there was a chance of finding him astir, I went in search of an old Parsee acquaintance, Hormusjee, whom I knew to have come down from Canton. He occupied the first floor of one of the most tumble-down-looking houses in the bazaar, a quite unnecessary affectation of poverty, for I knew as did many others that he had been making money hand over fist in the last two opium seasons, sending his profits back home in silver to Calcutta. I found him at home and succeeded in penetrating into his frowsty little hole which he had contrived to fill with a rich aroma that defeated the smells of the environment. Hormusjee asked me into his 'office', separated by a screen from the rest of the room. It consisted of one chair, on which I sat, and one chest, on which Hormusjee tucked up his feet. I came straight to the point. I wanted to go back to Bengal. Would Hormusjee finance me, and more, guarantee me when I landed up to—I named a sum which I could easily cover in a year. It was ludicrous to see the emotions chase each other across the merchant's face: incredulity, surprise, slow credulity, calculation—finally he spread his hands. 'Ah, Mr Chinnery, sir, it is too much money for a poor man like me. Besides, what for do you want to go back there? You only run your head into the tiger's mouth, as you say. Better stay in Macao. Macao is a very fine place. Plenty of money here, if you know how.' It was no good trying to shake him. If he could do it, I knew he would. But there was no need to give up hope: if Hormus-jee was not willing, there were others.

As I was coming back from this fruitless expedition, I passed through the square in front of the Leal Senado, usually a mass of Chinese humanity. Now it was empty, it had been swept and sanded, and black soldiers were posted at the entrances to turn back the populace. They let me through without difficulty, and I noticed something else. The private houses round the square have their ground floors blank to the street and only smaller windows above which are usually shuttered. Now these upper windows had been opened, and carpets and hangings had been draped over the sills. It was the same thing in the higher streets to which I mounted. For the first time it was possible to see through the open windows into the upper rooms of the houses, and servants were occupied in draping curtains and putting pots of flowering plants on the balconies. I could even see females moving to and fro within, and although none actually came out on to the veran-dahs while I was there, I was conscious from time to time of smothered laughter above me. Then from somewhere in another quarter of the town came the thump and toot of a band starting up, and it became apparent what was afoot. It was the day of the Portuguese carnival.

It was a weary afternoon shut up in my house listening to the bands playing in competition, and the firecrackers explod-ing as the many processions made their way through the streets. My house was off the route and I felt no desire to go out and watch. Late in the evening a comparative silence fell, and I do not know how late it was—it was quite dark—when my own front door opened and closed noisily and the voices of a man and woman talking loudly in Portuguese could be heard below. A burst of laughter followed which rolled up the stairs. 'This is too much,' thought I, and went out to investigate. Standing below were Augustine and his cousin. Augustine held a lighted candle in his hand and he was wearing some strange antiquated get-up, baggy breeches made of dark-coloured velvet and a doublet with slashed sleeves. On his head was an enormous hat. The light of the candle fell on his cousin, and she—she was superb. She too wore a costume of several centuries back. It was black, heavily spangled with gold, the full sleeves woven with gold thread and ending in frills of gold lace. The skirt was padded so as to stand out stiffly at the sides as one sees in old pictures of the Spanish court, and it was cut clear of the ankles so as to display her feet in high-heeled shoes. The bodice was so low in front as to show quite half of her breasts and more gold lace formed a sort of ruff behind her head. As a finishing touch she was masked, but there was no mistaking those magnificent eyes. Both of them turned to me as I came down the stairs. The lady raised her hand to her mask as if to assure herself that it was in position.

'Madam, this is a sight which merits the light of more than one candle. Permit me to see it more clearly.' I made the gesture of inviting her to walk upstairs and when she did not seem to understand it, I took her hand and drew her gently after me. She had to turn sideways to manœuvre her monstrous skirt. Augustine turned on his heel and disappeared into his quarters. Upstairs I led the lady into the middle of the room where she glinted and flashed like a goddess. So much gold would have overwhelmed most women: it made her look more queenly, and I reverently kissed the hand that I held before relinquishing it. 'Madam, I am your most profound and respectful admirer—so what's the need of the mask?' As I spoke, I advanced my hand to take it off—but my hand fell on the lady's waist. I could feel the heavy stuff of her dress under my fingers, and the metal ribs of the frame or cage on which it was suspended pressed into my legs, obliging me to remain at a respectful distance, while the square of white skin beckoned me on. Having got one hand firmly on her waist, I raised the other to take off the mask, but at this the goddess came to life. In spite of her cumbersome skirt, she slipped away from me like an eel and in a trice was on the stairs. She hurried down them and a few seconds later a door slammed somewhere below. Well, so much for that. I do not think she was angry, though, I am pretty certain that she was laughing at me. It was an agreeable contact with another human being which released me for five minutes from my thoughts, my obsession for Bengal, and Charlotte. The thoughts returned, however, to torment me through the night as they had the night before.

In the morning—this morning—I got up, filled with fresh determination. Again it was fine, and clear, and hot. The sky was a burning blue, the bay sparkled, the white houses baked in the sun as I hurried through the alleys towards Bowie's house. He heard me out, his face falling into heavy creases of concern and his eyes refusing to meet mine. 'It is no good, George,' he said. 'There is too much money involved, far more than I could put up, even if I were not in the same boat as yourself.'

'Hormusjee would come forward if he knew of your interest. I am quite sure he would agree to cover me for a year.'

'I doubt it. And besides, George, have you thought what would happen if you did go back? They would clap you into jail as soon as you landed: you would not be able to work and there would be precious little chance of your clearing your debts in a year or any other time.'

'I know I could do it, given the chance.'

'Ay, but who is going to give you the chance? George, you are crazy.' Bowie threw up his hands. 'You owe too many of them too much, my boy. And another thing you seem to forget: you will be right back in the arms of Mrs Chinnery.'

'She is getting to be an old woman now.'

'It is the old women who are the toughest,' retorted Bowie. He altered his tone and spoke almost with embarrassment. 'Why can't you make the best of it here, George? After all, it is not such a bad place, you know. We might both of us be much worse off. You ought to make up your mind to settle down and get somebody to look after you. We are both too old to go running round at nights.'

It was all so well meant, there was nothing I could say.

All the same, it was another hope gone. I crossed the square in front of the Senate House on my way home. The hawkers and beggars had drifted back in force, the clean sand of yesterday was now churned up with a mounting collection of debris, rejected fragments from the food stalls, the droppings of humanity. The shutters round the square had been closed again and the houses presented blank faces as before. Black soldiers stood on guard before the Leal Senado, ancient repository of the liberties of Macao. Behind it, through a sort of cloister, was the little building which housed the English library. I nearly turned into it, but the thought of meeting acquaintances, ladies possibly, restrained me. The next landmark was Doctor Anderson's Dispensary with the usual crowd of Chinese encamped in front of its doors. Then the shops left off and the region of private houses began, those select upper levels of which my own habitation was in the bottom-most. The narrow streets ran upwards in flights of steps, the high white walls on either side reflecting the sun unmercifully. I toiled up until I reached the mouth of my own lane. Here I wavered, and took the only other turning which ran down again, to the water. It was hot, blazing with sun, not an atom of shade. Not a single living soul was in sight: the quarter seemed deserted. I followed the road for fifty yards to the place where it widened slightly to form a little square with a church at one side. I do not know anything about this church, not even its name, if it has a name. It is simply one of the hundred empty churches of Macao, shut and deserted. A grille of ornamental ironwork enclosed the main door. I tried it, but it was locked. It looked as if there had been windows originally on either side of the door, which had been blocked with masonry at some later period. The builders had provided embrasures to sit in, let into the stonework by the porch, but iron spikes had been set in the stone so as to render them unusable. I sat on the steps in the shadow cast by the porch and wondered, what use was the church, to the Macaïstas, the Chinese or anybody else? I could not remember ever having seen it open. Whatever wonders of decoration adorned the interior, symbols of the Faith, gilding, leatherwork, sculpture, no one would ever see them. The doors would not open to permit a glimpse of the rolling clouds of incense, the vestments or the Host. Perhaps the church had been gutted, and was now an empty shell holding four old Chinamen gambling with a handful of pebbles. There were churches in Macao used as godowns. Whatever it was, it was dead. Beside the steps was a little pile of ordure, whether a dog's or human I could not tell, but quite dried and inoffensive. I could have taken it up in my hand, had I wished.

A clack-clacking of clogs at a distance announced the approach of a Chinese. It was a woman, dressed in the shiny black cloth of the lower classes. She hurried past me, turning her head away. From her hand dangled a bunch of chickens tied together by the feet. They were alive: I could see tiny frantic eyes rolling this way and that. The plumage was just the same as that of the feather-duster abominations which Augustine buys for the house. The colour reminded me for a moment of the ginger cat. Sitting on the steps of the church I felt my resolution stiffen. I will not give in without a fight. I will not be relegated. If Calcutta would mean a debtor's prison, what is Macao but a life sentence? If Bowie cannot help, I must find others who will.

I want so desperately to leave Macao and return to Bengal that it seems impossible this one simple wish can be refused, when so ardently desired. But it has been the same answer everywhere. I have been round my Indian acquaintances, my old Parsee friends. They all looked at me with their big sheep's eyes as if they thought I was mad. Perhaps I am. How should I know? Whatever the tale they tell, it comes always to the same end: no money. And without money I cannot get back to Calcutta. There still remains one possibility, though.

The same answer. I have tried everyone I can think of, and it is hopeless. I am nearly in despair.

I shall never get away from this place.

In the late afternoon I smelt the smoke rising from the fire on which the gardener boils his tea. I went down and demanded of Augustine where the firewood for the kitchen was kept. He pointed out the place, one of the downstairs rooms where a servant must also sleep, for there were bed-boards there, laid over two trestles, and a folded quilt. I took an armful of wood and dragged it outside. The gardener was squatting by the wall with his tea bowl, but the ashes of his little fire were still smouldering. I piled the wood on them: it caught and began to crackle. I went up into the studio and looked for the nearly-completed picture of the boat girl. It was behind others, I have not had the heart to work on it, and now it will never be finished. As I took it up I thought what a beautiful piece of work it was. I carried it outside, to where my fire was burning brightly, and I laid the picture on top of the flames.

They reached out for it at once, and a column of heat shot up in the air. For a moment the canvas seemed to remain suspended in the centre of the fire, then with a little plop! it shrivelled up into blackened fragments, and the flames devoured the stretcher. Turning round, I saw behind me Augustine, who had followed me quietly out of the house, and with him three or four of the Chinese servants. They stood and gazed in silence at the foreigner's strange offering, made without benefit of red paper, candles or fire-crackers. Nevertheless, it was the best I could do. I went back into the house and left them all standing there, like a gathering of black crows solemnly watching the last flutterings of breath.

The problem of support for myself and hangers-on is facing me once more. Every day the thermometer is dropping, and the wind has begun to blow from a new quarter. The gentlemen are off to Canton, their boats are leaving one after the other. No more commissions can be expected in that direction, and the occasional winter visitors as often as not go straight up-river to the Factories without stopping in Macao. In the painting-room there is a blank space by the wall where the unfinished portrait of the boat girl stood. I keep my eyes away from it, and force my mind to the question of putting something in its place.

Kind friends invited me to go up with them to Canton for a sojourn there, and I considered it, but in the end I refused. It was the prospect of the incarceration, of the inescapable formal dinners every night, which repelled me. One can have too much even of good company, and in the Factories every movement one makes is necessarily observed by a hundred eyes, friendly and unfriendly alike. Besides, I want my beautiful season in Macao, when it becomes once more a joy to walk about. There is the pleasure of revisiting old haunts quite a mile off, which I have been too languid to reach in the heat of the summer, and also of finding new ones. I have been to the boatyards to watch the building of a lorcha, a craft which is a speciality of Macao, a blend of east and west, and particularly favoured by pirates for its speed and capacity. The pirates' order must have been an express one, for the carpenters were at work from dawn to dusk, with their chests and shoulders bare, manipulating clumsy-seeming tools in ways very strange to our eyes, with miraculous results. They seem to need no guidelines, no measurements— all is done by eye alone (leaving, it has to be admitted, a good many gaps in the planking which have to be caulked). Their sweating bodies exuded the odours of garlic and Chinese cabbage, the air was redolent of shavings, oil (they rarely paint their craft here, applying an outer coating of oil instead) and cordage steeping in some concoction composed largely, I believe, of pigs' blood. But I could not get the picture I sought and came away.

On the way back I passed close by a drying ground for

246

fish, and was assailed by all the flies and smells of Asia. There was no way round, I had to run the gauntlet for the length of the street, making my way among the tribe of mangy dogs which haunt the area expectantly. On emerging once more into purer air, I was overtaken by a sedan chair. The occupant was Mrs Haverill. When the chair passed me, she bowed, I saluted. That was all. With my clothes empested with fishy and other smells I could not have approached a lady had I wanted to, but in any case there is nothing to be said between Mrs Haverill and myself, and we both know it. I fancied that she looked rather wan and disconsolate, but I had only a passing glimpse of her face. We have had no occasion to meet these last few weeks, and I shall take care that none presents itself.

My inability to settle to work is what troubles me most. I have scores and scores of sketches, but what I need is a big conception, and it refuses to come. The idea struck me of making a fancy portrait of Augustine's cousin, whom I still glimpse from time to time below stairs (where she seems to have taken upon herself the duty of ordering the servants), in her carnival costume, but she refused to sit to me. Perhaps she was ashamed of appearing in such an outlandish dress, except on an occasion of gala. A pity, as it could have been effective! I was fidgeting in the painting-room, trying and discarding ideas, when Augustine came and announced that a Chinese gentleman wished to see me, one Mr Lee Qua Loong, the son of the most highly respected old merchant whose portrait I had painted at Canton during my last visit.

Any distraction was welcome, so I had the visitor shown up at once. After a preliminary creaking and shuffling on the stairs, a delegation of no less than four Chinamen entered the room, young Mr Lee to the fore. I say young Mr Lee to distinguish him from the father, but in reality the son must be about fifty. Two of the other men were his attendants, and the third was dressed like an outside servant. This last was carrying in his arms a wooden box with big red labels pasted on it.

After a suitable exchange of salutations (via Augustine) there followed a long speech by Mr Lee, which Augustine translated to something like the following effect:

Last year (by Chinese reckoning) I had made the likeness of his respected father which was justly admired by all and hung in the great hall of the family mansion. Ten moons after completion of the work and its being put in position, heaven had blessed his father with yet another son. The happy coincidence had been remarked, and to mark the auspicious occasion and as a small token of his respect and esteem, Mr Lee senior had ventured to send me a small gift which he hoped I would honour him by accepting, unworthy as it was, etc.

Here the box was indicated, and the bearer put it down on the floor where the two superior minions proceeded to open the lid and to deal with a quantity of packing material which they laid aside. Finally there emerged an object wrapped in a piece of figured silk which with great reverence they handed to Mr Lee junior, who ceremoniously unveiled it before handing it to me. The object treated with so much care turned out to be a plain dark blue vase shaped like a bottle, with no decoration whatsoever, absolutely unfitted by reason of its design for any useful purpose I could think of. I took the thing in my hands and examined it. True, the glaze was smooth and perfect, not run down lumpily on the sides of the vessel as one sees quite often in Chinese productions, and the colour, though sombre, was pleasing to the eye, but I could not see any possible beauty in the thing. Yet the eyes of the company, including Augustine, were fixed on it in respectful admiration, and from the lips of all I heard the syllables put forth:

'Velly old!'

Those fatal sentiments which one hears so frequently from the Chinese! If the habit, the custom or the object is very old, it must be good. Their discriminative faculties are completely overborne by so much antiquity, and it would be a brave man who dared proclaim the truth, that the custom is oppressive or useless, and the object is hideous. The discrepancy between the solemnity of the occasion and comparative insignificance of the gift was so striking that I had great difficulty in maintaining my gravity and returning thanks in a proper manner. 'Young' Mr Lee added as a final recommendation that the vase had been in his family's possession for I forget how many generations, and I hope I gave the appearance of being suitably impressed. Young Mr Lee was a good-looking but rather heavy man, and his features bore an expression of habitual melancholy. He seemed to suffer greatly from the heat, and fanned himself incessantly. I could see in him no trace of the wizened but lively old man who had sat to me. I could clearly recall old Mr Lee posed in his carved blackwood chair, his feet shod in padded felt-soled slippers supported on a small table arranged as a footstool. The old gentleman's expression radiated mild benevolence, yet it was clear that his business faculties were as acute as ever, and in fact he struck a hard bargain with me over the fee. I did not doubt the genuineness of his intentions in sending me this belated addition, but if the vase had any monetary value (which I would have to find out) I would rather have taken cash down.

However, young Mr Lee was kind enough to tell me, when taking his leave, that should I come to Canton again I would find plenty of sitters, as his father would not fail in his recommendation of me. The idea of a portrait by Chinnery being in demand as a specific to procure potency in elderly Chinese gentlemen entertained me hugely, and as all these Hong merchants are immensely rich, I foresaw a harvest of remunerative commissions. It is a far cry from my early days in Calcutta when the rumour was—and who put it about I have never succeeded in finding out—that for an Indian to be painted by me would bring about his death within the year. It can be imagined what relief I felt when the first native sitter to submit himself to the process survived the magic period, and even after that I had a lingering prejudice to dispel which must have cost me dearly. Bengal! so cruel

249

to the young man making his way, so sycophantic to success, how can I forget you? Yet I cannot let myself think of Calcutta, or picture that world which I can never re-enter.

A few nights later I gave way and let all those crowding visions visit me which I had been keeping at bay. The moon progressed slowly across the sky. A night breeze had sprung up after a windless day, and the stiff banana fronds moved their arms up and down above the wall of my neighbour's garden. The Chinese say that a celestial Hare lives on the moon, where he pounds with pestle and mortar herbs to compound the elixir of long life, that goal of all their desires, and that on such nights as these he can be seen engaged on his futile task. For what virtue has long life, if that life be meaningless?

What I did was right, I know it, I have told myself this over and over again. My reason accepts the situation, but there are limits beyond which reason cannot command our nature. When I have already lost so much in my life I should have learned resignation, but what can reconcile a man to lost happiness? His death as a man, perhaps, but even that I doubt. While we breathe we must fight for our happiness. To have thrown mine away is more than I can bear to think of.

It was then that I remembered the bottles stacked at the bottom of the cupboard in the painting-room, otherwise given over as a repository for old rags, and as a place for Puss to make a nest for successive litters; bottles of claret probably of the finest vintage, the gift of some passing patron ignorant of my tastes. I had meant to give them away, but ended by forgetting about them. I got a bottle out and looked at it curiously before I opened it, as if it were a magician's potion to give oblivion.

The glass of wine which I poured out tasted like ink and ashes mixed. I had hardly got it down before I vomited. The draught acted as a purge and in the end, shivering and sick,

I wrapped myself in a cover and fell on to my bed, to lie like a log until the following morning.

Perhaps a purge was what my system needed, for the next day I woke feeling renewed and full of energy. Pausing only to instruct Augustine to pour the remaining bottles of wine away, for I was not prepared to take the risk of poisoning any of my acquaintance, I started out on my round. Shortly after passing the harbour, at a point of the shore where fishing junks often anchor, I found one lying close inshore. It was clear that she was being overhauled, for her deck was clear of the usual accumulation of duck and chicken coops and miscellaneous gear, her masts were down, and the mat sails, done up in bundles, were lying on the shore. It was a perfect chance to grasp the details of the craft clearly, and I settled down to make notes. The towering stern of all junks gives them their resemblance to floating castles, breasting their way forward through the water rather than riding on it, but none the less they are very seaworthy craft. The stern of a fishing junk is mostly taken up by a fish hold, but there are more dolls'-house-size compartments, or rather shelves, in which the twenty-odd men, women and children who make up the crew stow themselves. How they exist is a mystery. Their livestock look better housed. At this moment only a couple of old women and some children were visible on board the junk, and they took no notice of me at all. I would dearly have liked to venture on board but did not dare, in case indifference should give way to hostility. Even more than the old women and children I feared the dog, the usual black chow, which I could see was not tied up. I wondered where all the men could be, and then I saw one of them approaching along the shore. He was tall for a Chinese, a young man dressed in a suit of shiny black cloth. He also gave me an indifferent look. He put the basket on the deck and squatted on his heels beside it. One grandmother had started a fire in a box, and was cooking a meal (even with dry land at two paces these people prefer to live on their floating homes). A small half-naked child stood watching her, thumb in mouth.

251

I thought I had been there long enough, and made my way home, but next day as I passed the point again, I found the junk still at anchor, and work actively in progress. The rectangular sails had been spread out on a patch of open ground, and a number of women and one or two of the men were squatting over them repatching the worst holes. The rudder had been unshipped and brought on shore, and two of the men were working on it, which gave me an excellent opportunity of observing the extraordinary sight of a rudder with a pattern of holes deliberately cut in it. Even the dog had come ashore and was running round. He set up a frenzied barking when he saw me, but there was so much noise already that nobody took any notice of him. The workers were chatting at the tops of their voices and the young man in black tunic and trousers of the day before, who seemed to be the junk master, was directing activities. I was ignored when I placed myself some distance off and opened my sketch-book and sat in peace until I heard a dry cough and expectoration behind me.

I turned and saw a little old man, a respectable-looking old Chinaman with a black skull cap and soft cloth slippers. He approached me and peered over my shoulder, then he held out a hand. I guessed that he wanted to see the sketch-book and gave it to him, half apprehensive of the result. He examined it with care, holding it close to his face, but I doubt if he made anything of it. The smile with which he handed me back the book was one of politeness only. But it is enough for me if my sketching activities are tolerated, I don't hope to find appreciation. The old man sat down some distance away and set himself to watching the scene, including myself. I worked until the time came to prepare the evening rice, and the groups broke up.

Next morning I was impatient to get back to the water front. The picture was fixing in my mind, the grouped figures bending over their work, pigtailed heads together, the dog running in and out between them, the babies too young to be put to any work but released from being parcels on their

mothers' backs, waddling solemnly on the outskirts. I would
have liked to see again the junk master, the tall Chinese in the
black clothes, a young strong man, yet emaciated almost to
sickness, his face fined down to white bone. But when I
reached the place where the junk had been lying, the anchorage was empty. The junk had gone, and every man, woman
and child with her. Only a few broken baskets and bits of
old cordage remained. Those, and the old man sitting in the
same place as before, with his hands clasped round his staff.

His eyes flickered in my direction and he must have seen
my disappointment, for he sketched a gesture.

'Gone!' it said.

'Gone? Where to?' I gestured back.

'Anywhere.' His hands encompassed the islands, the way
leading ahead to the open sea, the creeks and rivers which
lay behind us.

'What for?' I asked out loud, although I could not hope
to make him understand me. But apparently he did, for in
answer he drew something in the dust with the point of his
staff. I came over to where he sat, and I saw quite clearly
what the dust scrawl represented. It was a fish, a fish with
an exaggerated hook nose which we call the jewfish (on
account of its appearance), or croaker (by reason of its noisy
habits). It is very good to eat, but it only comes into the
markets in the autumn, and is expensive. Augustine always
grumbles when I feed it to the cats.

The old man rubbed over the fish with his slippered foot,
and went off into a long speech in Chinese, nodding his head
earnestly towards me. He spoke slowly and distinctly, and he
was clearly imparting some valuable information, but of
course I could not understand one syllable. It was as frustra-
ting a situation as could be, but help arrived from an unexpected quarter. Hurrying along the path towards us I saw
Augustine. Now I have always suspected that although
Augustine never follows me, or inquires where I am going,
he is always informed by some means or other of my exact
whereabouts, and this was demonstrated when he panted up

to inform me that my presence was demanded urgently in the studio by an important tai-pan.

'Very well,' I said, 'I will come, but first ask this old man, the junk before-time here, where is she now?'

A long colloquy followed between Augustine and the old gentleman.

'That junk he go after fish, the fish that talks. Golden fish, these Chinese men call it.'

'Yes, but where has she sailed to?'

Again the old man launched on his dissertation, again the all-embracing gestures.

'He go everywhere, he go find the fish. He no can savvy what side fish come. He listen, he hear fish talkee, that way savvy what side fish go.'

And he explained, little by little, what the old man expounded. The shoals of jewfish, greatly esteemed for their eating qualities as well as the other fishy virtues they exhibit (conjugal fidelity, for fish always swim in pairs: perseverance, for they customarily swim against the current), come swarming up from the south in the autumn season. The fishing junks go hunting them, up and down the coastal waters, in and out of the creeks and river estuaries as far as saltwater runs, guided towards their quarry by the noise the fish make talking among themselves. The old man imitated the sounds of fish-talk, and explained what each noise meant, while Augustine looked on with respect. On each fishing boat there is one man, the master fisherman, who can hear and understand the voices of fish. It is he who listens, his ear pressed against the planking, and gives the directions to the crew. Once the shoal is located and its direction ascertained, the signal is given to the other junks cruising near by. The shoal is gently, little by little encircled: then the junks and the nets close the ring.

'This old man, he before-time savvy what fashion fish talk. He go with junk listen for fish.'

'Why does he not go out now with the junks? Is he too old?'

Augustine laughed with the old man as he translated the answer.

'He now have no need to go. This old man very rich man. He has many junks—one, two, three junks, maybe more. He wait, and by and by men bring the fish to him.'

The old man smiled benignly as he sat there, hands on knees, looking out to sea. Was he thinking of the golden profits now falling into his lap, profits which others had to struggle for, chasing the elusive fish in the dangerous waters of the South China Sea? Or was he recalling with nostalgia, in spite of his riches, the days when he too had listened for the voices, and sailed out in pursuit of the golden hordes, the shoals of golden fish?

I would have liked to know the answer to this and other questions, but Augustine, having by this time replied to all the old man's inquiries about myself (although I could not understand them, I knew the sequence by heart; place of origin, age, condition, number of children living, sex of children), was in no mood to linger, and would translate no more. He possessed himself of my sketch-book as the strongest hint that we should return.

To turn round was to quit the wider prospect and re-enter a smaller world. The vision of sea and sky gave way to a scene which was crowded, enclosed, familiar. Low tiled bazaars pullulating with children, alleyways where a bamboo pole stretched easily from side to side, and a ragged garment flapped as largely as a sail, homely shrines enclosing a domestic god in comfortable twilight, a deity content with the paper offerings of the poor. The Company's chief tea-taster's house with its pillared front stood up on a modest eminence like a palace. Farther on, the gleam of the Inner Harbour, a narrow strip of floating homes, and still more far, beyond the forbidden barriers, the green-checkered fields stretching on and on, parcelling out the vast province, with each village a nucleus of tidy, well-ordered life, each peasant living out the cycle pre-ordained, so exotic to our eyes, so every-day to him. Staggering under heavy weights expertly balanced, crying

255

strange wares in an unknown tongue, watching the hawker's fish flop in the pail, cramming rice into the children's mouths (gaping like birds), the people of China were all around us as we went deeper into the town. There was a woman, not old, not young, with a child strapped on her back. Too busy or too burdened with her load to mount the steps to the joss-house, she had paused in the street to make her little spiral of fragrant smoke, from a stick of incense thrust into a crevice of the stones. Her eyes were fixed on it, and she bowed and bowed again and mouthed her prayer.

I stopped the chair and called to Augustine for my sketch-book. The sleek black head of the woman, the soft black head of the baby clinging to her with arms and legs even as it slept, the shaven-scalped little boy at her heels, dressed in bright cotton rags, I wanted to get them down. But Augustine hurried me forward: the important tai-pan was waiting in the studio; commissions were precious and money was low.

Well, let me attend to the tai-pan and his important commission. After all, there is a lifetime for the rest.